My Summer

of WES

Missy Welsh

MY SUMMER OF WES © 2015 Missy Welsh. All rights reserved.

First edition published by Loose Id, August 2010.

Second edition published by Missy Welsh, November 2015.

ISBN: 978-1-51-919270-7

Edited by Echo Editorial, http://www.echoeditorial.com

Table of Contents

Table of Contents...i
Author's Note iii
Chapter One 1
Chapter Two...9
Chapter Three..17
Chapter Four..25
Chapter Five...35
Chapter Six...45
Chapter Seven 53
Chapter Eight 63
Chapter Nine..77
Chapter Ten..85
Chapter Eleven...93
Chapter Twelve 99
Chapter Thirteen 107
Chapter Fourteen 121
Chapter Fifteen 127
Chapter Sixteen...139
Chapter Seventeen 151
Chapter Eighteen..165
Chapter Nineteen..171
Chapter Twenty 177
Chapter Twenty-One...183
Chapter Twenty-Two 191
Chapter Twenty-Three 197
Chapter Twenty-Four...203

Chapter Twenty-Five 209
Chapter Twenty-Six 217
Chapter Twenty-Seven 225
Chapter Twenty-Eight 233
Chapter Twenty-Nine 241
Please Review 245
About the Author 247
Also By Missy Welsh 249

Author's Note

Originally published on August 10, 2010, *My Summer of Wes* was my very first written and published gay erotic romance. Back then, it was roughly 42,000 words, ended with a Happy For Now feeling, and had a lot of dangling threads to the plot. You see, it was always meant to have a sequel, but various things happened and the sequel was never accepted for publication.

This new version of *My Summer of Wes* that you are reading now is nearly double in length, has been extensively rewritten and professionally edited, and no longer has unanswered plot threads. In my humble opinion, anyway.

It was my goal to deliver a much smarter, more emotional, and successful novel about the coming-of-age of one Malcolm Small. Please turn the page and judge for yourself if that is the case.

Thank you very much for choosing this 2nd edition book.

For you, who waited so long.

Chapter One

The Sprinkle

I was going to go crazy over the next three months.

Being trapped in this sterile, gated community would seriously mess me up. I was floating in a pool of vanilla pudding, nothing to do and no one to do it with. Should've gotten a summer job before college started. Should've tried harder to make a friend.

Nah. Never would've worked before now.

The new neighbors across the street were not vanilla pudding kind of people. Maybe they could be my distraction. It wasn't much, but anything was better than sitting around doing nothing for another summer. Especially the summer before I would really reboot my life by going off to college on my own. Start over, you know? Brand new everything. Reinvent myself.

And here I was bored out of my mind and hoping strangers doing their thing would entertain me.

Ugh. I'm such a loser.

The neighbors did make my parents nuts, so that was nice. Father mostly. The man hated change and loved blandness. Our whole house was neutral, but I'd watched the people across the street move in all kinds of colorful pieces of furniture. A red couch, that was my favorite thing to go into the house.

My favorite outside thing was the wind chime on their porch. My father acted like it was a car alarm going off every few minutes, but me, I liked it. The tinkling little notes were soothing. I'd sit on our porch and try to anticipate if the breeze I felt would make the slim pipes ting against each other and send music my way.

Yep, slowly going crazy.

Except… The family over there had a son who looked like he was my age. That was… Well, what if I made a friend now? Instead of waiting until I was at The University of Akron, maybe I could be new right away. Something had to give because I'd been out of school for just two weeks and already I was twitchy.

Theoretically, it was a stupid plan. Trot over there and…what? Introduce myself and ask if he'd like to be my friend? Pretty sure that stopped working in seventh grade. Obviously, nothing would work if I couldn't bring myself to get off the porch and go talk to him. Even if I didn't know exactly what to say.

But it wouldn't be like in high school. There was nobody here to influence him with reputation-ruining gossip like before. I'd get way farther than saying "hi" this time. So maybe it *could* work. Maybe I'd make a friend. Get a life. Be a real person.

Right, so get to it.

I put my Kindle down, took my glasses off, and contemplated my clothes. Jeans and a T-shirt, no shoes—my rebellion for the day. Casual, nothing to make me stand out. Nothing to make me seem like what they all thought I was. What they'd yelled at me. The reason I had no friends. I took a fortifying breath and looked back across the street when I heard a door slam.

The neighbor boy came outside, and I tried to buck up. There really was no reason this shouldn't work. He wasn't familiar, so I doubted he was from around here. I had no idea how far and wide I might be known, of course, but still. And though he looked a little like a jock, I had heard him laugh and watched him play with his two younger siblings. He seemed nice. Friendly. He didn't seem like the meathead who would hate me on sight for my obvious total lack of athleticism. Maybe he'd be patient enough to teach me how to do something sporty. Like catch a baseball or dribble a basketball.

Wearing an old pair of cutoff sweatpants, tennis shoes, and no shirt was reason enough for my parents to dislike him. His muscles were clearly defined and he moved like he had complete confidence in himself. That was just awesome. Maybe he was into martial arts instead of sports? His hair was kind of crazy. Down to his shoulders and styled so all these wavy locks of blond and brown looked like a lion's mane around his face. He had chest hair and stubble along his jaw, too. When he put on aviator sunglasses? The dude just looked *cool*.

And here I was, his skinny opposite with no need to shave and no chest hair, fricking ringlet curls all over my head, and boring ol' brown hair and eyes. I had to wear *reading* glasses, for Pete's sake. My stomach cramped for a moment. *Loser, loser, loser.* Why was I even bothering to try?

I stood up, fists clenched. *I'm trying because I can't live like this anymore.* And, dammit, I deserved a friend. *I'm doing this.*

I tracked him as he went to his car, a bright yellow two-seater with a flat bed and historic plates. Maybe he'd inherited it from his granddad or something? He reached in and brought out an iPod or phone, then strapped it to his upper arm. Was he going running? I'd seen him do that once before. I walked to the porch steps, heart starting to race. I had to catch him before he got away again. Before I lost my nerve. Again.

That's when I heard *them*. I stopped cold on the first step down to the walk. Even though I hated my flight response, I stood there tense and staring. This pack of boys, my high school bullies, never came through my neighborhood. It was a dead end...with an entrance to the new park. *Shit.* They'd probably be through here a lot now. A shiver snaked down my spine.

I wanted to keep walking, ignore them, go over and make a friend like they didn't matter. But I couldn't. They'd never let me get past them, never let me ignore them. And they'd use the names they loved to yell at me, ruining any chance I'd ever have of meeting my neighbor with a clean slate. If they were in the right mood, he'd get to watch them beat me up, too.

I tip-toed back to my chair. Maybe they wouldn't notice me in the shadows of the porch. At least I had enough courage not to go inside and hide. Still, my hands shook and it was a little hard to breathe.

Neighbor Boy was looking at me as I sat back down. I almost

waved, but if I did, he might wave back, gaining their attention and passing it on to me. So I sat down and stayed there. *Cowardly loser.*

"Hey, man," Collin said to my neighbor. That one smiled like a news anchor and had a mean right hook.

Neighbor Boy draped his earbuds over his shoulder. "Hey."

"You new here?" Alex was tall and dark, with a tendency to spit when he yelled.

"Yeah. Few days ago."

"You play ball?" Todd nodded to the free-standing hoop now beside the garage. Shorter than the rest, Todd was still a bulldog. He'd never hit me, but he was always first to narc on me when I was hiding.

Neighbor Boy glanced at it and shrugged. "Some."

Then Rick, that big blond super-jock, said the first thing he'd ever said to me back in ninth grade. "What are you? Some kinda fag?" He pointed at the yellow car's chrome bumper. At the rainbow flag I hadn't noticed before.

Oh, great. Neighbor Boy's gay.

In the seconds before the others reacted, I wondered if I could get involved. There were four of them. Neighbor Boy wouldn't be able to fight them all. Could I go down there and, if nothing else, distract them enough for him to have a better chance of defeating a couple? Help him get away? I had gotten good at taking a punch and I could really run when I needed to.

Or should I just go inside and call 911 now?

But then Neighbor Boy actually took a step closer to Rick. Closer to the guy who had him by at least six inches and twenty pounds. Neighbor Boy cocked his head and grinned up at Rick. "I'm the kind of fag who'd love to thrust his cock into your tight ass. You interested, honey?"

I held my breath, expecting the beating to begin, but... Oh, my God, Rick actually took a quick step back. Rick had never backed down from me when I'd panicked and tried to defend myself those few times. This was like a miracle.

"Fuck you!" Rick yelled, then turned away. His face was bright, blazing red.

Neighbor Boy grinned and held out his arms like he was showing them what he had. "That's what I'm offering."

They grumbled too low for me to hear what they were saying, but they walked away.

They actually *walked away*.

My awe vanished quickly when I realized Neighbor Boy was now trotting over to me. I sighed and stared up at the white ceiling. It would just figure that the first chance I had to make a friend in four long years would be with a gay guy. Having a gay friend definitely wouldn't help me. It would probably make things worse.

"That was some crazy shit, huh?" He was standing in the flower bed, leaning on the porch railing, smiling at me.

"Um, yeah."

He opened his mouth to say something else, but I blurted, "You should take that sticker off your car."

"What?"

I dropped my eyes away from his sunglasses only to look at his groin. Was he free-balling it inside those sweats? And his pants rode really low on his hips. That darkness right there might just be the top of his pubes. I licked my lips, a little alarmed, and looked back up to his mirrored sunglasses. The reflection made me look weird. He grinned at me, and my cheeks heated.

Had I stared? I was forever being inappropriate with new people. What were we talking about? Oh.

"If you get rid of the rainbow sticker, they won't be able to spread around that you're— They won't be able to spread rumors because there's no more evidence." He didn't look gay at all, so maybe he could still salvage his reputation.

He snorted. "Hell no. I'm proud of who I am. I got that sticker when I went to my first Pride. It's staying where it is." He shrugged and took off his sunglasses, dangling them from his fingertips. His eyes were green. "Besides, one of them checked me out. Full head-to-toe once-over. With a grin. Can't believe he's hanging with a bunch of 'phobes, but that's his problem."

Sudden vertigo had me gripping the arms of my chair. "No. That's impossible."

"What is?"

"N-none of them would've done that. They aren't gay."

He frowned at me. "Well, one of them is."

I pointed after them with an arm that shook. "You're telling me that one of the assholes who's tortured me since I was thirteen is gay?" It was like he wasn't speaking real words. He couldn't be.

"Torturing you how?"

I was shaking. "That word they called you was spray painted onto my locker every day for six weeks in ninth grade. Someone wrote it on my backpack fifty-six times last year alone. And I can't remember how many ti—" My voice cracked as tears burned my eyes. "How many times they beat the shit out of me in four goddamned years."

I clenched my jaw and crossed my arms, closing my eyes tight. I couldn't take the shocked pity on his face. And I would not cry.

"God, man, I'm so sorry."

"Save it." I sniffed my damn nose and wiped at my traitorous eyes. "It's over now."

And it was. I'd graduated high school and never had to go back. I could let it go, move on. I could.

"They do anything else," he said in a firm voice, "you let me know."

I shook my head, staring at my knees. "Yeah, right. That'll really help."

"Hey, man, didn't you see me out there? Not one punch thrown, but you know I won that shit."

I snorted. "Yeah, okay."

"We'll stick together."

Wait a second. I stared him in the eyes. He couldn't possibly mean... "What?"

"Safety in numbers."

Why... Just... Dammit, *why* did he even think that?

"I'm not gay," I said, clearly pronouncing each word.

He stared at me, eyebrows raised, and there was a sick twist in my gut. Why did no one ever believe me? Not since Rick accused me of it in ninth grade had anyone ever believed me when I denied it.

Finally, he shrugged and said, "Okay."

"I'm serious. I'm not gay."

"Fine. It bother you that I am?"

I didn't even have to think about how to answer that. They had to be born that way because nobody would choose to get beat up like I had. That was all I needed to know about being gay. "No, I don't care. But are you sure you are? You don't look gay."

He grinned at me. "We don't all dress in drag, you know."

My blush flared again. "Well... I mean, you seem so—"

"Oh, God, man," he said with a chuckle. "Don't you dare say I seem *normal*."

I gulped and I kept my mouth shut.

"Believe me, I'm sure. I think women are great, but I don't want to fuck them. There's nothing I like better than hairy legs, hard muscles, and taking a long, hot dick into my—"

"Okay!" I held up a hand. "I believe you."

His laugh was wicked, like he enjoyed making me squirm. I laughed a little, too. I couldn't remember the last time teasing had felt like I was in on the joke and not what the joke was about. That was kind of a nice feeling.

Then someone hollered, "Wesley," from across the street. A woman stood in the doorway of his house, waving a phone. "Sorry, honey, but it's Grandma Belle."

"All right. Be right there." He turned back to me. "Gram Belle just got out of the hospital from a hip replacement. I'm her favorite grandson." He took a few steps back, leaving footprints in the mulch. "Well, I'll see you around, then..." He raised his eyebrows.

"Malcolm," I said, realizing he wanted my name. "Mal."

He nodded. "See you, Mal."

"See you, Wesley."

He seemed happier for some reason as he turned to trot away. "Call me Wes."

"See you, Wes," I whispered.

Had I done it—made a friend? I hoped I had even as I wondered if it was a mistake. If nothing else, I supposed, one good thing had come from all this. Now there was a colorful sprinkle on the vanilla pudding of my life. Maybe I wouldn't go crazy after all.

My Summer of Wes

Chapter Two

Call Him Ted

Two days later, I'd just sat down on the porch with my Kindle, when I heard the stomp of footsteps coming toward me. Before I looked up, I heard, "Hey, Mal."

I jumped a little, and he chuckled at me from the flower bed.

"Hey, Wes." I cleared my throat and took off my reading glasses. "What's up?"

"You interested in cars at all?" He squinted at me.

He had on a pair of jeans that were smudged and torn from hours doing something filthy—under a car?—an equally destroyed T-shirt that might have always been gray, and a pair of scuffed and worn cowboy boots. Even all messed up like that, he still looked cool.

In comparison, I looked like a choirboy in my khaki slacks, navy polo, and loafers.

Man, I'm such a geek.

"Um, I don't know much about cars, but I like your El Camino." I nodded at his yellow muscle car. I knew the name of it only because of an exhaustive Internet search of car photos. I'd heard the engine yesterday evening as he drove off. It had sounded thrilling.

"Awesome. I restore cars. Would you like to see my newest acquisition?"

I hesitated.

"She's in a garage in Maple Heights. Sorta near Cleveland? You're the only person I know in Fairlawn—or any part of Akron, really—so how about you come have a look at her, smile and nod while I babble, and I'll get you a smoothie afterward?"

I chuckled, both at his words and his pleading puppy-dog expression. He was difficult to resist. I bet this was something friends would do. "Yeah, okay, I'll go with you."

If nothing else, I'd get to ride in that cool car for a while and practice small talk—maybe even car talk since I'd been reading up on them.

"Fantastic." He looked me over as I stood up. "You have something to wear that you wouldn't mind, you know, getting dirty? I'm not going to make you roll around on the shop floor or anything, but shit happens."

"Uh, yeah. I can change."

"Cool." He gripped the porch railing and jumped up and over it in one leap. "What?" he asked as I stared at him.

"Nothing." I made myself turn away because I was blushing. He'd done that so easily! "I'll be right back. In a minute. After I change."

He grinned. "Okay. I'll wait here." He walked around and sat on the top step, taking out his phone.

Even though he flustered me, I wished that he'd been at my school with me. Then, maybe, I'd have been able to learn something about making Rick and the rest leave me alone. I'd had nightmares for four years, but last night, Wes had jumped in and beat the hell out of all those bastards. The dream me had been so surprised, I'd woken myself up.

After digging through the back of my closet, I settled on a T-shirt with a bleach stain across the front and an old pair of jeans that were a little big on me, sitting lower on my hips than normal. They made me self-conscious since I'd show skin if I raised my arms too much, but wearing a belt would be weird while trying to look laid back and grungy. Right? I dug up an old pair of tennis shoes and dropped my glasses into my pocket. I'd need them if he wanted me to read anything. Annoying, but a fact of my geeky life. Looking at myself in my mirror, I thought I'd managed to pull off... Well, something close to messy boy-ness.

How sad was it that I barely knew how to be just an average guy? *Loser.*

Wes was still sitting on that step, now surveying the neighborhood. He waved at Mr. Ellison as he stalked by, his cane smacking the sidewalk like gunshots. Mr. Ellison didn't wave back, as usual, just kept walking and glaring. Wes raised both arms and waved like a madman. I laughed and turned to lock the door.

When I turned around, Wes was right there, grinning at me again. "Christ, you're cute." He shook his head at me, those green eyes roving up and down my body.

"What? My clothes?" My face heated up. "I don't really...you know, um..."

"It's fine, Mal." He put his arm around me, his big hand on the back of my neck, and guided me toward the stairs. "I'm gonna have to get you dirty now. You know that, right? I'm *seriously* not going to be able to resist until you're filthy."

That sounded all right. But having him hold onto me like that, so casual and companionable, built a little lump in my throat. No one had touched me in any way for a really long time. It was shocking that I hadn't noticed until then how I'd been missing out on such simple human contact. It was kind of a relief when he let me go to get into his car.

Movement at the front window of the house caught my attention. His mom smiled at me and waved. She had Wes's wavy blonde-brown hair, but darker eyes. I waved back and got in the passenger side just as Wes started the car, making it growl ferociously.

Impulsively, I said, "I love this sound."

He smiled at me, and then popped it into reverse and eased down the drive. He drove like he moved, easy and confident. He didn't do anything wild, but the sound of the car, and the way people looked at us, made me feel like we could, at any second, become criminals, leading the police on a three-state chase.

"I'm really loving your car." The black leather seat was hot from sitting in the sun, but the air swirling around us through the open windows took away the burn.

He watched the traffic as we headed north. "It's the first car I restored. My dad helped in the beginning, but it's been all me for the past few years. It was little more than the frame when we bought it, but we could see the potential."

Wes went on about all they'd had to do to the car, talking about parts and theories—*cars had theories?*—and different designs. I acted as he'd said to, smiling and nodding, understanding only his passion for this, his love for his father, and, for whatever reason, his desire to draw me into this world.

Which was just weird. I couldn't have pointed out where washer fluid went or known where to find the dipstick to check the oil level—or what the level should be—let alone whether all the bits were there for an engine to be complete. Yet he seemed perfectly happy to tell me all about it.

And I liked listening to him, even if I didn't understand everything he said. This was a first for me. No one had ever been so excited about something they'd wanted to share it with me.

About a half hour later, we pulled into the lot of a run-down garage in Maple Heights. I'd never been here before, and it was nothing like Fairlawn. I got out of the car feeling like I stuck out horribly, but Wes was all confidence, calling out greetings to a few of the people hanging around. He knew their names, and they knew his. I tried to relax.

Suddenly, someone called out something in Spanish. *"Es tu novio?"*

Wes winced and his eyes cut toward me.

"I took French," I said with a shrug.

"En mis sueños," Wes hollered back, making him laugh and give Wes a thumbs-up.

I frowned as I followed Wes into the garage. Were they talking about me? I tried for a neutral tone, like it didn't really matter, when I asked, "What were you two talking about?"

Wes was quick to say, "Nothing."

They had been talking about me. Dammit. Probably about how ridiculous I looked, that I was trying too hard, forever the scrawny geek who'd never fit in, and maybe even the gay thing, too. And here I was stuck with this guy I didn't even really know, who obviously didn't mind lying to me, until he finally decided to take me back home. This had been a stupid idea. I should've known.

When Wes put his hand on the back of my neck, I flinched and stopped walking, looking up. "Hey," he said, "Hector was teasing *me*. Asking if you were my boyfriend."

"Oh." I blushed, but that wasn't so bad. It sucked because yet another stranger was assuming something about me without even knowing me. But Hector hadn't seemed like he was being mean about it. Of course... "You told him I'm not, right?"

"Yep." He looked away and urged me closer to a totally wrecked car. "And here's my newest baby." He sounded crazy proud of it.

I wasn't sure what reaction he might've been expecting from me. I mean, I knew it was a Dodge from the emblem, but that was about it. The front was smashed nearly back into the driver's seat. No tires, so it sat on the kind of lift they use to raise a car. A lot of it was orange and brown rust, but it had once been a slightly sparkling dark blue. The seats were missing in the back of it, letting me see right on into the dark trunk.

"Wow, so that... It, um, must have been one hell of an accident." Should I have been impressed by the car? Was it a classic something or other?

Wes leaned on me, his arm around my shoulders now. "Yeah, but he walked away from it. That's the old steel frame for you. The other car was totaled."

This *wasn't* totaled? "Looks like it needs a lot of work." I figured he'd do the theories and designs thing now and let me off the hook.

"She," he said. "Like most other man toys, we refer to cars as female."

I looked at him, and he waggled his eyebrows at me. What was that for?

Wes leaned close and whispered in my ear, "I call him Ted."

"Oh, I get it." Straight men called them girl names, so since Wes was gay... I rolled my eyes. Whatever.

He jogged over to something hidden under a sheet. "This is my baby's heart."

With a flourish, he took the sheet off, revealing a shiny engine. No idea if it was anything special, but it looked impressive sitting there with thick pipes and whatnot all over it. If it ended up letting the poor car make the same powerful noises as the El Camino, I could be a fan of a car engine.

"I bought it last month with some of the money from the last one I restored."

"Yeah? Was it expensive?" I went over for a closer look and put my glasses on. The engine seemed designed to look like a piece of art. There were words on some of the parts, but they didn't mean much to me.

When he didn't answer, I looked up over the top rim of my glasses at him. There was an odd little smile lifting his lips. He wiped a hand down his face and chuckled in a way that made me think he was...strained? Was I, like, trying his patience somehow? I stuffed my glasses back in my pocket.

"So, uh, no," he said, "it wasn't too expensive, considering I got a hundred for the car."

"A hundred?" That seemed really low, unless— "One hundred *thousand?*"

He nodded. "Think of them as collectables. People spend their lives looking for them or building them, holding on to them, fighting wills over them." He gestured at the wreck. "The guy who had this one kept it in his garage for twenty-eight years just like this, hoping to fix him up someday."

"Then why'd he get rid of him?"

"He didn't, really. He owns forty percent of him, so when I sell him, Doug'll get that much of the price. He'll need the money more than the car now that he's the father of triplets."

"Oh, well, yeah. How much do you think you can get for him? I mean the car."

He shrugged one shoulder, tilting his head toward it. "Maybe eighty, eighty-five."

I did some mental math and realized Wes would be, like, a *millionaire* in no time, even with putting some of the money into the next car. That was pretty awesome.

"Hell of a way to save for college," I said with envy. My parents were paying for me. "Or are you not going?" Because he had a career right here.

"Oh, I'm going. I want a business degree so I can get my own shop someday and know what I'm doing in the office, too."

I nodded. "That's smart. Good idea."

"What about you?" He hitched a hip on the passenger side of Ted's hood.

I shrugged and crossed my arms. "College, but I don't know why. I mean, for what. It's just expected, so I'm going to go." I'd figure out what to take eventually.

"What do you have a passion for?"

"A passion?" I let my gaze wander away to stare at nothing in particular. Did I have a passion? I might have been able to mumble about liking some subject, but a was I really crazy enthusiastic about something? I shook my head. "I don't know."

He leaned, catching my eye, and smiled a little. "What would you rather do than anything else if you had all day to do it?"

"Is that what cars are like for you?"

He chuckled and rocked back against the car. "Dude, I can work on a car and forget to eat, sleep, piss. If I didn't have any other responsibilities, I'd be right here 24/7." He looked proud of that.

What was something I did that made me forget the world around me and that I was in it? It shouldn't be that hard to think of something. But it was because... God, because most everything I did was designed to escape the reality of my existence. Reading took me away. Video games. The Internet. I didn't have a passion for anything because everything I did in a day was stuff I used to waste time until I went back to sleep.

"Shit," I mumbled and tucked my arms tighter around my chest. I squeezed my eyes shut to fight back the burn of tears.

I'd wasted so much time, so much of my life, trying to escape being me because those assholes had made me hate myself. I had no idea who I really was because I'd never wanted to be me.

Warm fingers touched my elbows. I opened my eyes, and Wes was there, urging me closer to him. He was frowning, but not like he was frustrated or upset. When he put an arm around my shoulders and kept me moving to the back of Ted, near the wall, I sniffed and realized with complete humiliation that I hadn't fought anything back. I was crying.

I swiped at my cheeks and faced the wall, my face scorching hot.

"It's okay," he said quietly, his hand rubbing circles on my back.

"No one's looking."

"Sorry." I cleared my throat and swallowed, trying to get a grip.

Wes gave me a sideways hug. "No, I'm sorry, Mal. It's hard to find a passion when you're fighting bullies all the time."

His hand went to the back of my neck again, and I found it oddly comforting as he massaged my tense muscles and just stood there beside me.

"But maybe now you can fix that," he said in a gentle tone. "And I'd like to help."

I really had made a friend. "Thanks, Wes."

He bumped me into his side and said nothing, but his smile was encouraging.

Chapter Three

Scratched to Second Base

We spent hours wiggling around inside Ted. Apparently, Wes had removed the backseats because he needed to strip the whole car down to the frame to take care of all the rust. He gave me odd jobs, correctly guessing I didn't know what I was doing and shouldn't be trusted with anything important. Eventually, I looked up, moved forward, and suddenly found myself facedown through the backseat area and half into the trunk. My ears rang from the bang of me on metal and then the twang of more metal hitting the cement floor.

"Oh, shit! What'd I break? I'm *so sorry*."

Oh, my God, I'd broken Wes's car. He'd hate me. He loved his cars, and I'd destroyed this one. I'd have to buy it from him. *Oh, my God.*

"Easy, Mal. Seriously, it's fine."

I got up on my hands and knees. "Are you sure?" I looked back at him over my shoulder.

His green eyes flicked up to the ceiling and he mumbled a prayer for strength.

I winced. "I'm *really* sorry. I'll fix it. Or buy a new part or whatever it needs. I promise."

He did that strained chuckle thing again. "Just come on out of there. I'm sure it's not that bad."

,rabbed one of my belt loops and nearly took my pants down. .:hed at the waist of my jeans with one hand, and he let me go .ediately. Almost face-planting again, I widened my knees to .ep my jeans from leaving my hips. Apparently, that belt might not .ave been such a bad idea.

Wes snorted a laugh that grew to one of those uncontrollable things that make you double over, get tears in your eyes, and struggle for breath. I laughed, too, because he was starting to sound like an asthmatic goose. Shaking my head at the both of us, I very carefully backed out of the trunk and into the space beside him.

It was when I sat down that I noticed my shirt was slashed across my chest. *How'd that happen?* I touched the open edges, and then widened them to look at my chest. "Oh, shit," I whispered and fixed my eyes on Ted's ceiling. I flapped my hands. "Wes! Wes, shut up, I need *help*."

He sobered up fast, crawling closer. "What's wrong?"

My waving hands fluttered near my chest. I couldn't catch a deep breath. "I'm bleeding. There's blood." I had to swallow hard. "Um, I'm not good with blood. Like at all."

He caught my hands and pressed them down against my thighs. "I can't tell how bad it is. Let me see." There might be tear tracks on his face from laughing so hard, but he was all seriousness now.

"What do I do?"

"Mal, you're not gushing or anything. I think it's fine."

I closed my eyes when I felt him move the torn shirt around. I had to tell him. "Wes, I faint."

"What?"

"At the sight of blood. My own. *I faint.*"

"*Oh*. Okay. Close your eyes then." He took hold of the hem of my completely non-protective shirt. "Lift your arms up so I can take your shirt off and get a better look."

I raised my arms and gasped when the material snagged on my wounds. If rust got in my bloodstream, would I need a tetanus shot? Had I ever had one? What was tetanus? Was it fatal? "Maybe we should go to the hospital. Or call an ambulance.

"Breathe, Mal," he said, firmly but softly. "I swear it's not bad, but don't look at it."

"If it's not bad, why can't I look?"

"Because you *are* bleeding."

"Oh, God." I heard a muffled laugh. The bastard. "Wes, I'm not kidding around here."

"I know, but it's okay. I'm helping." He lightly held both my hands and pulled a little. "Let's get out of here, and I'll take a look at it in the washroom, where there's better light."

"Okay. Then we'll call 911?"

He cleared his throat. "If necessary. Come on. Just keep your eyes closed and let me guide you."

I knew I was grinding the bones in his hands, but I couldn't relax and he didn't complain. Getting out of the car was tricky with my eyes closed. I wanted to open them, but fainting in the garage with a bunch of macho mechanics around? I wouldn't ever be able to come back. Assuming I didn't die of tetanus.

In a little back room, Wes backed me up until my butt connected with a horizontal surface. "It's a stool. Sit on it, while I get the first aid kit."

I heard him running water at a sink, though I looked at the paint peeling from the ceiling. "Do I need—" I gulped down a swell of bile "—stitches?"

He finally came over to me and set a box in my hands. I held on to it.

"You don't need stitches."

"Wes, no offense, but you're not a doctor."

"But I've watched them on TV."

The box rattled in my hands, so I redoubled my efforts to keep still. "This *isn't* funny."

"It's a little funny. You've had a tetanus shot, right?"

"I don't *know*." Oh, my voice cracked there. I was losing it. The heat of tears swamped my eyes and nose.

He took hold of my chin, and I opened my eyes. He was so close to my face, I saw the golden specks in the green of his irises. "I promise, Mal, you're okay. There are three scratches across your chest. They're not deep, so you don't need stitches or doctors or 911. Let me clean you up some, and then you can see for yourself."

"Okay," I said a little too breathlessly, so I tried to take deeper u trust me?"

es."

Wes smiled, clearly pleased. He cupped my cheek in his palm and gave me a little pat. "Then don't worry. Everything's going to be fine."

I swallowed and nodded. Friends trusted friends. He wasn't laughing—okay, he'd laughed earlier, but not meanly—and he got it that this was a big deal for me. But it was fine. He'd said so, and I would believe him. *Fine, fine. Everything's fine.* Except for the spider hanging out in the corner of the ceiling. That was *not* fine. But hey, I'd keep an eye on it and that would distract me from whatever Wes needed to do with the very mild, nothing-to-it injury across my chest.

I'd bolt if that eight-legged nightmare came down, though. No way was I dealing with blood *and* spiders. No way.

Wes swiped a damp cloth across my skin a few times. I twitched with each pass. Then he set the cloth down and rummaged in the box. A cap popped open. "This might sting," he said before spritzing me with something cold.

It stung. I bit my bottom lip, refusing to make a sound. He leaned in and blew on me, his breath making the sting stop, but... *Oh, awesome.* My nipples tightened right up, the exposure and gusting air just too much for them. My cheeks flushed hot, which at least meant I wouldn't faint right now. No problems with my circulation.

Would Wes say anything? Perfect opportunity to make a crack about the fact that I was reacting in a sort of sexual way to something he'd done to me.

But he didn't say anything, stopped blowing on my skin, and reached for something else. "You can look," he said, his voice a little gravelly now. "No more blood, just long red lines."

I shook my head. "Nah, I'm good."

"I promise, Mal."

"I know. Just...in a minute."

"Okay."

He smoothed something cool across my chest, following the line of the cut. I nearly groaned, but from the goose bumps breaking out all over me and the way my stomach muscles kept clenching. I cleared my throat and tried to get back control of my breathing again.

"So, Mal, you do know I just got to second base with you, right?"

I choked on a laugh, blushing brighter, of course.

"Don't worry," he said, his tone pure wicked. "I won't tell anybody you're so easy."

I kicked his leg. "Shut up, jerk. I'm not easy."

"Please." He cocked his hip out and planted his fist on it. "You *jumped* at the chance to take your clothes off."

I snorted. "So you could see my injuries."

When I looked at him, he winked at me, his mouth quirked up in a bad boy grin.

I mock-glared at him. "You're the one feeling up the straight boy."

"Ha! Like I'd pass up that chance."

I almost looked down to see what he could mean, but I knew I was all skinny and undefined. Working out hadn't been one of my distractions from life because it put me too much inside my own head. And when I got nervous, I got clumsy, so if I went to a gym, I'd probably die in a freak treadmill accident. Wasn't worth the risk.

Wes patted my shoulder. "I think it would be better if we left it uncovered. We don't have a bandage big enough anyway."

I resisted questioning that and just nodded, trusting his judgment. I could swaddle myself in gauze when I got home.

"There's some blood on your shirt and the tear really wrecked it. What do you want to do with it?" He took the box and turned back to the sink.

I grinned as it suddenly occurred to me that maybe I could tease him, too. "You just want me to walk around shirtless in front of you."

He made a breathy sound, and blushed a light pink high on his cheekbones. He didn't look at me in the mirror, though.

My breath caught. Was Wes actually *attracted* to me? *Seriously?* But…why? I was nervous and scared and a total freak. It couldn't even be a physical thing. I looked down at my pasty skin, thin muscles, and oh hey, *my wound*.

Okay, so it wasn't bad. Fine, it was barely a thing. Just a few thin, red lines. Before I wasn't allowed to visit her anymore, my grandmother's cat had scratched me. My big, bad injury wasn't much worse than that. They'd probably be faded or gone in less than a week.

See? I was a twerp and a head case. He couldn't possibly be attracted to *me*.

"Whoa, hey," Wes said and gripped my arms, getting in my face. "You all right?"

"What? Yeah. Why?"

He raised one eyebrow. "The blood? Fainting?"

"Oh." *Nuclear blush commencing.* "It's no big. Um, you were right." I forced a smile.

Wes didn't say anything, but his hands slid up my arms and around to my shoulders. I wasn't sure what he was doing until he leaned in closer.

He *hugged* me.

It was gentle, our collarbones barely touched, and he sort of pressed his scruffy cheek against mine. His hands were warm on my shoulder blades, and I was just figuring out maybe I should hug him back, when he pulled away.

I didn't know what was written on my face, but it made him stop smiling and say, "Sorry. You looked like you could use a hug."

"Oh. No, it was fine. Thank you." God, I made *everything* awkward.

He handed me my shirt. *Should I put it on?* There was a tiny bit of mildly disturbing blood on it and the tear was like a lion had come after me. I really wanted to cover up, but he'd said it would be better to leave my cuts uncovered. Plus it was filthy from the crap all over that part of the car. That could get in my scratches and give me an infection.

No shirt wins.

"Here," Wes suddenly said. I looked up in time to see him whip his T-shirt up over his head. Muscles, hair... He was like a poster boy for lean and masculine. "Now it won't look weird," he said and tucked part of his shirt into the back pocket of his jeans.

I frowned and looked away. That wasn't *better*. Now everyone would be able to see how awful I was by comparison. I couldn't say that because he thought he was being nice, so I was stuck. With a sigh, I stood up and did the same tuck with my own shirt. Immediately, I wanted to cross my arms and hunch over or something, but I'd get the salve on me and I'd still be half-naked.

This sucks.

"So now that you've broken my car and injured yourself, how about we go for that smoothie?"

I looked up. Was he pretending not to be upset when he really was mad about the car?

"Seriously, Mal, it's fine." A patient smile now. "Shit like that happens all the time. You probably discovered a rusted out bolt."

"So I kind of helped?"

"Yep, totally assisted. So let me buy you a smoothie to compensate for the blood-letting."

It was easier to smile this time. "I could use a smoothie, yeah."

"Then come on, my little grease monkey. I'm hungry."

I rolled my eyes as I followed him back to Ted. We spent a few minutes putting tools away and covering things up again. No one seemed to care that we'd come out of the washroom together and shirtless. A couple of the guys looked over, but no one said anything or pointed or laughed. Maybe they were just too busy.

Outside, just before we got into Wes's bright yellow El Camino—which he called Juan—the same guy from before called out in Spanish again. *"No quiere decir no, hombrecito."*

Wes closed his eyes briefly and grinned, then cut his gaze toward me. "That was for you."

"What'd he say?" I glanced back at the guy.

"No means no."

"Huh?"

Wes pressed the back of one hand to his forehead and pushed the other against my shoulder. "No, no," he said, "don't you force yourself on me, you mean man."

"Oh, my God." I batted his hand away and covered my face. Wes snickered, and that guy's laughter practically echoed in the parking lot. I dropped my hand, gave in to a grin, and then sprinted for the car.

Yeah, sure, the guy was implying I'd hit on Wes and he'd refused, scratching me to get away. But whatever. That was harmless friend kind of joking, right? Wes's friend joked with him, passed it on to me, and it just meant one really great thing: I had a friend.

Chapter Four

Sprinkles and the Survivor

I was so exposed walking around without a shirt on in a trendy little shopping area not far from the garage. I never did this and I was acutely aware of being half-naked in public. Wes seemed perfectly comfortable sauntering around with his shirt off, so I tried to emulate him and not care either. I very much doubted it was working because people stared.

I watched their eyes go to my chest first, and bet they were probably wondering who'd scratched me. Then they looked between Wes and I, no doubt trying to gauge how we knew each other. Some people didn't seem to care after that, but then I noticed a few girls openly staring at me. Two pointed and giggled, making me blush hotly. Why couldn't they mind their own business? Why did they have to be mean?

"You're causing quite a stir, Malcolm Small," Wes murmured as we walked into an ice cream shop promising smoothies, too.

"Yeah," I said, keeping my head down.

"Don't you want the girls checking you out?"

"What?" I got in line behind him, but looked back outside. Both girls were still watching, smiling and giggling, their heads close together as they talked. "That's not checking me out. They're making fun of me."

He stared at me with disbelief. "You really need to learn what it looks like when someone's interested in you."

My face felt like it was on fire, so I ducked my head down and just shrugged. Someone like him would never understand. I turned away. "I'm going to wait in the car."

Wes got in front of me. "You haven't ordered yet."

"I don't want anything." I stepped around him.

He caught my forearm. "Come on, Mal."

"Come on, what?" I tried to shake him off. "I'm just going to wait in the—"

"No one's making fun of you." He moved in closer and whispered, "I swear, Mal, that's flirting."

Couldn't be. I shook my head, and then glanced back at those girls. They weren't looking in the ice cream shop anymore, but they... Well, all right, they looked happy. No squinty eyes or curled lips or hands held near their throats like I might have something contagious. So not mean, not disgusted. I stood up a little straighter and had to consider if I wanted to flirt back. I'd never had the chance to think about it before.

"You're a good looking guy, Mal."

My gaze snapped up to Wes's face. He didn't look like he was teasing either.

"Don't look at me like that," he said with a grin. "You *are*. Big brown eyes, curly hair, some freckles... You're pretty. I mean, like, in a handsome way. Just, you know, you—"

"I'd fuck ya."

I flinched and looked at the ice cream guy leaning on the counter. He had his arms resting on the top, his chin on his hands, and gave me smile and a wink. He had a piercing in his bottom lip and a tattoo on his neck. I gulped and looked away, crossing my arms and not caring that I got sticky salve on them.

"Dude," Wes said and moved to stand between me and the counter.

"What?" the guy said with a cruel chuckle. "I bet fucking his tight, little ass is—"

"Stop. Now." Wes sounded pissed.

An older guy came over and told the first to go finish unpacking boxes in the back. I watched him roll his eyes and saunter off.

"Sorry about that," this guy said. "I'll be with you in just a minute." He opened the sliders above the ice cream and began scooping, presumably for the mother and two kids in line in front of us. They weren't looking at us, but had everyone heard what that guy said to me?

Quietly, Wes asked, "You okay?"

I nodded. I wasn't really, but there wasn't anything he could do about it. Other guys had said they'd wanted to fuck me up, but this guy wanted to fuck me, period. And he'd looked like he'd make it hurt. What was wrong with people? They made me want to disappear. The only one who didn't was Wes.

I didn't realize I'd moved closer to him until he put his arm around my shoulders. "Don't worry about it, Mal. He's just an asshole looking for attention."

"Sure."

I excelled at worry, though. And that guy saw something that made him think it was okay to say that to me. Everyone thought it was fine to bully me. Again, though, not Wes. I leaned a little into him, hoping it was acceptable to do that. Being gay, he wouldn't freak out if we touched, right? That was kind of a good thing. I couldn't remember the last time someone let me do that.

Wes cleared his throat, and I almost moved away, but then he squeezed my shoulder. "So, you know, with girls sometimes their flirting looks like they're just talking behind your back, but it's not. I mean, they're talking about you, but in a good way. What they like about you. What makes you cute."

I nodded but frowned a little. "How do you know?"

Looking up, I saw him wearing that wicked grin again. "Female cousins who liked to use me for recon."

"Recon?"

"They'd send me into a pack of guys to find out what I could about them and report back. Guys'll talk to other guys easier than they will to a girl, so in I went." He looked kind of proud. "Of course, my cousins eventually stopped using my services when I started keeping the best guys for myself."

Why was it when Wes winked at me, I smiled? That other guy

winked and it freaked me out. Not with Wes, though. His winking made me feel…included.

"So what'll you guys have?"

The ice cream guy—the nice one—was smiling at us. Wes walked over and, since he kept his arm around my shoulders, I went with him. Despite wanting a smoothie all day, Wes ordered two scoops of vanilla rolled in sprinkles.

"That's so you," I said before I really thought about it.

"What is?"

Thankfully, the guy had moved off to get Wes's cone.

"Um, I was… Before we met, I figured out the neighborhood was kind of vanilla. But, um, you have that red couch and yellow car, and you're kind of…colorful sort of, so it's like, you know…" I gulped at how stupid this was. "You're the sprinkles."

I didn't look up at him. I couldn't. It had sounded a lot less weird in my head. He probably thought I was a freak or something. I sighed and rubbed at my eyes.

But then I felt him breathe into the hair above my ear. He gave me a sideways hug and it was possible he'd just kissed my hair. "Thank you, Mal."

What? Why was he thanking me? I mean, it was great that he was okay with my ridiculous imagination, but… Maybe I was overthinking it; I did that sometimes. Maybe… "Did I just give you a nickname?" I peeked up at him.

Wes laughed like it was startled out of him. "Sprinkles? Don't you dare."

The guy came back and offered Wes's cone to him. "Sprinkles for Sprinkles," he said. It was the gayest ice cream cone I'd ever seen.

Wes went to get his cone. Then he stood there with his hand on his hip, that hip cocked out, and licked up the side of his cone. I snorted a laugh. Wes savored his lick and rolled his eyes at me.

"Lemme guess," the guy said, looking at me. "You want something with chocolate curls on top." He gestured to my corkscrew hair.

Only because he smiled and Wes barked a laugh did I smile back. "Um, no. I'll have a strawberry-passion fruit smoothie."

When the guy moved off to get that, Wes reached for me. I fit myself back against his side, glad for the soothing touch and his heat since the air conditioning was making me cold. But Wes pulled me into his chest, making us bump together, and I stared up at him as he grinned.

"You are so damn adorable," Wes said before kissing my forehead with cold lips.

A shivery sort of thing happened inside me. I just blinked at him, my mouth hanging open until I remembered to close it and take a breath. I had to look away from him, jumping slightly when I saw the guy offering me my smoothie. I moved out of Wes's...embrace and accepted my plastic cup. The smoothie was frighteningly pink with a huge green straw. *Good grief.* My fingers started going numb already, so I grabbed a handful of napkins.

When I heard the guy say the price, I realized Wes was paying.

"I can get mine, Wes," I said, reaching for my wallet.

"My treat." He shoved his change into the tip jar. "I mean, I kidnapped you, forced you to do manual labor, caused a *catastrophic injury*... A free strawberry-passion fruit smoothie is definitely in order here."

This time, I rolled my eyes, but I also let him pay. Maybe there'd be a next time and then I could pay for us. That seemed like a friends thing to do.

We decided to eat outside so the sun could warm us back up from all that air conditioning. The humidity wasn't bad today, so it didn't feel like walking through soup, but it was early in the summer yet. I'd wilt outside come July. As it was, I'd probably get a mild sunburn while sitting out here now.

After a few minutes of watching Wes systematically work his way through his ice cream and then the cone, I realized the silence didn't feel awkward at all. I was comfortable with Wes, and it was becoming obvious to me that he felt the same about me. So I figured I could say, "It's been a great day. I'd be happy to repeat it."

"How about we let you heal up"—he bit into his cone—"and head back to the garage on Friday?"

"Sure."

What was I supposed to do tomorrow? Weird how it felt like what I normally did—reading, computer, TV—wouldn't be enough

29

now. I wanted to be out, to interact, see and do.

"I have a friend's birthday party in Cleveland tonight," he said. "I'm sure it'll be an all-nighter. I'll be useless tomorrow."

"Sounds like a blast," I said because I didn't know what else to say. I'd never been to a party like that. In fact, there'd been a clown at the last birthday party I'd gone to.

"Want to come with me?"

I stared at him. Go with him to a party full of strangers? *Jesus, no.* "I, um, can't. I've got…stuff." *Lame.* I closed my eyes and pulled my feet up onto the seat. Wrapping my arms around my legs made me feel a little less exposed. I lay my head on my knees so I didn't have to look at Wes.

He touched the back of my hand. "It's okay, Mal. Maybe some other time."

I nodded and grabbed my smoothie from the table beside me, drinking it so I wouldn't have to say anything else. At least Wes didn't try to convince me to go. I tried not to let it bother me that it was so obvious how freaked his offer made me feel.

We ate in silence for a while. It was less comfortable for me now, but I made the effort to loosen up when I realized how withdrawn I probably looked, sitting there hugging my knees. I put my feet down and sat up straighter, busying myself with my smoothie until it was gone.

Wes finished his cone, leaned back, and laced his fingers on his chest. With his legs stretched out and crossed at the ankles, his feet nearly touched mine. Would I ever be able to be that chill?

"Yesterday, when you said those guys beat you," he said, "did you mean that?"

I nodded and pretended to be very interested in the smudge of something dark on my jeans.

"Did you fight back?"

"Sometimes." I crossed my arms and looked over at the car. Couldn't we just go?

"Your friends didn't help you? Your parents?"

I glared at him. "Nobody wanted to be friends with the weak, crybaby faggot, okay? In the beginning, when somebody tried to help, they just got shit on, too. Nobody sticks around for that. And my parents don't care. Can we not talk about this?"

He didn't move, his expression neutral, and his voice was soft as he said, "So you've been on your own through all of it?"

"Enough. Stop it." I stood up. I'd walk home or get a bus or something. "I don't have to explain anything and you don't know me, so—"

He sat up and caught my wrist. "No, but I can see you. You've been kicked down a lot, but you still get up." He let me go and leaned on his elbows. "Mal, I think you're a lot stronger than you think you are."

Was he serious? I stared at his face, and he kept looking up at me like he wanted me to see everything. But I didn't know what I was seeing. Why was he doing this?

"You're a survivor," he said. "And that's really something."

Still frowning, I sat back down on the edge of my seat. Was that, like, pride? He was proud of me for getting back up every time they knocked me down? *Oh.* I'd never really thought of it like that. It had been more like there was no other option but to keep going and someday, like now, I'd be free of them and could start again. There just hadn't been any other choice.

Wes sighed and stared down at the concrete between his feet. "I knew this guy in school who got bullied all the time. He wasn't a friend, but I had a few classes with him. Gym was one of them." He shook his head. "God, he was skinny as hell, and we had to wear these uniforms that didn't fit anyone, but they hung on him, making him look like a little kid. He couldn't do hardly anything. Sucked at sports, couldn't lift more than forty pounds, couldn't do a pull-up to save his life." He sighed again and rubbed at the back of his neck. "One day he asks me how I do it. How I'm out and nobody messes with me about it. So I told him I wouldn't let anyone intimidate me out of being myself. They don't like it, that's fine, but I'm not going to hide. I'm not gonna take it."

I hid. I took it. *Fuck you, Wes.* I couldn't look at him.

"So two days later he comes to school with his granddad's .45 and killed the one guy who always picked on him before he killed himself."

I gasped. "Jesus, Wes!" Did he think I— "I'd *never* do anything like that."

He looked at me, a sad little smile curling his lips. "I know, Mal. That's why I think you're strong. Did it ever even occur to you to do that?"

I shook my head, mouth open, just shocked. "Not that. I mean, I wanted them to stop and I'd sort of fantasize about making them leave me alone, but never like that. I'd wish I was bigger or stronger or something. Like a... Like a superhero." I shrugged because yeah, Mighty Mal swooping in to save the day? Please. But it had helped sometimes to imagine myself as him.

"See?" Wes reached over and held my hand for a moment, rubbed the back of it with his thumb before he let go. "Stronger and smarter. You're trying to make a better life for yourself."

"I guess I never thought of it like that."

"You should."

I nodded, then realized— "You don't blame yourself, do you? I mean, you know it's not your fault he did that, right?"

"I don't." He shrugged. "Well, not anymore. My dad talked to his aunt and found out he'd left a note. He'd taken what I said and turned it crazy-side up, you know? Twisted it. I still wish someone had paid attention to him. Neither of them deserved what happened." He sat back in his chair, looking exhausted. "I'm sorry you're parents didn't pay attention to you, but I'm really glad you've stuck around."

I smiled just a bit. That was nice. It was pretty much the first time in maybe ever that someone was glad I was alive. Which was kind of awful, but still... This was friendship. Wes might actually miss me if I wasn't around. Not at all upset now, I wanted to share.

"My father doesn't like weakness or change or quitting," I said. "If I came home hurt, he'd ignore whatever it was except to tell me to take care of it myself." I dropped my voice to imitate him and said, "Buck up. Be a man." I shook my head. "My mother wasn't much better. She did take me to the emergency room for the broken noses, but just to make sure they'd set well." I rubbed at the little bump on the bridge of my nose that I'd always have now.

"I can hardly tell," Wes said and smiled encouragingly.

"Thanks. I tried to get them to let me go to another school. Like to start over? But my father insisted I stay there because it was the best school and I just needed to toughen up." I shook my head, looking down at that smudge again and frowning at it.

"You're tough, Mal," Wes whispered. "You survived when others couldn't handle half what you did."

My nose itched and my eyes burned. I sniffed and only looked up because he stood and put a hand on my shoulder.

"Come on," he said and patted me. "Let's get outta here."

I got up and it was nice when he put his arm around me again. "Thanks, Wes."

"Sure."

"For, you know, everything."

He smiled and sideways hugged me before we walked back to his car.

This had been one of the best days of my life and I owed it all to Wes.

My high from spending the whole day with Wes crashed completely when I came through my front door to see my father just easing down into his favorite chair. He stopped before his backside met the seat and his eyes widened. I gulped.

There I stood in crappy jeans, shirtless, scratched and smudged. What would he go after first?

He sat down with a heavy sigh. "Shut the damn door. I'm not paying to cool the whole neighborhood."

Money. Figures. I stepped fully inside and shut the door behind me. As it occurred to me that maybe he meant for me to be on the other side of it, I glanced at him. He eyed me critically.

"Honestly, Malcolm. Can't you just man up?"

I looked down and realized I'd left my tattered shirt in the backseat of Wes's car. I wanted it now so I could cover up. I crossed my arms over my chest and stared at the carpeting.

"Did they steal your shirt this time?" he went on. "The frequency of these fights is—"

I looked up. "I wasn't in a fight."

"—Getting ridiculous," he finished over me. "Explain yourself."

It was my turn to sigh. "I made a friend. He took me to this garage where he restores, um, antique cars and stuff." Maybe that would sound better to my father than calling them "muscle cars" might.

"You went off with someone who works in a garage?"

Or he'd just focus on his white collar son mingling with blue collar people.

"He makes great money doing it." I looked away, frowning. "The last one sold at auction for over a hundred thousand. It's a good job." And Wes didn't deserve my father's judgment at all.

"It's the position of an uneducated person. No son of mine is going to associate with that level of people. Go clean up."

"He's smart. He—"

My father huffed and waved his hand before he picked up the newspaper. I was dismissed. Damn him. I straightened up, bit back any further defense of my friend, and stomped up the stairs to my room.

How dare he? Wes wasn't uneducated. He might've learned things about cars in a garage, but he knew those things. He could do a lot of amazing stuff that I had no idea about. How did that make him less than me? Oh, no, I knew. I closed my bedroom door and leaned against it heavily. In my father's world, Wes was the kind of people best suited to manual labor. They were *the help.*

And I'd just been told not to see Wes again.

"No way," I said to the empty room. "*Absolutely* no way."

Wes was my friend. The first one I'd had in forever. I wasn't going to throw that away just because my stupid father didn't like mechanics. Or didn't like me hanging out with one. *Whatever!* It wasn't happening. I could do whatever I wanted while my parents were off at their corporate drone jobs all day. They'd never know. They sure as hell never asked what I did with my day. I was eighteen now and in charge of myself.

I'd keep seeing Wes, and there was nothing they could do about it.

Chapter Five

Mr. Fix-it

Wes called me on Friday and asked me to come over to his place. He said he was finishing up a design concept that would give me a clearer picture of what Ted would look like when he was finished. As I walked across the street—fully embracing my decision to defy my father—I hoped Wes wasn't doing the design thing because he'd seen how unimpressed I'd been with the destroyed version of Ted. I really had liked working on that car with him and didn't want him thinking it was some kind of chore for me to do it again.

With all of Thursday to replay and overanalyze our time together, I was a little nervous to see him again. After everything we'd talked about, I couldn't help wondering if anything had changed between us. He'd insisted I was strong, but he had to see I wasn't that confident. He was right that I was trying, but some things, like college... I mean, God only knew what that would do to me.

I pushed that thought away. College would be fine. I wasn't the socially disabled freak I'd thought I was because I could make friends. It had happened a little by accident, but we were friends and he even knew everything about me that had made other people avoid me. That was huge. So, yeah, I could be normal.

Feeling braver, I knocked on his front door.

"Mal?" he called from somewhere inside.

"Yeah, it's me!"

"Door's open! Come on in!"

The red couch was just inside, on the left. I smiled at it because even in a room where it was coordinated to match, it stood out like a rebel. *You go, couch.*

"Up here, Mal!"

I went up the stairs where the walls were lined with framed photographs of the Kinneys. I stopped a few times to watch Wes grow up, one shot at a time. He was always smiling or goofing off in the candid shots. The requisite class pictures showed his hair getting longer and longer, braces on and off, and only one pretty glum shot of him in a suit. I grinned because he looked so wrong like that, totally not him at all.

About halfway up, there was a shot of him holding his baby brother and sister, twins, as newborns, one in the crook of each arm. He was looking at them with such love, like they took his breath away.

"They felt like mine."

I looked up at him, seeing that same smile on his face now as he looked at the photo. It was really sweet, but kind of made me sad. Had my parents ever looked at me like that?

Then I realized Wes's red T-shirt was, like, two sizes too small or something. He looked even more muscular than he had without a shirt on. Why was I even noticing? Envy, probably. I'd have to shop in the kid's section to find a shirt too small for me. I wished I'd thought to wear sweatpants too because he looked a lot more casual than I did in khakis. I was all geeky again.

"They were cute like that," he said, "for about a month before they learned how to synchronize their wailing and drive us all insane." He bugged out his eyes and pointed at a photo of the babies in little seats with their fists tight, mouths open, and faces red. I could only imagine the sound, but winced anyway.

"Still annoying?" I asked and walked up a couple of steps until another photo stopped me. Wes held the hands of both toddlers, walking away from the camera and down a forested path. Why did that tug at my heart so much?

"Nah. Sometimes they're pretty cool."

"Do you want to have kids someday?" I didn't know how I might be as a father since I barely knew what to do with myself and didn't think I had any kind of a good role model in my own father. But Wes... He would probably be great at it.

He shrugged and nodded. "Someday."

"So does that mean, like, adoption?"

"Or a surrogate."

"Oh, sure. You should definitely donate."

He raised his eyebrows.

"I mean, because you're... Um, you know, you're..." What the hell *did* I mean?

He chuckled. "Super hot and completely awesome?"

My face heated up, but I laughed. "Sure."

He planted a hand on his hip and looked down his nose at me. "You could *try* saying it like you mean it, Malcolm."

I snorted. "Okay. You, Wes, should definitely pass on your DNA because you're super hot and completely awesome." I rolled my eyes because oh my God that sounded so gay. "But I really just meant, you know, like, the world needs more people like you. That's all."

When I looked up at him this time, I realized there was something warm about his expression. A small smile, and a look in his eyes that was just...warm. I didn't have the words for it, really, but it made me smile, too. Like this banter was good and right. Maybe it was just about clicking with someone, a best friend.

"You're nice," I said and shrugged. "That's all."

"Thanks, Mal." That look remained and his cheeks were pinker as he waved me up. "Come on."

I followed him into his bedroom. It was sparse like mine. Nothing much on the walls and just a double bed, desk, and dresser. Car magazines, along with clothes, littered a few surfaces, so he was sort of a slob. I tried to care, since order and cleanliness were quirks of mine, but I was too caught up in being in Wes's domain. Where he slept, dressed, hung out... Why did that make me feel like laughing?

"I was just finishing up." He gestured to the PC on his desk. "But then my computer decided to freak out again, so it's still not done."

I eyed the CRT monitor and huge CPU tower. "How old is this thing?"

"I know. It's ancient, but it still works…pretty well."

"What's it running on?"

He blinked at me.

"Memory? Speed?"

The right side of his mouth curled up and he blinked again. He had no idea what I was talking about.

"Okay, then." I sat down at his desk and took a look around the poor PC's specs. "Wow, more memory might help, and it's pretty cheap nowadays. If you can find it, of course."

He sat on the end of his bed, leaning close. "You one of those mobile computer-repair guys?"

"My parents won't let me work." I updated and then ran a malware-removal program I was glad to see he had. "Not while I was in school or now. And you know, now that I think about it, how were you working on your cars and going to school? You must have never—"

A laugh kind of barked out of him.

"What?" I asked, blushing. I sighed. "Am I being cute again?"

"You're always cute, Mal. But I'm smiling because it just occurred to me that you might think we're the same age."

"We're not?"

"Nope. I'm twenty-four."

Six years older? "Seriously?"

He nodded, still looking so amused.

"Oh. Huh. But then, why do you still live at home?"

He slumped down, the grin fading. "I moved back because I couldn't stand my crappy apartment anymore."

I sighed with longing. "God, what I'd give for a crappy apartment."

"It wasn't so much the actual place as the neighbors. They didn't approve of my *alternative lifestyle*."

I snorted. "And you couldn't charm them into changing their minds?"

He huffed out a breath. "Unfortunately, no. The Hispanic community is not very accommodating." There was something in his eyes, a seriousness I hadn't seen before. But then he sat back, grinning wickedly. "Which is a damn shame, since they have some really hot gay guys."

"I'm guessing they didn't like you finding those guys."

"Or taking them home with me." He waggled his eyebrows at me.

I laughed, but then imagining Wes sneaking men into his apartment through the fire escape in the dead of night left me frowning. I didn't like imagining that. *Why?*

"You know," he said, "you look like there's some Latino somewhere in you."

I leaned close, whispering, "There is, but we don't talk about them."

He leaned in, too. "Oh, yeah?"

"It seems my great-grandfather committed the unforgivable crime of falling in love with and marrying a Mexican woman while vacationing in Mexico City."

"Oh, the scandal!" Wes pretended to faint back onto the bed with his hand to his forehead.

I rolled my eyes at him. "I was actually *forbidden* to learn Spanish in high school."

He groaned, no doubt at my father's idiotic prejudice over not being one hundred percent vanilla. I'd never understood why it mattered and thought it was cool I could trace my ancestry at all.

Then I realized that, if Wes's neighbors hadn't liked him being gay, it was possible they'd tried to hurt him. That was awful. He was so strong; I didn't know if I wanted to think of him as ever being scared. But maybe he had been, and maybe he wanted to talk about it.

"Did they threaten you? Your neighbors?"

The mirth left his face as that seriousness returned. "Yeah, they did. It wasn't violent, but I think it might've gotten there if I hadn't left when I did." He ran his hand through his hair, and I was surprised all those kinky waves didn't make a knot. "Mostly I hated the fear the guys I'd see would feel. There wasn't anything I could do to help them, save them. And I don't want to hide. I never have, and I never will. So watching them hide and having them beg me to do it, too, was just too much."

I nodded, understanding that. I couldn't imagine Wes trying to pretend he was anything but himself. I mean, he wasn't at all effeminate or flashy, but I very much doubted it was in him to deny wanting what he wanted. I bet he might've tried for the sake of the guys he dated, but I also bet it hadn't lasted long. Unless he'd been in love.

"Have you ever been in love?" I whispered.

He looked me in the eyes and gave me this tiny little smile that made my heart pound.

"Yes, I think I…have been."

I nodded, but had to look away as I cleared my throat. What had that reaction been about? He'd just smiled, for Pete's sake. Thinking about the man he'd loved and, I guessed, lost. Maybe I was just sympathetic. Nice guys deserved love, right? So he should have someone just like I should. Someday. Yeah, that was all it was.

The computer's test results dinged, and I happily refocused. I knew what I was doing with computers. They always made sense to me. Never any surpri— I gasped at the display on the screen. Well, okay, *that* was a surprise.

Looking over my shoulder, Wes said, "I'm guessing that high a number is bad."

"You think? I'm amazed it can still turn on with over two hundred instances of malware. What kind of websites are you visiting?"

He sighed. "Probably all the porn sites."

"Porn?"

He grinned at me. "People having sex in front of a camera so anyone can watch, too?"

My face flushed and I had to gulp before I could say, "Yes, I know *that*. I just—"

"The gay part." He rolled his eyes and kind of looked…disappointed?

"No. I mean, not really. I just…" I glanced around, unable to look at him. "It's just so embarrassing."

"What is?"

I settled on picking at my fingernail. "Watching."

"Watching porn embarrasses you?"

I sighed and glared at him.

He chuckled. "It's fine, Mal. I guess it's not for everyone."

I shrugged and turned back to the computer. That was full of porn-related malware. Gay porn. Would I find something—a photo or a video—while I cleaned up? If I did, I couldn't react. I really was fine with him being gay, nothing wrong there, but I didn't think I wanted to see anything. A kiss might be okay, but more? Naked guys? Doing things?

What exactly did gay guys do with each other?

Why the hell do you want to know?

"So I guess I need a new computer, huh?"

"What? Oh, no, it's not broken." I refocused—again—and clicked to make the software get to work. "Let's let the program finish, and then I'll see what else I can do."

"You mean, you can fix it?"

"Look at me. I practically scream computer geek without saying a word."

He chuckled. "Yeah, that you do. And you know, that's actually a good career choice. Computer science, I think it's called. You could be the guy who makes the computers in the Pentagon secure and all that."

"Yeah, okay." Right, *me* in the Pentagon. I'd probably get nervous, trip, and set off a nuclear weapon aimed at Kansas. I laughed as the program finished with the malware. Then I went in to update his virus protection.

"Seriously, Mal, you might want to think about it. Computer science could be your passion. I mean, if nothing else, you just saved me a bunch of time and money."

I opened my mouth to agree that it was a possibility I could do something like that, but— "You haven't updated your virus protection for over *two years?*"

"I have to update it?"

I looked over at him. Yep, he honestly didn't know. I leveled him with a glare. "Tell me you don't do any online banking on this gigantic security risk."

"No, nothing like that," he said, his green eyes wide. "I use the app on my phone or actually go to the bank. The computer's just for designing, finding auctions, and..." He grinned. "Other recreational activities."

I rolled my eyes. "Well, that's good, at least."

I turned back around, then opened the software and set it to update automatically, which it would do the next time he turned the computer on. I tried to make it to update now, but of course, it acted like I hadn't done a thing. He probably had a virus preventing updates.

Shaking my head, I took out my key ring and popped my USB drive into his PC. It took a few minutes for the poor thing to recognize the new drive, but then I was able to access my own files.

"What're you doing?" he whispered near my ear.

I jumped a little. He was so close he could've rested his chin on my shoulder. He smelled good. I cleared my throat and managed to tell him about the potential virus and that I had work-arounds on my USB drive.

Grinning again, he said, "You just carry around one of those on your keys?"

"Yes, I do." I gestured up and down my torso. "Geek."

He chuckled, held the other side of my head, and planted a kiss on my cheek. *Oh, my God.* And not OMG because he did it, but because I... I kinda liked it.

But I shouldn't. Guys didn't do that. Straight guys anyway. Right?

He settled onto his bed again to watch me, like nothing weird had just happened. Okay, so, it was fine. Wes was just super friendly. Probably did that kind of thing with all his friends. No problem. *Moving on...*

What had I been doing?

Right, yes. Find the virus—probably more than one—and clean them up.

Wes asked, "How do you feel about bowling?"

"Uh, fine, I guess." He could change the subject like flipping a switch. "You don't want me on a league, but I think it's fun." At least, I had when I was twelve.

"I discovered an alley last week that has a live band on Saturday nights."

"Yeah, I know that place. It's—" I gasped at the screen. "Six viruses! And they're still coming." I turned to frown at him. "I feel like I should wear gloves to touch this keyboard."

He looked confused. "Why?"

"You're not just infected—you have a full-blown infestation."

"Six—seven—is bad, huh?"

"One is bad, dumbass."

He chuckled. "Well, thank God you're here. Super Mal to the rescue!" He made a sound like a crowd cheering.

"When I'm done here, we're going to have a discussion about protection."

I turned back around while he kept on laughing and reached for his bedside table. He might not be paying attention now, but I'd get him listening later. Even if I didn't visit porn sites, I knew all about how bad some of them were about spreading malware, computer viruses, and letting hackers sail right in. "Nine viruses," I announced and held my hand toward the monitor because there was my proof.

A condom smacked into the monitor, and then landed in my palm. For a second, I was stunned since that was an unexpected first for me. But then I cracked up, turning around to toss it back at him. "Not *that* kind of protection."

He was sitting on the end of the bed again, inches away from me. "Shoot, because you could've had that one. It's cherry flavored. I hate that flavor."

I squinted at him, frowning. Why would taste matter with a—

"When you're sucking cock, you don't really want to think of cough medicine." He did a slow lick across his lips and grinned.

I stared at his mouth. I'd wondered about blowjobs. Even though I'd done my best to disappear in the locker room before and after gym classes, I still managed to hear the guys talk. Some had given pretty graphic descriptions of what girls had done to them. I didn't think they were lying about how amazing it could be. Did gay guys maybe know even more about doing it? I mean, they had the same equipment, so they knew both sides of it. And Wes had an agile tongue; not one single sprinkle on that ice cream had gotten away from it. Nice lips, too, actually. He was probably good at blowjobs, being older and experienced and all that.

Wes cleared his throat and stood up, wandering over to look out his window, and I realized I'd just been staring at his mouth and wondering things I had zero business wondering about. My stomach felt like it flipped over, making me swallow hard.

Holy shit.

After a few minutes of him over there and me focusing on the computer, Wes asked, "So, you have lunch yet?"

I peeked over at him and shook my head. He didn't look weirded out or upset or anything.

"Then let's find a pizza place, okay?"

Relieved, I said, "There's a great one just a few blocks from here."

"Then let's walk. I could use some air."

Yeah, me, too. I met him at the door. "Do you still want to work on Ted today?"

He smiled, and I felt better, more grounded.

"Definitely."

I think he might've meant for me to miss seeing him do it, but he tossed the cherry condom in the trash as he sent me through the door first. It was kind of nice that he made the effort not to freak me out with that thing. I didn't want to go there again.

Chapter Six

Click!

"I am a complete klutz."

Wes laughed and gave my shoulder a pat as I passed him, flexing my hand. I don't know how, but I'd somehow managed to whack the back of my throwing hand with the bowling ball. Of course, then it went on down the lane to be my fourth gutter ball.

"Poor Mal," he said, fluffing my curls as I slumped beside him.

"And you won't even get me a beer," I grumbled.

"Ask me again in a few years, kiddo."

"Ha-ha." I got up again. "I'm going to go get another Coke."

"Make it caffeine-free so you don't ruin your bedtime."

I knocked his head forward as I walked by. He was quick with the one-liners tonight.

And he had really soft hair.

"Stop it already," I mumbled to myself as I wandered over toward the concession area in the center of the bowling alley. I'd been having weird thoughts like that a lot tonight. Noticing things about Wes that were... Well, inappropriate, I guess. How well his jeans fit him. The way his arm muscles flexed when he bowled. How his eyes sort of sparkled when I made him laugh. And now I wanted to fondle his hair? I rolled my eyes at myself and got in line.

Was it normal to be so super conscious of someone? Because sometimes it felt like I was checking him out, but it couldn't be that. That was... Well, it just wasn't that because I wasn't gay, so I wouldn't be interested in Wes. Period. But my eyes totally strayed back to Wes like he was the best thing to look at here.

He was standing now, holding his beer and talking to a guy with military-short dark hair and a sleeveless shirt that showed off his muscles. Wes looked small compared to him. The guy laughed at something Wes said, then reached out and cupped Wes's elbow in his palm as he rocked toward him. Wes laughed, too, and didn't seem to mind being touched at all.

I frowned even as I blushed. No, not blushed, flushed, like with anger. With...jealousy?

What? No, I wasn't.

Just then, Wes looked at me and his smile faded. He stepped back, away from the guy. He followed Wes's gaze, and I looked away because I was blushing in embarrassment now.

What was wrong with me? If Wes wanted to hook up with someone here, so what? Good for him.

But I didn't want him to.

Why? He was my friend, but that didn't mean he couldn't make more friends or get himself a boyfriend. I wanted Wes to be happy.

Just not with someone else.

What? I put a shaky hand to my forehead and stared with wide eyes at the floor.

"Help you?"

I jerked and looked up. Somehow, I'd managed to follow the line up until I was at the counter. And the woman was glaring at me for being such a flake.

"Um." Why was I here? "Oh. A, uh, Coke, please. Sorry."

"Whatever. Four-fifty."

I handed it over the ridiculous amount and accepted my drink a few seconds later. Should I hover up here for a while? I mean, if Wes was working on getting a date, I didn't want to butt in. He'd probably already had to say something to the guy about me. *Don't worry, that's just my freaky little friend.* I sighed, but chanced a look in his direction. *Crap.* The guy was gone and Wes was selecting his ball from the line. Yeah, I'd messed it up. Would he be upset?

I walked back down to our station and set my Coke in the holder. Wes got into position and swung. Damn, he made it look so effortless. He was graceful about throwing a bowling ball. And he got yet another strike, making the lane light up and our little scoring area flash colored lights, sirens blaring.

I blushed and sat down, ducking my head. I loved that he was so good at this—it gave me something to aspire to—but I hated the attention it drew. With how I'd already ruined Wes's date, made that woman at the drink counter glare at me, and now with the whole room staring at me… I closed my eyes and hugged my arms tight around me until the noise stopped.

Wes laid his hand on my shoulder. "Hey, you okay?"

I looked up. Well, at least he wasn't upset that I'd made that guy go away.

I shook my head, not able to lie to him and say I was fine. Three days together and he could already read me better than anyone else I knew. Besides, it wasn't the first time I'd freaked since we'd been here. As if it wasn't enough to want to hide when he got a strike like this, I'd also scared the hell out of myself when a bunch of guys came into the bathroom behind me. Not one thing happened, but I'd, like, had a flashback and come running back out here. *Big baby.*

He sat down beside me and looped his arm around my shoulders, drawing me close to his hard body. *Dammit, just his body. Not his hard body. Knock it off!*

"No one's paying attention, Mal. They're all getting ready to watch the band."

I sighed, trying to rein myself in again. Why did having him touch me make that so much easier to do?

"This is your last one," he said. "You want me to take it?"

I wanted to do it myself, I really did. But my one knee was jumping and the other leg felt boneless. I'd just get another gutter ball anyway. "You don't mind?"

"Nope." He gave my shoulder a squeeze and went to get my bowling ball.

Then the big dork walked right up to the line, held the ball in both hands, bent over and threw it from between his knees. The ball promptly went into the gutter, my streak of not hitting a single pin the entire game still unbroken.

"You dick! You couldn't have let me go out with a strike?"

"And ruin your game? I wouldn't *dream* of it, Malcolm."

I rolled my eyes and picked up our drinks as our final scores flashed on the screen. You would've thought he'd been playing against a toddler. I groaned, and he laughed.

Taking his beer from me, he said, "Want to stay for the band or get going?"

I looked behind him at the crowd and saw a few empty tables near the back. We could sit there and still see the band fine. I wanted to stay. I wanted to be able to sit over there with people all around me and actually ignore them to enjoy the music. I looked back at Wes, seeing his patient smile, and felt a little braver. He'd stick by me. I could do this.

"Let's stay. I mean, if you want to, too."

He smiled brighter. "You know I love hanging out with you."

Yeah, I could do this.

"Now let's turn in these godawful shoes and find a table." He rested his hand on the back of my neck and guided me toward the rental area.

We stood in line, sipping our drinks and waiting, and I found myself watching him again. I couldn't seem to stop. And I knew it wasn't envy anymore that made me notice things about him. I didn't feel any burning need to suddenly have green eyes, but I could look into his and see that there were a lot of shades of green and gold. He was really handsome. Did anyone think I was? Did he? I stared at his strong jaw and watched his mouth move, those lips so pink. Were they as soft as they looked? Envy wasn't what made me want to find out.

"Mal?"

"Huh?" *Shit*. He'd been moving his mouth because he was *talking* to me.

He blinked and cleared his throat, blushing a bit. Then he held up the receipt and said, "They gave us half-off for—"

"Me sucking so monumentally?" Awesome. A discount for the idiot kid.

He glanced up at the ceiling, his blush deepening. My blush kicked in because, wow, after all my weird ass wondering, I'd gone and said I was great at *sucking*. At least all he did was loop his arm around me again and turn us toward one of those empty tables.

We sat down, and I noticed that guy Wes had talked to was in my line of sight, looking at me. He gave me a small smile and held up his drink like he was congratulating me. *Oh, my God.* Did he think Wes and I were *together?* And if *he* did, how many *others* did, too? Was that why he'd walked away?

Wes was leaning back in his chair, bobbing his head to the beat as the band started rocking, and his arm rested along the back of my chair. Even with everything I now suspected, I let him do it. I let Wes look possessive of me. Let him maybe *feel* that way about me.

Let him because, dammit, I liked it.

Gasping, I opened my eyes. *Where am I?* My bedroom. Okay, that was where I should be at—I glanced at the clock—two in the morning. The streetlights through the closed shades made the room a soft orange color. I lay back, blinking at the ceiling, my heart racing and breathing fast. It hadn't been a nightmare, and that was unusual. My dreams were always pretty vivid, but I didn't have a lot of sexual fantasy ones. At least none that I could remember. This dream, I'd remember forever. It had been about Wes.

In real life, we'd gone swimming in his backyard pool that afternoon. The heat had been climbing, the humidity up, and we'd decided to play and hang out instead of working on Ted. And the dream had been us laughing and splashing—me well past any issues about Wes seeing me all scrawny in nothing but a really old pair of swim trunks. But then the dream went sideways.

Wes definitely hadn't kissed me or held me close or slid his hands down my trunks at any time during our swim. And I sure hadn't kissed him back or pulled him to me or begged him to make me come. But, in the dream, he had and so had I. Now here I was with my aching cock straining my sleep pants, shaking with the need to come, and...and I was scared.

What did it all really mean? Was it just because he was the first and only person to pay attention to me since puberty? He was comfortable with, like, physical affection and all that, but he'd never done anything in my waking life like he'd done in my dream. I didn't mind his arm around my shoulders or his hand on the back of my neck. That always helped calm me down and made me feel more confident.

But after the way he made my heart trip when I fixed his computer and the insanity at the bowling alley, well... What if this was more than reacting to someone who was nice to me?

Could I actually be gay after all? *Oh, my God.*

I groaned and covered my face with my hands. It didn't have to mean *that*, did it? Maybe my stupid dick didn't care who touched it so long as *someone* did. It was reacting like it was supposed to. Perfectly normal. Maybe my little fantasy was some crossed wire in my brain dredging up what was available. It wasn't like I had a lot of personal contact moments to choose from. So this could be nothing.

I took a deep breath and let it out, reaching down to relieve the pressure so I wouldn't wake up with sticky sheets in the morning. I fisted my cock and tried to remember those girls from the ice cream shop. The guy with the smirk popped into my head instead. And then there was Wes stepping in to protect me. *Dammit.*

The memory of Wes's tongue swiping those sprinkles off his ice cream cone smacked into my brain. I squeezed myself and forced a grunt out. Not good. Well, yeah, it felt good, but no, I shouldn't think about Wes. Not like that.

Should I?

I opened my eyes and stared at the ceiling again. Pumping faster, hitting the crown more often, I reached down to play with my balls, and goddamn, there was Wes in my head again. That mouth maybe sucking, definitely licking, and it was not some girl's but Wes's lips and tongue and grin... *That* was doing it for me. Seeing *Wes* in my mind was pushing me over the edge.

"No," I sobbed, but didn't stop, couldn't, and then I grunted and shook, coming hard all over my hand and stomach.

Gasping and vibrating from way more than the orgasm, I held

onto myself and realized this was it. I'd just come while fantasizing about a guy. About a gay guy. That had to mean... Well, it didn't mean straight, for shit's sake.

I grabbed some tissues and cleaned up as much as I could. I sort of wanted to go wash my hands, but that wouldn't make any of this go away and I didn't want to see my reflection right now. I closed my eyes and covered them with my forearm.

How was I going to face Wes? I'd blush, he'd ask, and I'd say what? *Oh, you know, I had a sex dream about you and then jerked off to the idea of you sucking my cock. You know, no big.*

Was this seriously who I was? Gay? After all my denials, had I actually been wrong?

But why? Weren't they—we—supposed to be born knowing?
I never really had a chance. Oh, God, I really hadn't.

A gawky, little tween had walked into that high school with wide, innocent eyes, just starting to wonder about kissing and touching. I hadn't had the chance to consider who it was I wanted to do anything with, because Rick had found me staring at him and accused me of being gay that very first day. He'd labeled me before I could figure out my own label. Fear had made me deny it and fear had made others stay away, so I'd never had a chance to find out if I was gay before I'd had to fight not to be, so I could try and fit in.

I hadn't even been able to explore one single thing. Never had the chance to know myself and maybe consider saying, "Yes, you asshole, I am gay," and make a stand against them.

Nah, that wouldn't have happened. If I had admitted to being gay that first day, I still would've gotten the shit kicked out of me. No one could know if it would've kept on like it had or been different.

Okay, so I was attracted to Wes. I knew I had been mentally interested in him before now. I sought him out because I was happy when I was with him and he made me feel good about my sorry self. Now, I knew I was attracted to him physically, too. And I hadn't just pulled out of thin air that vivid scene of us making out in his pool. I'd wondered about his mouth, been in his arms, and my subconscious had wrapped it all together into my own personal midnight revelation.

Could I really know without knowing? I rolled over to hug my pillow. Yeah, I thought maybe I had known all along.

So what was I going to do about it now?

Chapter Seven

Is This a Date?

"Hey, you got a minute?" Wes said over the phone.

I ignored the little flutter in my belly at hearing his voice so intimately in my ear and went over to close my bedroom door. "Sure. What's up?"

"My parents want to meet you."

"What? Why? What'd I do?"

He laughed all throaty and loud. "You didn't do anything. I've just told them about you, and they want to meet you themselves. It's no big deal."

A bark of so-not-amused sound leapt out of me.

"Well," he said, "it *shouldn't* be a big deal."

But, of course it was, since I was his freaky little friend who couldn't handle the simplest social situations and now had a crush on him, too. *Let's party!*

"Mal, they already like you. Trust me."

"Yeah?" I sat down on the corner of my bed, but then popped up again. It felt weird to talk to him while on my bed, the scene of the revelation. I went and sat at my desk instead.

"Yep. They just want to put the real person to the stories."

I groaned. "What stories?"

He chuckled through saying, "Good ones, I promise."

"Good like he can't bowl and don't let him near sharp objects and sometimes sandpaper?" I looked at my knuckle. One little slip while sanding away rust, and I had scraped the back of my finger.

Wes cleared his throat, and I knew that was him trying to hide another laugh. "My mom's just as bad with stuff like that, and Dad thought it was funny. The twins are jealous that I let you touch my tools."

His tools... I sighed because it wasn't that wrenchy thing that loosened bolts that I thought of right then. I'd seen the outline of his cock in his wet swim trunks three days ago and my brain was *not* going to let me forget it.

"Okay, fine," I said and braced myself. "When?"

"At six."

"What day?"

"Tonight."

I froze for a moment. I couldn't have heard him right. "Excuse me?"

"Yes, I waited to ask until the last minute so you wouldn't have very long to work yourself up over it."

"Oh, my God." I put a hand over my heart as it started galloping. "Wesley, you're evil."

"Evil genius, yeah, I know. Now," he said sharply, "go get all adorable and preppy, wear a tie if you can't stand not to, and get your cute butt over here at six."

I held my phone away and wiped a hand down my face. Was I already sweating? *Oh, my God.*

And did he really just say I had a cute butt?

"Come on, Mal," his distant voice said. "You can do this."

I held the phone to my mouth and said, "Fine, but I might die before I get there from heart failure or a stroke and it'll totally be *your fault.*"

I ended the call to the sound of him laughing. For a moment, happiness for making him laugh filled me up before—*ah crap*—the anxiety of meeting his parents and having dinner with him and this being the first time I'd see him since realizing I was gay, too, and that I wanted him and—

I slid out of my desk chair and onto the floor just in case I was about to pass out.

I'd stolen my mother's cupcakes.

After changing my clothes four times only to settle on the first polo and the last pair of slacks, I realized I'd fiddle and twitch if I didn't have something in my hands when I went across the street. And there had been the cupcakes my mother had gotten from a local gourmet shop just yesterday. I figured the note saying I'd gone elsewhere for dinner would shock her out of wondering where the sweets went.

I was slightly less than seconds away from exploding by the time I closed the front door. Wes had sent me encouraging texts that held clues to the line of questioning I might be in for. Mr. Kinney wanted to know my opinion on Ted since Wes hadn't let him see the car yet. Mrs. Kinney was cooking as thanks for fixing Wes's computer and saving him money. I wasn't sure what to expect from a couple of kids, but Wes had said they kept themselves entertained most of the time, so I shouldn't worry about the twins being a pain.

As I trotted across the street clutching my box of cupcakes, I realized I wasn't worried about any of the Kinneys. Not really. I mean, these were the people who had helped shape Wes into the man he was today, so they had to be pretty cool people. When we'd been lounging by the pool, he'd told me that when he'd come out to his parents at fifteen, both of them had been completely supportive. That was pretty awesome. When I worked up the nerve to tell mine I was gay, they'd either start screaming or keel over dead.

I stopped on the walk up to the Kinney's front porch.

When I told my parents I was gay? *When?* I pinched the bridge of my nose and sighed. Man, these thoughts were just shooting out on autopilot now. No hesitation. Like I'd already accepted it. And after the dreams and the two days of thinking… And while I might not have seen the real Wes for a few days because he'd driven over to Detroit to get parts for Ted, I'd seen the fantasy Wes every night and sometimes more than once. I was going to go blind at this rate.

So was it official, then? Was I really gay?

I'd tried dredging up memories of girls from high school, but they were always less than real. I remembered one who wore a ponytail every day, the glittery-lipstick girl, the one who wore cowboy boots every Friday. Little stupid things that stuck with me. No sexy bodies or anything like that. It wasn't like they'd ever really figured in my fantasies, though. I usually watched myself when I jacked off, either looking down at my hand on my dick or standing in front of the mirror on the back of my bedroom door. I'd wanted to see someone, *anyone* touch me.

But whose hand had I been imagining? Because, nowadays, I could close my eyes, think about Wes, and *boing, bang, splat!*

Shaking my head at myself, I finished walking to their door. With a deep breath, I reached out and rang the bell. Hey, maybe tonight would be a sort of test for me. I could see if all of this was just a weird trip my head was taking, or if I was really all about Wes now. Maybe in person he'd be a lot less enthralling.

I gulped when Mrs. Kinney answered the door, but then I pushed out a smile since she looked thrilled to see me. "It's so good to meet you, Malcolm," she said before ignoring my out-thrust hand and pulling me into a hug instead.

I leaned in and gave her a back pat. "It's great to meet you, too."

She'd obviously given Wes his green eyes and the wild, curly, blond-streaked brown hair, though hers was down her back. After the hug, she took my hand and held it through pulling me inside and closing the door. When I handed her the cupcake box, she gasped and hugged me again, tighter this time.

"I love these," she said and smoothed her fingers across the bakery's label. "What a sweetheart you are."

I had to clear my throat before I could thank her. Nothing could stop my blushing.

Well, that wasn't true because when Mr. Kinney walked over, I felt a little faint so I probably paled fast. He looked like Wes. Not the hair, and his eyes were darker, but he'd passed down his facial features and his build. Seeing an older version of Wes did thumping and warming things to my insides. Wes would only improve with age.

Of course, this realization had me nearly fumbling a simple handshake with the man. Blush restored and nerves jangled, I smiled apologetically even though he just chuckled and patted my back.

"How's it going at the garage?" he asked. "Wes says it's going well, but that much damage..." He shook his head doubtfully.

"Um, I think Wes is making great progress."

I had to swallow hard when Mr. Kinney showed me Wes got his big, happy smile from his dad.

That was when Wes himself finally walked in. Peripherally, I was aware of the twins screaming into the room and distracting their parents, but I was lost watching Wes.

He'd dressed up. It was odd seeing him in navy slacks and a pale yellow polo. He filled both out much better than I did mine, of course, and oh hell, there were those thoughts again. Wes looked *good*. Really good. I'd seen him half-naked in swim trunks, wearing ratty sweatpants, or grubby garage clothes. Clean and pressed was new...and thoroughly distracting. I had to look away so I could breathe.

"You okay?" he asked quietly and touched my arm.

Did I imagine the static pop between us? "Yes," I said and it came out breathless.

His smile faltered a little as he stared into my eyes. Did he know? Could he tell?

How did gaydar actually work?

I don't know how long we stood there, but eventually Wes gave me a possibly flirty sort of grin. I tried smiling back, not at all sure what to do, but it helped when he looped an arm around my shoulders and led me over to the living area.

Mr. Kinney asked, "You like baseball, Mal?" The TV showed a game in progress.

"I guess." I moved forward, acutely aware of Wes now following me.

"We're Dodgers fans here." His dad settled into a recliner with a cup holder built into the arm of it.

I stared at the screen as Wes and I sat down on the red couch. Well, I perched on the edge and Wes sort of sprawled beside me, all confident male with his legs spread and his arm along the back. If I sat back, he'd have his arm around me.

Suddenly, I very much wanted to sit back.

"Mal?"

I shot to my feet and spun around to face Mrs. Kinney. "Yes?"

She grinned at me. "Wes didn't think you had any food allergies, but I wanted to make sure."

"No, no allergies."

"Okay, good. Food's on the table, then, boys." Over her shoulder as she walked toward the dining room, she said, "Give it up, Marshall. They're gonna lose."

"Bite your tongue, Carol," he hollered back. Then to me, he said, "Okay, we're not *all* Dodgers fans."

From a distance, Mrs. Kinney called, "I'd rather bite yours."

Mr. Kinney got up out of his chair with a wicked grin on his face and raced out of the room. A moment later, I heard a girlish squeal and masculine laughter.

"They're like that a lot," Wes said as he stood up beside me.

"It's nice." It was. My parents certainly never played with each other. I couldn't even remember seeing them kiss.

"Not when you walk in on them making out." He closed one eye and stuck out his tongue, his face scrunched up like a kid who thought kissing was gross.

I chuckled at him, but didn't agree that it would be bad to really know your parents liked each other that much. Honestly, I couldn't remember the last time I'd seen mine touch. Did they care about each other at all? Because I couldn't think of a time when I'd heard them say anything loving either.

Suddenly, Wes's hand was at the small of my back. I looked up at him, very aware of his size and... Was he wearing cologne? He smelled spicy. I shivered.

Wes rubbed that hand up and down. "You're doing great," he whispered near my ear.

I sighed, loving the contact and that he noticed I was nervous and offered reassurance. He really cared. While he might be completely misinterpreting what was making me nuts right now, he wanted me to be at ease here with his family.

Looking over my shoulder, I smiled at him smiling at me.

"Thanks," I whispered back and let him lead me to a seat at the table beside his.

After that, my blush felt constant since I'd brush fingers with Wes every time we passed plates and bowls of food. Though his parents kept up a steady stream of conversation, I couldn't really follow it. The harder I tried to focus and calm down, the more awkward and desperate I felt.

I even ended up making Wes feel self-conscious because I sucked in a breath when he put my napkin back in my lap for me. He'd looked at me questioningly, offered up an apology, and my attempt to wave it off made me feel even more like a freak. I knew I was making a mess of things for sure when we reached for the salt at the same time and he snatched his hand back like he was afraid to touch me. But how was I supposed to fix it?

As we dug into the cupcakes, Katie said, "You're boyfriend's cute, Wes." She grinned across the table at me as her twin, Carter, snickered beside her.

Oh, boy. I gulped a little, but liked the sound of that.

"He's not my boyfriend, Katie."

"He isn't?"

"No."

"How come?"

To his plate, Wes said, "I'm not his type."

She frowned at me, her cute little face all puckered up. "What's your type?"

It felt like the perfect opening, but this wasn't some Hallmark movie of the week. I wasn't about to announce my newfound gayness at the dinner table over cupcakes. Though now that I looked down at my pink one that glittered with sugar, it seemed pretty appropriate.

But Mrs. Kinney said, "Let it go, Katie."

"Why? Mal's smart and funny and cute and he likes Wes's cars. Wes's *other* boyfriends never liked his cars as much as Mal does. Mal actually *works* on them with him."

Wes had never had someone work on his cars with him? I peeked at Wes and found him blushing as he drank his water with his eyes closed. Did that make me special? I wanted to be special to Wes.

Mrs. Kinney was smiling at me. Did she know? I knew she wouldn't be upset if Wes did bring a boyfriend to dinner; they completely accepted him. When she nodded at me before promptly distracting both kids by bringing up their upcoming trip to summer camp, it felt like she'd confirmed or shared something with me. I just didn't know what.

I wanted to say something to Wes. But what? And then I couldn't because he had turned in his seat just enough to give me his back while he talked to his dad about Ted.

I'd screwed something up. Maybe I should've confirmed Katie's assumption. I could probably be up in Wes's room celebrating or something right now.

Mrs. Kinney got the twins to help her take dishes into the kitchen. When Wes and his dad got up and walked back toward the living room, I wasn't sure if I should follow them or help with cleaning up. So now that familiar feeling of being invisible and forgotten layered on top of my uncertainty and regret. I could probably leave now, and no one would notice. But, for the first time, I didn't want to disappear.

I stood up and followed Wes.

Mr. Kinney knew more about cars than me, so their conversation was over my head. But my name came up a couple times as Wes mentioned things I'd helped with, and Mr. Kinney shared how he'd once discovered a rusted out bolt, too. I smiled and chuckled, glad to share something with him. So I wasn't excluded, but I didn't know how to be more active.

Eventually, Mrs. Kinney and the twins came in, raising the noise level. I withdrew from it all and realized this was usually when Wes was there with a touch and a smile. Not this time, though, and it was my fault. How could I fix it? Wes was the only person I could ask, but not here in front of everyone.

When the landline rang and Mrs. Kinney handed the call off to Katie to talk to Grandma Belle, I decided it was time to leave and regroup. I could try this stuff again sometime, maybe after asking Wes what I'd done wrong. I stood up.

"Mal?" Mrs. Kinney asked.

"Um, it's getting kind of late, so… Tha-thank you very much for dinner. It was great. I really liked the—" Shit, I didn't know what they were called. "The green things. They were good."

She smiled at me. "Asparagus."

"Right. Okay."

"Mal," Mr. Kinney said, getting up to shake my hand. "Great meeting you. Come on back over anytime."

"Thanks." At least this time I managed a real handshake.

Wes led me to the door. With his shoulders slumped, head bowed, and fingers fidgeting in his pockets, it was like he was a whole different person. For God's sake, I'd managed to make confident, awesome Wes nervous and tense! I didn't know what to do, so I just blurted, "See you tomorrow?"

He looked up, his surprise clear before he beamed. "Yeah, of course."

I smiled back, nodding, and it felt like maybe things were okay now. He waved at me when I turned to look, the last person at the door, and I waved back.

My porch light wasn't on and I had to knock so someone would let me in. Instantly, my mood plummeted. They were glad to have me across the street, but my own family turned out the lights and locked me out. Even if they didn't mean it, I didn't feel welcome.

"How was dinner?" my mother asked as she opened the door. She was still dressed for work with a ruffled purple blouse, pencil skirt, and hose, but she had on her slippers instead of heels. It occurred to me that she never really dressed like Mrs. Kinney had in a T-shirt and jeans shorts.

"Good," I said. "I discovered I like asparagus."

"Your father doesn't like asparagus."

I resisted sighing. If he didn't like something, we didn't have anything to do with it.

"Goodnight," I said and turned toward the stairs.

"Goodnight."

She walked away, and I went upstairs to my room.

What made families the way they were? As I changed and got ready for reading in bed, I knew enough to recognize that Wes had a better family than I did. They were warm and happy and glad to see each other. More real than a sitcom family, but about as unattainable.

Or were they? I bet if I was Wes's boyfriend, his family would adopt me. It made me smile to imagine being loved by so many people.

Chapter Eight

Teach Me

Sunday afternoon, I watched Mr. Kinney and the twins get in the family car and drive away. I couldn't wait another second to talk to Wes, and with both my own parents lurking in the silence of the house, I didn't want to risk a phone call. Besides, one of these conversations we needed to have was the kind of thing you talked about in person.

That Mrs. Kinney was still home over there made me nervous, but hey, I was already sick to my stomach, so what was a little more queasiness, right? And she might know or at least have an idea of what was going on with me. It would be better if she overheard something than if my own mother did.

"Hey, Mal." Mrs. Kinney hugged me at the door again. "Here to see Wes?"

I nodded. "Thanks again for dinner last night."

"Oh, of course, honey. You're so sweet." She rubbed at my back like Wes did while guiding me toward the stairs. "I'll be down here catching up on my shows, so you boys can have some privacy up there."

A weak smile was all I managed before escaping upstairs. Privacy to talk? So she did suspect something. Which was fine. Really.

When I looked into Wes's room, I realized that privacy might be good for something besides talking.

He was shirtless and had on those gray sweatpants he'd worn the day we met. The pants molded to his thighs and…groin. Was he wearing underwear? Because that was a lot of detail right there. Thin pants. Thick…cock. *Oh, wow.* I stood there, half in the doorway and half in shadow, just watching him bob his head to the pop song on the radio while he flipped through the pages of a magazine.

I *did* want him. Maybe not just any guy, but definitely Wes. My dreams had been kind of vague because I knew what a lot of him looked like, but I didn't know how he felt. And I wanted to know. I stood still, but imagined going in there to trail my fingers over his cobbled abs and the hair on his chest. How would he react? Would he smile? Sigh?

Could I make him moan?

What if I slid my hand under the waistband of his sweats and pushed them down to his thighs? If I found out how big his cock was and how hairy his balls were? Was his ass really as firm as it looked covered up?

Could I make him come?

"Oh, hey, Mal," he said, startling me.

I opened my mouth to say something as he stood up and grabbed a blue T-shirt, but nothing came out. How should I start this whole thing? I looked down at my sneakers and gasped when I saw just how much my dick was pushing out my khakis. *Well, that's one way to open the discussion.* Rolling my eyes, I twined my fingers together in front of myself and tried to look casual.

He was fluffing his hair back up when I looked at him again. The blue shirt changed the color of his eyes, making them look darker even from across the room. Didn't change the appeal of his body, though. And I swear to God, he couldn't possibly be wearing underwear with the freedom to sway he had down there.

"Mal, about last night—"

I winced and stopped staring. "I know. I'm sorry."

"You are?"

"I made everyone feel so awkward." I couldn't look at him frowning at me. At least my embarrassment was helping my boner go away. "Every time I tried harder, it all got worse."

"Hey," he said, and I realized he'd moved in close. I could smell his soap or maybe his shampoo, something clean and fresh. I wanted to lean into him.

"Last night was a great first try." His kind smile eased out and had me smiling back. "So you were nervous. You still showed up, you talked, and Katie's smitten with you. She's not easy to win over."

"Oh? That's cool. Good to know most of the freak show was in my head." Or maybe he was just being nice about it all.

"I am sorry about what Katie said. That she assumed you're gay? I know you hate that, but I didn't—"

That was my opening. I'd do it now. Oh, my God. I squeezed my fingers tighter and kept my eyes on Wes's face. "No, that was fine."

His mouth hung open for a moment, frozen in his aborted sentence. Then he frowned and said, "Fine?"

Do it! "I didn't understand until recently, but... I am gay, Wes."

His chuckle was breathy as he put a hand over his heart and smiled. "Yeah, I know."

"What?" I croaked. "What do you mean, you know?"

He waved me into the room, and I came in on wobbly legs. I'd expected him to be surprised. While he closed his door, I asked him again, "How did you know?"

"I've known since, like, ten seconds after meeting you."

"But...but how? And why didn't you say anything sooner?" Shit, I'd actually just stomped my foot.

He snorted. "After the way you reacted? After everything you've been through? No way. We come out when we come out, and you were pretty deep in the closet until, what? Like last week?"

"You knew *when?*" I cried, my voice cracking.

He put his hands on my shoulders like he was trying to hold me together. "You always look people in the eye when they talk to you. It's kind of unnerving at first, but then it's really great because I always know I have your full attention."

"I do that?"

"Yep." His voice went softer to say, "But then, last week, you kept looking somewhere else when I talked to you. *That's* when I knew you were getting it."

"Where did I look?" I whispered, betting I already knew.

He licked his lips. I closed my eyes and nodded. I'd given myself away here in this room and at the bowling alley by staring at his mouth.

"Hey," he said, squeezing my tense shoulders. "This is a good thing, Mal. No more denial, no more hiding. You can be yourself now."

I frowned. "I thought I *was* being myself."

"Well, yes." He shrugged. "This adds a new layer, then."

I looked down, saw his cock again, and chose to keep my eyes on his face because... "I don't really know what to do with all of this, Wes."

"Come here."

He pulled me in and held me tight, his strong arms restricting but feeling so safe. I was completely wrapped in Wes, protected and secure, like everything would be fine. My shaking eased, and I was finally able to take a deep breath. It was a Wes-scented breath, though, and suddenly having him wrapped all around me, so warm and strong... I bit my lip to keep from moaning because, man oh man, I was getting hard again, and I still didn't know if he was just offering comfort to a friend in need or if I could tilt my head here on his shoulder and taste his skin.

"It isn't like there's a time limit." The heat of his breath washed down my jaw and neck to make me shiver. "You get to figure everything out on your own schedule. This here, Mal, is a great first step. Now you know you're not alone. I'm absolutely on your side from here on out."

I tightened my arms around him, snuggling into the solid heat of him. It was great to know he was my ally, to have this assurance and promise, but I couldn't help wanting more. I just wasn't so brave that I could ask him directly if he wanted me back, so I took another tactic. Maybe he could guide me without knowing I wanted directions to him.

"So what should I do first?" I asked him. "Find some guy who's willing to kiss me?"

Was it telling that he gave me a sudden squeeze?

"I could—" He let me go and sat down on the corner of his bed. "Yeah, I could take you out to a club or something, if you want. See how a dance feels before you"—he waved a hand, not looking at me—"you know, get physical. In *any* way."

Oh, this was definitely telling. He'd take me out, mentor me, but I didn't think he actually wanted to. I bit my lip to keep from smiling. What'll he do if I say... "Will it be a turnoff to guys that I'm a virgin?"

Quietly, he said, "Ah fuck," and leaned on his elbows, his head in his hands. "No, Mal, that's not a bad thing." He sighed. "A lot of guys'll love that." His hands fisted in his hair.

Was he trying not to take advantage? Like, be a gentleman or something?

That was my answer, wasn't it?

So I laughed. It was giggly and it just bubbled up out of me. When he looked up at me with a frown and squinted eyes, I was suddenly confident and brave like never before.

I sat down beside him. "The only guy I'm interested in is you, Wes."

His smile slowly stretched his lovely lips. Shaking his head, he looped his arm behind my neck and pulled me close. "You little shit," he said, and then he used his other hand to tip my chin up and give me my first kiss.

My arms found their way around him again as his lips pressed to mine, lifted away, pressed again. It was a light, sweet kiss. He was so gentle, so patient. This felt right. Beautiful, in fact. Tears burned my eyes as I opened my mouth and leaned in, desperate for him to teach me how to kiss him back.

And he did. Those soft lips showed me what to do by wonderful example. He cradled me in his arms as I did what he did back to him. He was thorough but slow, making me feel cherished even as I realized I was aching for him. His hair was silky, his skin warm, and the stubble on his cheeks scratched so nicely. I was definitely kissing a man, and I definitely liked it.

He held me tight, and I never wanted to be anywhere else. He felt like what home should be—a warm, safe place where no one could hurt me.

When his tongue slid past my lips to stroke over mine I moaned from that delicious feeling. He moaned back, and my cock was hot and aching and confined. I wiggled, seeking relief, and he chuckled into my mouth.

"Oh!" I hollered as he sort of tackled me back on the bed. He came down on top of me, pressed to my chest, and then used one knee to push mine apart and settle his hips on me so he straddled one of my thighs.

"You're hard," I whispered up into his devilishly grinning face. Of course, I immediately blushed because my dick liked that his was so nearby now.

"I am," he said and there was a growl to his voice now. "For you, Mal."

"Oh, man."

He rocked his hips against mine, humming in my ear. I gasped at that wonderful feeling. Then he rolled us over, and I sprawled in surprise on top of him. His hand slid down my back to press on my butt, fingers splayed, as he arched up into me. He did it again, and I rubbed back this time. The friction and pressure felt fantastic, but it was the low-lidded look on his face that was the really awesome part.

"I've dreamt of this." He looked so pleased. "Woken up aching for you, having to finish myself off quick because it hurts so much." He pressed close and stayed there. "I've been waiting for you, Mal."

Really? My chest ached a little at that. "I-I've been fantasizing about you, too."

He gripped my ass and smiled at me while his other hand slid up my back beneath my shirt. I shivered for having his hot palm on my skin and didn't really think, just pushed my hand between us and reached down until I had him in my hand. Cupping him, feeling the softness of his sweats at odds with the steel rod beneath them, I watched him groan like he was dying.

He rolled again, pressing me into the bed, and found my mouth for a new kind of kiss. Not so lazy, definitely not sweet—this kiss was *sex*. I moaned because it just felt so damn good as heat and need sizzled through me. I wrapped my arms around him again, holding on and grinding up into him as he rocked down against me. Whatever he wanted was his.

"Teach me everything," I said when we broke for air.

He rested his head on my shoulder, his quick breaths and the fast thump of his heart making everything so very real.

"I won't say I think we should take this slowly, even though I bet we probably should." He turned his head, his stubble making my skin feel so alive. "I honestly don't know what to do here, Mal. I want you *so much*, but I don't want to do anything that scares you away."

I gulped a little. "I don't know what to do either, but I trust you, Wes."

"Yeah?" He lifted his head, smiling sweetly.

I nodded, smiling, too. I was scared, sure, but this wasn't a chance I wanted to miss. Being here with Wes was good. I was scared only because I'd never done anything with someone before. I didn't want to mess up or be terrible at anything. So I said, "Tell me what to do."

His grin went a little wicked. "Sure. Lie here. Breathe. Let me get you naked and spend a few hours doing really naughty things to you."

I laughed, but then... "Wait. Hours?"

He leaned in and nipped at my bottom lip, sucked on it. My breathing went shaky. If he could do that to my lip... "Yeah, okay," I said. "Let's do that."

"No, Mal," he said and framed my face with his hands. "We don't have to do anything. I was teasing you."

I frowned at him. "But you said you want to."

"Well, yeah. You're beautiful, and you've been driving me crazy, but—"

I thrust my hips up, rubbing hard into him because he was doing that gentlemanly thing again. He gasped—I did, too, actually—and the way he pressed into me seemed instinctual. *Good to know.* "I want to, too. I mean, also. Whatever you want, I want."

Now I watched his eyes searching my face. I relaxed beneath him, a little amazed that it really did feel just fine. Normal. Natural. Man, I was so gay. It was crazy what I'd talked myself out of when I was scared.

Finally, he nodded and eased away from me, getting off the bed at the end of it. "You want to stop, you just say so. Any reason, anytime. Okay?"

I nodded as he took off my shoes and socks. My fingers were a little uncooperative when it came to undoing my pants, but Wes's eyebrow waggle and grin helped. He tugged my pants off, while I sat up and lifted my shirt over my head. When he took off his, I bit my lip with the knowledge that I could now touch those abs, feel all that hair. And oh my God, he wanted to touch me, too! My heart tripped over itself inside me. Then he tipped his chin toward my lap and with one of those wicked grins said, "Go on. Show me."

The tiny hairs on my body stood up. Would he think I was weird for being uncircumcised? They'd thought I was in school, when we'd had to shower after gym. But maybe when guys liked penises, they liked variety? *Just do it. It's Wes.* I lay back, lifting my hips, wiggling free before I untangled my legs and tossed my briefs at him. He caught them, but his gaze aimed at my dick standing tall just for him.

"Malcolm Small, you need to change your name. You are not small."

I blushed and lay back, so many worries just vanishing. Then my heart kicked up when he put his hands on the waistband of his sweats and pushed them slowly down. I knew it, no underwear. And oh, wow, there was a naked man in front of me, and I was really excited about that because... "Wes, you're beautiful."

He smiled at me, cocking his head to the side, letting me look at him. I'd known he was lean and toned, but seeing him naked and hard—*for me, for me, for me!*—was absolutely intoxicating. I mean, holy God, he was fucking awesome. He ran those big hands over his chest and stomach, still smiling at me as I stared. Then he reached one hand down to cup himself, to slowly stroke from root to tip as he sighed, those green eyes fluttering closed.

I understood porn then. It had always seemed too rough and kind of gross when I'd tried watching it online. But this? Watching Wes touch himself? This made me reach down to stroke in time with him, my cock growing longer and harder.

But I didn't want to just watch. Not now that I didn't have to.

"Wes, please." I reached for him.

He crawled over, and I pulled him down on top of me, wanting to kiss him. Skin to skin, he felt even more amazing than before. The heat of him was like a bonfire, his kiss slow but deep. His tongue danced on mine as if he liked my taste and wanted more. *Wanted more...* I ran my hands down his back, my fingers tracing his spine, before I found his very firm ass. Wes moaned as I gripped him in both hands and lifted my hips up, pressing into him again. *So good.*

He reached down and ran his hand over my thigh, and then brought my leg up. I hooked it around his waist, holding tight to him. How heavy he was and the way he pressed into me was exciting. The pressure of our dicks side-by-side and snug between us throbbed pleasure through me. Wes shifted, his lips kissing over my jaw to my throat, my shoulder. He laved and sucked at my skin like he needed to.

I gasped as his mouth settled on my left nipple. "Oh, damn, that's nice," I said and threaded a hand into his hair, looking down at what he did to me.

Watching his perfect lips brush over me, that tongue lick and twirl, made me moan as much as feeling those subtle sensations. Someone was finally touching me. *Wes* was touching me. His thumb teased my other nipple, the different sensations making me ache, making it impossible to keep quiet. I bit my lip, suddenly afraid of sounding all wrong.

"Don't go quiet on me now. Let me hear you, Mal. I love it."

He gave me a wicked smile before looking me in the eyes and licking a line down my stomach to my navel. A groan welled out of me because, damn, that was sexy. Then he angled his head, and my cock got a rub from his prickly cheek. I *squealed*.

Wes chuckled at me, sitting back on his knees and looking me over. Was it wrong not to give one shiny shit about the fact I lay there like a complete slut with my hands by my head, my legs spread around him, and my dick weeping for him already? Oh, who was I kidding. I didn't care.

"I've never been with a guy who wasn't circumcised." He tilted his head and caressed my thigh. "I've heard it makes you more sensitive since the head's always protected. Is that true?"

When he touched the slippery crown of my cock, a small wail left me and I clutched at my hair and the pillow, just needing an anchor.

Heart thumping chaotically, I was fast losing control.

"Well, look at that. Like a turtle coming out of its shell."

My laugh sounded like a whine because, yeah, my dick was so full the veins stood out and my foreskin was stretched to the limit. I wanted to reach down, make myself come, but I didn't want this to end yet. It was the most perfect agony I'd ever felt.

Wes gripped my cock and pumped his hand up, then down, moving my foreskin. I panted, rocking my hips with him. When he pinched my foreskin over the head like I loved, a deep moan rumbled out of me only to pitch higher the longer he did it.

He chuckled at me. "You're not going to last much longer."

Yeah, no. Dammit, I was already gasping. I shook my head, panicking a little because I really did want to last, really did want to enjoy this for hours, not minutes. Or, hell, *seconds*. And what would happen afterward?

I gasped a breath to say, "Sorry."

"Don't worry, Mal. I'll take care of you." He leaned over me and gave me a little kiss. "Just go with it, baby. Relax."

Baby. I liked that. I closed my eyes, taking a deep breath and letting it out slowly, trying to find that nice, calm place to let me back off the edge. But then something soft and wet slid around the head of my dick. I gasped and jerked almost upright because that was his tongue. Wes had *licked* my cock.

"The good thing about virgins..." He smiled. "Well, in my opinion, there are *a lot* of good things about virgins. But right now, the good thing is I don't need a condom on you before I can suck you off."

Safe sex. I should've thought about that. But I hadn't ever thought I'd get laid so... "I'll get some. Somehow." Because I didn't think it was something I could put on the grocery list.

"*I'll* get some," he said, "and until then..." He opened his mouth and swallowed my dick.

"Wes!"

Oh, I was gonna die. His lips sliding down, his tongue pressing up, and my heart was going to explode from beating so hard and fast. I couldn't catch a full breath because he was down there teasing my cock with his tongue. All sides, base to crown, he slid all over me. And then he looked me in the eyes and sucked me into his mouth again. I cried out, thoughts stopping completely for a moment as sensation took over. Dark, wet, dizzying pleasure.

I collapsed back, twitching and writhing. I couldn't stop making little *uh, uh, uh* noises as he bobbed his head, sucking his way along my cock. It was wet and warm and oh so good. I spread my legs wider, giving myself permission to run with whatever my instincts wanted to do. The reward was instant when Wes fondled my sac in his palm and one long finger—"Oh, fuck."—massaged my hole.

That was a little startling, made me too aware of the possibility he might want to fuck me. But then my cock was in his throat and the swirl and press of his fingers was making me soar. It was good, *so good*, and oh, my God, I was *coming*.

I howled and shook, coming in waves of heat and bliss that only got better when I realized Wes was staying down there, sucking and *swallowing*. I'd come in his mouth, and he'd wanted that. "Wes... Oh, my God."

He drew out every last drop and sensation as I moaned and slowly melted, boneless, into the bed. I was undone, ravished. I might've read a sex scene or two in a book, but now I knew what they really meant. And his care continued because he was down there bathing my dick with his perfect tongue. It felt heavenly, all soft and gentle. Loving. After a smile and a kiss to my belly, Wes moved back over me.

He was still hard, so it was my turn to make him feel like this. "What do you want me to do for you?" I asked.

He shook his head. "What do *you* want to do?"

I didn't analyze it, just pulled him down on top of me. His weight and his heat felt fantastic, and I sighed when his hard dick pressed into my stomach. He reached down for a moment, adjusting us so our dicks were side-by-side, and damn if mine didn't start aching all over again. I arched up, rubbing, feeling the slick softness of his leaking dick against my own.

"Oh, shit, that's good," he murmured, rubbing with me.

"Yes."

Despite the fact he was probably going out of his mind with wanting to come, it was like he waited for me to catch back up. We kissed slow but deep, tongues and lips devouring. Then he got on his knees between my legs and thrust his hips faster while still leaning on me. I clutched at him, moaning and straining even as I realized again how we imitated fucking. He could do it, slam deep into me with that thick rod now only rubbing against my belly. Right here and now, I wanted that; I wasn't afraid. My hands were everywhere on his body—shoulders, back, ass—because I wanted him closer, wanted him to be a part of me.

It felt so good to do this while holding on to him! It was desperate and primal and so unbelievably thrilling to feel him wanting me, hear him loving this, too. How he made me feel was fantastic, but knowing how *I* made *him* feel was even better.

I panted, staring at Wes, feeling my orgasm tightening my balls and tingling down my spine. Tendrils of his hair stuck to his forehead and cheek, his skin flushed, eyes so dilated I could barely see the green, and he was the most beautiful thing I'd ever seen.

"Come, Mal." He clenched his jaw and growled. "Lemme feel it."

I cried out, arching up and holding tight to him as heat burst between us, mine then his. Holy shit, that was amazing! We'd come at the same time. Together. I buried my face in his neck as he squeezed me to him, both of us trembling and gasping and sweaty. God, even the scent of us was thrilling!

He kissed my shoulder and sighed. "You were so worth the wait."

I hummed with happiness, hugging him and smiling as the seconds ticked by and a lovely feeling of... What? Was this how love felt? Could I be in love with Wes?

Eventually, my sweat cooled and I started to feel chilly even with Wes still draped on top of me. Before I could say something, he untangled us and sat up. "Better clean up before we fall asleep, and then end up glued together."

What covered us was the evidence of change. I'd just jumped off a fucking cliff, Wes holding my hand the whole way down. Now here I was, a gay guy with the proof of it all over me. I wanted to take a photo or something, preserve this moment, but I just smiled instead.

"Don't move." He walked into his bathroom.

I put my hands behind my head, still feeling that inner glow as I listened to him run water and splash around. Did I feel different? Definitely happy and satisfied, so that was new. Sex with Wes had to be at the very top of the all-time favorite moments of my life. So I was gay. It wouldn't be all sunshine and orgasms, but if Wes was with me all the way? I could do it. I could be this guy.

The water went off, and I watched Wes walk back to me. It was cute how he wiped me off with the warm and damp washcloth. He seemed a little shy about it, but I just sighed and admired his grin and blush.

But... Was I supposed to leave now? Should I suggest we go work on Ted? It had been the original plan. I watched Wes walk back into the bathroom and bit my lip. Did coming out and having sex change all the friend things we did?

I didn't say anything when Wes came back. He knew I had no idea what to do with all these things and he'd be nice about explaining if I did something wrong. I sat up, watching his face and ready to get up or lie back down.

It was a huge relief when he got on the bed. In seconds, he'd settled in beside me and encouraged me to cuddle into him. Cocooned in Wes. Oh, it felt *so good*.

"Thank you," I whispered. "I've never felt so amazing."

He kissed my forehead. "I wanted you in my life from the beginning, Mal. Any way I could have you." He snuggled me closer. "Even if it meant just as friends."

I couldn't help snorting. "Thank God that's not the case."

"Amen, my friend."

Chapter Nine

Vanilla Condoms

Wanting to get home before my parents seemed like a lame reason to leave Wes naked and warm in his rumpled bed. It was probably good he was still napping because I knew he'd have easily convinced me to stay longer with only a few kisses. I got dressed while watching him snore softly, and then wrote on a bright pink sticky note for him to call me later. I stuck it to the pillow beside his head, wanting to make sure he saw it right away when he woke.

It wasn't until I got to the bottom of the stairs that I remembered his mother was home. I froze. Had she heard us? How loud had all my embarrassing squealing really been?

She picked up the remote, aimed it at the TV, and paused the show on the screen. "You heading home, honey?" she asked with a smile.

I had to gulp a couple times. "Uh, yeah."

"Okay. Don't be a stranger," she said cheerfully. She started her show up again.

Well, alrighty then. At least she hadn't said "come again." I didn't hesitate to hustle out of there and across the street.

It was so strange to eat dinner with my parents after that. I was this whole new person, but they didn't have a clue. Neither of them asked me about my day, like, ever—and my father still wasn't speaking to me because I'd had dinner at the Kinneys last night. Nothing new there. It was almost funny to me, how much they didn't know about me.

After dinner, I got online and looked up everything I could find on safe gay sex. I tried hard to ignore the really porno sites and instead got caught up in the medical information. The number of diseases and what they'd do to a body were seriously disturbing. Torpedoed the fun of it all. My takeaways were that I needed to have a conversation with Wes about his health and that condom shopping was now at the top of my to-do list. If he got them, cool, but if he didn't, I would— *Ugh...* I would say *no* to any more sex until we had them. Because he'd been right about me not ever being exposed to anything that could hurt him, but even a blowjob could mess me up if he hadn't always been careful.

I did wonder about the trust in sex. How could people just jump into it with strangers? I got the need and excitement and everything about it now—boy, did I—but all the things that could happen still made it maybe not worth the risks. Sure, drugs took care of a lot of things, and *maybe* I wouldn't die from AIDS complications nowadays, but some of those illnesses were forever. I couldn't ignore that.

I wanted to trust Wes completely. I liked him, he was great, and he'd been so amazing to me. I'd definitely try to trust him and a conversation about his status would be where that could really start. It had to happen.

The next morning, when the doorbell rang, I used the walk downstairs from my bedroom to answer it to psych myself up. Wes had called last night to say he wanted to see me again today. Maybe go out for breakfast together. So this might be the perfect time to have that safe sex talk.

Afterward, I'd be getting laid again.

I opened the door and—*oh, man*—how had I not caught on to my desires sooner? *Just look at him.* Tall, broad shoulders, lean muscles, that friggin' tight T-shirt showing off sculpted pecs and a flat stomach, jeans riding low enough that I could see the top of the fascinating muscle that pointed to his groin...and his grin! Yeah, it was really the expression on his face that did it all because he knew he could have me. *Oh. My. God.* I got hard so fast, I was a little dizzy.

He stepped inside, crowding me back. "Anyone else home?"

I shook my head, the blood filling my cock leaving my brain empty.

He grabbed me up and devoured me.

Wow. Just… Damn. And wow. So this was what it felt like to have someone want me.

I clung to him, holding on to those shoulders and that neck as he kissed me like he was trying to crawl inside me. *Oh damn.* He could actually do that. I didn't know much, but I knew his cock could go up my ass. I moaned into his mouth, his tongue curling with mine, and hauled our hips together, grinding into him.

He lifted his head and sucked in a lungful of air. "Jesus, baby." He panted, his hand holding me tight and still against him. "You keep that up, you'll have me coming in my jeans."

I got him just as worked up as he got me. That was cool.

"Oh, you like that idea?" He chuckled, wrapping his arms around my shoulders, a big hand holding the back of my head.

"Yeah, I do." I held him around his waist, petting the muscles of his back.

He nipped at the tip of my nose, making me laugh. "I was going to whisk you away for something sticky and sweet at the café, but I'm thinking now I might prefer the cream-filled treat you've got in your jeans." His voice dropped to a growl by the time he got to the end of that sentence.

I shivered, pressing in tighter to him, trying to ease the increasing ache of my dick.

He dipped his head, running his lips over my jaw before nibbling on my neck. I was learning that he had a very talented mouth. "Let me?" he whispered right into my ear.

Oh, God, he was really asking to suck me off right here in my living room. *The conversation!* We had to talk about this first. *Say something!* "One condition," I managed to say.

"Name it."

"Did you get the condoms?"

"Yep. You thinking you want to try giving a blowjob, Malcolm?" His grin was pure wicked.

"Yeah. Yes. Okay?"

He chuckled. "Honey, nobody says no to a blowjob." He dug a packet out of his pocket. "How's vanilla sound?"

I shrugged and dropped to my knees.

Wes's chuckle sounded breathless. "Zero to sixty, huh?"

A wicked laugh left *me* this time as I unbuttoned his fly. I could do this. I really wanted to. It was exciting and— Okay, he just didn't wear underwear. Twice now, I'd gotten to see him undress, and both times he'd been naked inside his pants. Knowing he was so accessible was just real damn sexy.

And then it was a little scary.

"It's okay," he whispered, threading his fingers into the hair at my temple.

"Um. What should I do? I mean—"

"Remember how it felt yesterday? What you saw me do?"

I snorted and grinned. "Man, do I ever. I remembered twice last night and again this morning."

While he chuckled, I caught the scent of him. He smelled a little like soap and sex. Musky maleness. I think he might've said something to me, but I was so totally focused on the flushed, hard cock in front of my face that I couldn't hear anything except my own heartbeat. I leaned and breathed him in, before kissing the base. I licked it. He was a tiny bit salty, and I liked that. I heard him gasp, felt him shiver.

"C-condom, Mal." He handed it over.

Right. Time to be serious. I opened it up, being careful since it felt slippery in there. My school had been all about abstinence, but a video had gone around about how to put one of these on a banana. I got it right side up and set it on the tip of his dick, realizing I'd have to hold him still while I rolled it down. Wes pinched the tip, making me look up.

"Gotta leave room for me to come."

I nodded and finished rolling the condom down. He was circumcised, the scar subtle, and his cock had more prominent veins and a fatter crown. With the rubber on, he was a milky white color, and there was lubrication all over my hand. I sniffed at it. Yep, it was vanilla. Licking my fingers clean, I thought it was a little weird tasting and slippery, but not terrible. It kind of made me think I was licking vanilla lotion.

Wes groaned. I looked up and, by the tortured look on his face, I realized I was actually being a tease, licking my fingers while he waited. I grinned at him.

He snorted a laugh. "Whenever you're ready. You know, no rush. I'm not losing my mind or anything." He scrunched up his face and shrugged.

I smoothed my palms up his abs, reveling just a little longer in this newfound power I had acquired. He'd faked a crowd cheering when he'd thought I'd make a great computer geek. What would he do if I turned out to be a fantastic cock-sucker? Chuckling at myself, I leaned in and swirled my tongue around the glans.

"Oh, Jesus." He gripped the back of my head, his fingers massaging roughly. Though he didn't pull me closer, I moved in for more anyway.

The point was probably to create a warm, wet place that could grip him tight, slide over him, and suck with a rhythm like a pulse. Those had been the fantastic things he'd let me feel. So I closed my eyes, opened my mouth, and let whatever instinct I had guide me. Listening to him helped, too. Wes was definitely not quiet during sex.

He tried to say different things a few times, starting and stopping. Mostly things that sounded like amazement and mumbles of my name. Over and over. I loved it and would've smiled a lot if my mouth hadn't been so full of him. I really wished I could taste him instead of plastic-y vanilla.

Eventually, I decided to find out how deep I could take him and earned a "holy Christ!" for my efforts as he bumped the back of my throat. That wasn't even difficult. I just relaxed and swallowed, holding my breath. He was like a really big tongue-depressor. His thigh muscles jumped against my palms.

I pulled back, watching him staring down at me with low-lidded eyes. While his pubes were trimmed, his balls were bare. The silky skin wrinkled or stretched as I fondled him, rolling his nuts around. That made his eyes flutter closed and his mouth pop open. He panted and groaned, and I sucked harder each time I bobbed my head.

This was brilliant. I knew with complete certainty that he loved what I did to him. I didn't have any doubts or worries about whether I was doing the right thing. Everything I did was good for him. That power I'd felt before was nothing compared to the knowledge that I was making him feel so amazing.

It was getting me going, too. I reached down and rubbed at my trapped cock as I took him in deep again.

"Mal. Oh, fuck. *Baby...*" He gasped and his fingers pulled at my hair as he made a fist. His cock sort of shimmied a little in my mouth, hot and stiff, and I realized he was coming.

And apparently that was all I needed to dive over the edge myself. I pulled back, pressed my forehead into his thigh, and came in my damn pants. I'd barely touched myself, for Pete's sake.

"Damn, Mal." He smoothed both of his hands over my hair. "You are gifted, my friend."

Okay, that's nice. "Thank you." I lifted my head and smiled up at him. Then I kissed that intriguing spot where groin, belly, and hip met before resting my cheek there. *Yay, me.* I gave good head. And enjoyed doing it!

But what would it be like to do it without the condom and taste Wes's real flavor?

"Mal," he asked with a chuckle, "did you come?"

My face burned. "Um. Yes."

He laughed and tipped my head back so he could bend down and kiss me. "Then I'll owe you one." He kissed me deeper, and my lips felt swollen and tingly.

I stood up on wobbly legs, grimacing at the wet mess in my briefs that wilted my chance of being able to tell him I'd be ready in a minute or two for him to do whatever he wanted.

"Go on and change," he said, "while I lean here and remember how to breathe."

He did look wiped out. And totally gorgeous. I carefully pulled off the condom, then tucked him back into his jeans and buttoned them up for him. He cupped my cheek, pulling me close.

Man, I liked his kisses. These soft ones were the killers, too. The rough ones could get my blood boiling, but the gentleness in these made me think about love.

We sighed together, staring into each other's eyes. His smile was small and quiet as he stroked my cheek with his thumb.

"It's a shame cock-sucking isn't a degree, because you—"

I howled with laughter and covered his mouth so he couldn't say any more.

Chapter Ten

Ambushed

We ate breakfast at his place by ourselves, and then drove up to the garage. I hadn't really thought about it, but when we got out and Wes held my hand... That was gay, and everyone could see us. I didn't know what to do about that. I might've squeezed his hand, but my nerves kicked in and I started shaking.

I tried to follow his lead. Wes wasn't hiding anything, so maybe I didn't need to worry about it. But by the time we got to Ted inside the garage, I could barely breathe. When Wes figured out I was losing it, he pulled me into his arms. I was such a pathetic loser right then.

"What's wrong?"

I hid my face in his neck and whispered, "They're looking."

"Who?"

"Everyone."

"Are you... Do you not want people to know we're together?"

Dammit, I couldn't do that to him. I couldn't make him hide like his exes had.

"No, that's not it. I mean, it is, but... Wes, I got beat up because people *thought* I was gay." I gripped the back of his T-shirt and leaned on him. "What'll they do when they *know* I am?"

He hugged me tightly. "Aw, Mal. I know, that is scary. Some

places aren't safe to be out in. Here, though, it's okay. Hector doesn't care. And Ben—the guy who does the paint?—he's gay, too. We're pretty sure Leon's gay or bi, but he's not talking."

I pulled back to look at him. "So we can do this and touch and stuff, and it's okay? Nobody'll get upset?" That was actually really encouraging.

Wes slid his hand up under my shirt, stroking slow circles into my skin. I relaxed under his gentle touch. Even after such a short time, he knew me so well.

"Nobody'll get upset. This is fine." That grin of his peeked out. "Probably shouldn't have sex here or anything. Unless you like an audience."

I snorted. "So not sharing you."

"No?"

I looked up at him, frowning. "No."

Okay, apparently, I was a little possessive.

He smiled. "Good." He pressed his forehead to mine. "Me neither."

"Good." Warmth pooled in my belly. We didn't want anyone but each other.

He gave me a quick kiss, and then rubbed my arms up and down. "So, what do you want to break on Ted today?"

"Oh, shut up." I socked him in the kidney before moving away.

He laughed, smacking at my butt and heading for his tools.

And just like that, I was fine.

I got it that some places were safer than others for gay people— for us. I knew about marriage equality and how some states were passing laws to protect even more right for everybody under the rainbow. I knew about how soldiers could be out while serving instead of getting dishonorably discharged anymore. Sure, none of that had been on my radar much before, but I should pay more attention now. Those laws were about *me*, about *Wes*, and about what we could do together. If there were places in my own city where it wasn't safe to hold his hand, I needed to know about them.

But so I could avoid them, not fight to achieve acceptance. My God, I couldn't even *think* about confronting someone who hated us. I hadn't been able to stand up to high school boys, how could I do anything about church groups, school officials, or politicians? *No. Just no.*

So I concentrated on helping Wes sand rust spots and enjoyed my first day as an out gay guy in a safe place. It was a little bit surreal. I kept catching Wes looking at me, a familiar expression on his face, and it would hit me that he'd been looking at me like that all along. Wes *liked* me, even before I liked him back. He'd hoped for me to come around. When he'd touch me as he walked by or sneak a kiss, it was crazy amazing that this was *real*.

I was floating on a cloud all the way until I was outside the ice cream shop and on my way to the table Wes had snagged for us.

"Well, well, if it isn't Malcolm Small."

Fear slithered through me as my old nemesis Rick gave me that psycho smile of his. I stepped back instinctively but bumped into the glass door of the shop, trapped.

But wait a minute. This wasn't school. He hadn't caught me alone in a stairwell or a corner of the locker room. I was in public, and Wes was right over there, sitting at our table in the sun. Fine, he didn't see me right this second, but he was there, and so were a dozen other people. And I hadn't even done anything gay.

"Leave me alone." I moved to step around him, but he slammed me back against the door. I dropped my smoothie, splashing red all over the ground. Oh, God, it looked like blood.

"You don't talk to me like that, you little fa—"

I shoved at him. "Shut up! *You* don't talk to *me* like that. Not anymore!"

For a moment, I think we were both shocked at me fighting back. Not ready to take on a cause? Well, maybe I was, and I was gonna start with asshole bullies.

But Rick was a lot bigger than me and didn't stay shocked. He grabbed my throat with one hand. His other punched me in the gut. I couldn't holler and pain radiated everywhere. I tore at his hand around my neck and tried to twist away. He hit me in the ribs, the force of the blow knocking me free of his grip. I hit the ground on my hands and knees, gasping a breath only to scream it back out.

"Stupid little faggot."

I scrambled up, but I couldn't move fast enough. Rick grabbed my shirt and swung me around, sending me stumbling toward a picnic table. I put my hands out, tried to catch myself, but my head still collided with the corner. I heard a thunk and was dazed as I fell onto the grass.

"You son of a bitch!"

That was Wes. *Oh, thank God.*

My head throbbing, I rolled to my side and saw them.

Wes was hauling Rick away from me by his shirt, both their faces contorted with rage. I knew Rick's face, had seen it like that a thousand times, but seeing Wes that way was awful. He was smiles and teasing, not snarls and curses. And what if he got hurt, too? I had to make this stop.

"Wes, don't." I got on my knees and reached out to use the picnic table to get to my feet. My balance was shot and my knees really hurt.

A gray-haired woman caught my arm. "Sit down here, honey." She helped me onto the bench. "That's a nasty cut on your head there. You're bleeding."

I was suddenly aware of warmth seeping down my face.

"Shit," I muttered, my stomach roiling. "Can't do blood."

"I called the police," the ice cream guy said as he came out. "Should we stop them?"

"Doesn't look like he needs any help," some other guy said. "How's that one?"

"Not too bad," the woman said, reaching for me with a tissue. "You know how head wounds are, though."

Oh, God. Wounds. On my head. And when she pressed that tissue to me, it felt like she was pressing it against my brain.

"Wes!" I reached out for him as the world flipped over and went dark.

From very close by, Wes said, "No, you can treat him right where he is."

Someone pressed on my head, and pain made me jerk and gasp.

"Mal? Baby, you awake?"

I blinked and realized Wes held me against his chest, tipping my head back so he could see my face.

"Yeah. You okay?" Wait. Why wouldn't he be okay?

He smiled, his hand now cradling the side of my head. "Me? Yeah, honey, I'm fine. It's you we're worried about. You've been unconscious for, like, forever."

I noticed an older man, a paramedic, hovering. We were in the back of an ambulance with the doors open, facing outside. "Look over here, son," he said, shining a penlight in my eyes.

"I'm telling you," Wes said, "he fainted because he saw his blood. He does that."

Why was Wes acting so defensively?

"Just to be on the safe side," the paramedic said, "I recommend you go to the hospital so you know he doesn't have a concussion."

"My head does hurt," I muttered.

"Okay, Mal," Wes said, his voice softer. "We'll go to the hospital. But not in the ambulance."

"That's fine, son. Let me get the paperwork. How old are you?"

"He's eighteen."

Man, it was nice lying there against Wes, letting him take care of me. My head pounded, but it felt better when I leaned into Wes and closed my eyes. He was warm and solid and sure beneath my cheek. He smelled like sweat and spicy laundry detergent, and that was nice, too.

"Hey." He jostled me. "Mal, baby, keep your eyes open for a while, okay? For me?"

I opened my eyes. He looked scared.

"I'm okay, Wes," I whispered and managed a smile. "Just fuzzy."

He grinned at me and tugged on a curl. "You're always fuzzy."

"That's frizzy."

Suddenly, like with a snap of someone's fingers, things became a whole lot clearer. I grabbed a handful of Wes's shirt and looked around, my head throbbing as I scanned the area. "Where's Rick?"

"It's fine," Wes said softly, rubbing my arm. "I knocked him out, and he was arrested for assault."

I swung back to look at him, surprised. "You knocked him out?"

He chuckled self-consciously. "I think I'm lucky there were so many witnesses who saw what he did to you, or I'd be the one arrested."

I sat up enough to hug him, my words of thanks lodged in my throat as tears burned my eyes. He'd protected me, just like he'd said he would. I'd doubted him that first day, hadn't wanted his help. Now I squeezed him tightly and saw that the arm he'd had behind me was actually resting on the floor of the ambulance, an ice pack over his knuckles. My hero.

"Thank you, Wes," I managed to whisper into his ear.

He shivered, his arm tight around me. "I just wish I'd seen him earlier," he whispered back in a sad little voice.

I pulled away to look into his green eyes. "It could've been so much worse if you hadn't been here. Rick's broken my nose twice. Bruised ribs, broken fingers, dislocated—"

He tugged me back to him, both arms crushing me close. Wes shivered again, and I knew he cared about me. Who would've thought I'd have a knight in shining armor? Sir Wesley.

"I'll never let anyone get to you again, Mal." He swallowed hard. "Because I love you."

I gasped. *He loves me?*

"Excuse me," someone said, making me turn around as Wes relaxed his arms. It was a cop, a young blond guy with kind eyes. "Some of the witnesses are saying this was a hate crime."

A hate crime? *Oh, my God.* I looked at Wes.

"What did he say to you, Mal? Anything about being gay?"

I swallowed hard and nodded. "Rick called me a… He called me a faggot before he hit me." I touched my forehead and discovered a bandage tapped there.

The cop asked, "And who provoked the confrontation?"

"He did."

"Do you know him?"

"We went to high school together." Were they always hate crimes? Was bullying a hate crime? "This isn't the first time he's attacked me either," I said to maybe find out.

"Did you report the other times?"

And there was the problem. "No, my parents wouldn't let me."

He blinked at me like he couldn't imagine why. "Are they taking you to the hospital?"

"No, but we're going on our own."

He handed me a business card. "Have them fax over the medical report so we can add it to the file, and give me a call if you want to add anything else."

I nodded and thanked him, tucking the card into my pocket as I finally stood up from Wes's lap. Wes kept his hands on me, offering support.

"Mal, I already talked to them, but I didn't know that part of things." His green eyes were round and worried. "Honey, they're going to write up that you're gay."

I nodded. "I don't really care." I looked up into his concerned eyes. "Rick needs to be punished for trying to hurt me because of that. And... And I'm not going to be a victim anymore."

The pride in his smile made me blush. But he wasn't just proud of me, was he? Because Wes Kinney loved me.

Chapter Eleven

Sit Down or Stand Up?

We went to an urgent care facility instead of a hospital emergency room since nothing about my injuries screamed emergency to me. I figured that if I didn't need an ambulance, I'd probably end up waiting for hours and hours to be seen if I went to a hospital. Besides, I was familiar with this urgent care place since I'd been here three times since January.

I waited near the entrance while Wes parked the car. He'd said to go sign in, but when seven pairs of eyes snapped to me as I walked in, I... Well, that old feeling of being exposed chilled my blood and had me shivering because this time wasn't the same as last time. Then, I'd just said it was a fight at school. But now? Was I really going to explain to these people that I'd been beaten up for being gay? I gulped so hard I nearly choked myself.

What had I been thinking? Just because I didn't want to be a victim anymore didn't mean I had to come out. Right? Because everyone was looking at me, trying to guess what happened, and any minute my *boyfriend* would come in here and it might get obvious. This wasn't a safe space like Hector's garage.

I wanted to go home. Turning around, I bumped right into Wes.

He steadied me with hands on both my shoulders. "Did you sign in?"

Staring up at his face, I shook my head.

A little wrinkle formed between his brows, and then it smoothed out again. He smiled patiently and his hands rubbed up and down my arms. "Breathe, Mal. It's okay."

"But is it?" I glanced over my shoulder. A woman reading on her phone quickly looked away. "I'm not feeling so brave about...about coming out anymore."

"Regardless of what you tell anyone, we have every right to be here." There was conviction in his tone, but more than that, it was him walking away toward the sign-in window that made me follow. I didn't want to be alone with this target on me now and I already knew Wes could handle so much more than I could.

I hesitated again when I had the pen poised over the sign-in sheet. Did I want to give them my name? Why couldn't it be anonymous?

Wes casually leaned on the ledge beside the clipboard and whispered, "If you don't want them to know it's you, use my name and I'll give you my insurance card."

"Isn't that fraud?" I kept my eyes on the paper.

"It's either use yours or mine, honey."

I sighed. I'd have to use insurance because I couldn't afford this without it, and then they'd know who I was anyway. "I'll just use mine. My parents won't notice."

I filled in the few boxes of information before obediently following Wes over to find a seat. The room was fairly large, but the double rows of connected seats made it seem way smaller. Thankfully, it also wasn't crowded. Just the reading woman, a really fat guy in loose clothing, a ragged looking mom with two bouncy kids, and two guys in dusty overalls who might have been sleeping.

Plus there was the cop who came out from the exam area to loiter near the door. That was new. I couldn't remember seeing a cop in full gear doing any kind of security before. Maybe it was a good thing.

Wes leaned back in his seat and confiscated my armrest with his elbow. In that same quiet tone, he asked, "You have a co-pay for something like this?"

"Yeah, I think it's fifty." I took out my wallet only to find I had fifteen dollars.

Wes got out his. "I can make up the difference."

"You don't—"

"Hush." He handed over the two twenties he had.

I tucked them in my wallet, and then put that away, slumping in my seat. I'd pay him back somehow. Maybe I could get a job in secret. It wasn't like my parents knew what I did all day while they were at work. If I left after they did and got back before they did, then I'd never have to say anything. I could ride my bike back and forth. Or take the city bus. Or maybe Wes wouldn't mind dropping me off and picking me up sometimes.

"How you feeling?"

I turned in my seat enough to face him, putting my back to the rest of the room. "Knees hurt, my stomach aches, my head's throbbing, but, you know, I'll live."

Wes gave me that tiny smile and reached up to bop my nose. It was cute and affectionate and, for a moment, I just smiled back at the sweet look in his eyes.

"Hey!"

I flinched and so did Wes.

Down a few seats and in the opposite row was that sloppy, fat guy wedged into a seat and leaning toward us. He looked pissed, his pale skin turning red.

"You some of those gays?"

Oh, my God. I looked at Wes as my heartbeat galloped. Wes glared at the guy.

"Goddamnit. I can't stand you little fags coming in here for your goddamn blood tests." He shoved himself up onto his feet, clothes billowing and fat jiggling. "What you got, the AIDS? I am not sitting here with that shit floating around." He stomped over to the cop.

I scooted to the edge of my seat. A quick look at Wes showed me he was still settled in, arms crossed and leaning back. The only things that said he wasn't happy were his narrowed eyes and hard scowl.

When I looked back at the guy and the cop, I saw the cop walking toward the check-in window. The fat guy looked smug as hell. He stayed where he was but crossed his flabby arms over his man boobs while he smiled toward us like he had succeeded at something.

Were we going to get kicked out? Could they do that?

"Wes," I whispered.

He shook his head, staring past me. "We're *not* leaving. We have every right to be here, same as anyone else. And if they dare, they'll find out just what a kick-ass civil rights lawyer my dad is."

I gulped and looked again at the cop. He was walking toward us now. I couldn't read the expression on his face, it was so neutral. Would he back down at the threat of a lawyer? I stood up and stepped to the other side of Wes. He could talk if he wanted to, but I was going to run if the cop tried to throw us out.

"Hey, guys," the cop said and now he smiled a little. "They've got an open exam room, but the doctor's not available yet. Would you like to wait in there?"

My mouth fell open and all I could do was blink at him. They were letting us cut in line? They were getting us out of the waiting area? I looked down at Wes.

His eyes searched my face. I didn't know what he was looking for. I just wanted to leave one way or another. Wes sighed before saying, "That's fine."

Neither of us said anything as we followed the cop to the door to the exam area. He opened it, and then a short, brunette nurse kept it open for us from the other side. She had a much bigger and more welcoming smile. Just before the door closed, I heard that fat asshole holler his outrage again. Guess this wasn't the door he'd expected us to go through. Maybe they'd ask *him* to leave for being a belligerent jerk.

The nurse settled us in a tiny room with an exam table, a guest chair, and a wheeled stool. An ugly pastel print of a pond and a hand sanitizing gel dispenser were the only things on the white walls. Based on that pond, I was pretty sure I'd been in this room before. There was another one with a field and a deer's silhouette in the—

"Sometimes you have to stand up, Mal."

From my seat on the exam table, I looked down at Wes sitting in the chair. He went from looking at the floor to at me, a sort of sad expression on his face.

I didn't know what he meant. "Stand up?"

"Stand up, fight back, resist. It's easier to duck and run, but then nothing will ever change." He frowned and shook his head like he was disappointed. "I thought you understood that when you pressed charges against what's-his-name."

He *was* disappointed...in me. I blushed hot and looked back at the painting. "That's different."

"How so?"

"He'd already attacked?"

"So'd fatso out there."

I stared at my hands. "It just didn't feel safe. And the cop—"

"Which is why we stand up for ourselves."

"But we didn't have to."

He sighed loudly. "If I'd been here by myself, I'd have stayed out there. I'd have told the cop I wasn't going to get sent away just because some bigot didn't like having me in the same room with him."

"I thought you *were* going to do something like that. Why didn't you?"

Before he even said it, I could see the answer on his face. He didn't because of me.

"I was afraid of what you'd do if I did. You looked like you were about to run away."

Slumping down, I stared at my knees. Cowards ran away. That's what he meant. Was I a coward? I'd felt like one before, but I'd also thought I'd been getting braver and stronger since knowing Wes. I'd fought Rick, hadn't I? But maybe it'd been reactionary and not really taking a stand. He'd cornered me, and any trapped animal fought back, even squirrels.

Wes came over and cupped my face, tilting my head up so he could press a kiss to my forehead. "Baby, I'm not criticizing. Not really. Maybe, right now, your first instinct is to run. And that's okay because you've only been out for a little while." He made me look him in the eye. "But what if you stayed and backed me up next time? Like I'm your backup?"

"Oh." I blinked a few times as that clicked into place in my head. "I could do that. Actually, I was going to do that when you met Rick in your driveway that first day." I shrugged. "I mean, either jump in or call 911."

Wes smiled and gave me a quick kiss. "Either way, that's taking a stand."

What I'd done before when faced with these conflicts wasn't going to work anymore. Well, maybe sometimes. I was sure Wes didn't mean for me to stay and fight when I was outnumbered and blood might spill. But I could raise my voice and demand...equality. We should've stayed out in the waiting room with everyone else. My stomach clenched as I squeezed my eyes closed. It hadn't occurred to me to fight for that.

I wrapped my arms around his shoulders and kissed him. "I'll do better," I whispered against his lips. "I promise."

"I know, baby. I'm sorry if that hurt you. I couldn't think how else to say it."

I shook my head. "You woke me up. I didn't understand, but I do now."

I just wasn't sure what to do with this new knowledge.

Chapter Twelve

Learning by Doing Him

When we left the urgent care facility, the fat guy wasn't there anymore. I wanted to know, but I didn't ask if he'd been kicked out. While Wes ignored the cop's smile and nod, I'd waved in a show of thanks. He'd thought he'd been doing the right thing for us, and that was okay with me. I realized then that I wanted stand up for my equality when someone did the *wrong* thing, not when they tried to do the right one.

When we got back to Wes's place, we both took some painkillers for our bruises. My throat was sore, neck stiff, and Wes's knuckles were angry looking but not really damaged exactly. I had a butterfly bandage on my forehead—no need for stitches, thank goodness. Since we both smelled like the garage and sweat and now hospital grade antiseptic, we decided to take a shower.

Despite the pain and trauma of the day's events, I couldn't help grinning. Showering was such a normal thing to do, but now I was going to get naked, wet, and soapy with another person. One who thought I was hot. How many showers had I taken and gotten myself off while thinking about someone being in there with me?

But when Wes looked back at me after adjusting the water, he was trying to hide a frown.

I groaned. "What'd I do wrong now?"

He huffed a laugh. "Nothing."

I planted my hands on my hips and frowned at him.

Wes came close to kiss me gently. "I don't like seeing you covered in bruises." He petted my hair back and stared into my eyes. "You've been hurt enough," he whispered and the skin around his eyes got red. Like he might cry?

I shook my head. "I'm okay. This isn't so bad."

He ducked his head and sniffed, so I wrapped my arms around his neck and pressed us together from cheeks to knees. My heart beat hard because this was someone really, truly caring about me. It hurt him to see me injured. That was just monumental to me. It meant love. Wes loved me. And since it would have devastated me if Rick hurt Wes, that must have meant...

"I love you, too," I whispered.

He pulled back to look at me intent and close again. I knew what he was looking for when his green eyes searched mine. If there was a way to let him see my love for him in my gaze, I didn't know how to do it. But when he smiled, it was bright and happy. Maybe he'd seen my love after all. This was his face knowing I loved him back. He'd never been more beautiful.

I drew him down for more kisses, and he wrapped me in his arms. He had a hand on my shoulder blade and one on my ass, keeping us pressed tight together. I started getting hard, but it was a slow, easy kind of feeling. Just heat spreading lazily outward, and I didn't need more or faster. I only wanted to stay close to him, touch him.

To *show him* I loved him. *Oh, yes.* That was what I wanted to do now.

Easing away, I took his hand and led him into the shower. The water was perfectly warm and the way it tapped at my skin and slithered down added to the sensations arousing me. I tipped my head back and wet my hair while Wes closed the curtain. When I opened my eyes again, I easily recognized the sexual need in Wes's expression. I grinned at him and turned around to get the shampoo, and then peeked at him over my shoulder.

He stared at my ass. I was pretty sure he knew exactly what to do with that part of me. I took a few deep breaths as I turned back around and concentrated on washing my hair. Rationally, it was, of course, a good thing that Wes wanted all kinds of sex with me. But up my ass? It seemed like a gross place to want to be. Could anyone really clean it that thoroughly?

Except... Well, putting his penis in my mouth wouldn't seem like the best idea either, but I'd liked that a heck of a lot. Liked it when he'd sucked on mine, too, of course. All that wet and heat and pressure was amazing. If sticking his dick up my butt would feel as good or maybe even better... Okay, so I had some thinking to do, but I had a ton of questions, too. I rinsed my hair and rolled my eyes behind my closed lids. That be a fun conversation. *So what's it like to have a penis stuffed up your ass, Wes?*

Behind me, I heard a growl. "Do you have any idea how much you're teasing me right now?"

I pushed my hair from my eyes and turned to look at him. He had soap suds all over him and stroked one hand up and down his stiff cock. I grinned. "Oops?"

He snorted and made me switch places with him. I picked up the soap and watched him wet his hair while the white bubbles glided down his body. I might not have meant tease him, but seeing his muscles flex while he unconsciously posed under the spray was definitely erotic. I reached down with a soap-slick hand and slowly jacked myself while taking stock of his every dip and groove of muscle, and all the hairy and flushed patches of his skin.

While there were awesome things to see, I'd spent way too long looking in from the outside. He was here, he loved me, and it was fine with him if I moved in close and touched him. I had a flash of worry as I got closer. What if now wasn't the time? What if he wasn't actually interested despite the physical evidence? But he'd say something and he wouldn't crush me doing it. I could trust in that.

My dick made first contact, poking him in his butt cheek. *How apropos.* Wes looked over his shoulder, already grinning, so I held my dick up and stepped in against him. I slid my arms around him and could hear the hum in his sigh over the sound of the shower. He leaned against me, tipping his head back, and bent his knees while I glided my fingers all over his chest and belly. With a little shimmy of his hips, he got my dick into the groove of his ass and groaned as he rocked his hips to rub us together.

My mouth popped open, but I was too shocked to gasp or speak.

I hadn't even considered that Wes might want me to do him. I'd figured he'd know about being the do-ee from being the do-er. Did I want to, you know, fuck him?

I kind of thought I did.

"Let's see how you like this," he said with wicked look over his shoulder.

I gasped when he pointed my stiff cock down and then guided me between this thighs. Was this... Did he... *Now?*

"Just hug me, Mal, and rock those lean hips of yours."

I caught on real quick when he pressed his legs together, trapping my dick between them. There was a tight space where thighs and ass cheeks came together. When I bumped forward mostly in surprise, I was pretty sure I poked the back of his scrotum with my cockhead.

"Oh, my God." I wrapped both arms around his torso and rocked my hips back and forth, driving into that spot in an imitation of exactly what I'd been thinking about.

I was fucking Wes, and the *sort of* part didn't matter.

By the sounds coming out of him and the way his hand kept pace on his cock, I knew he liked doing this. My height was in the length of my legs, so we lined up nicely. I couldn't kiss higher than the base of his neck, but if I used my teeth, he groaned like that was the best thing ever.

I'd been after something sweet to reconnect us, but this was happening and I *wanted* it. I even pushed Wes's hand off himself and took over jacking him. I wanted to be the entire reason he got off right now. He seemed to be cool with that because he braced his hands on the wall and moved to rub his ass against me, thrusting his cock through my fist.

I could barely catch a breath between the warm spray hitting my face and the hard pace of my heart. My own moans combined with his sounded so hot. We were going to set the water on fire.

When Wes cried out, head flung back, ass tilted up, I exclaimed, too, because his legs and cheeks tightened on me to the point I couldn't keep thrusting. His cock pulsed in my hand, and mine shot against his sac. While I panted through it, he made these whining sounds like that orgasm had been ripped out of him. I pressed my face to his shoulder blade and smiled.

After a while, Wes spread his legs, bracing himself up. My knees felt a little wobbly, too, as I backed away. I petted a hand up and down his back.

He turned around. "You sure know how to make bath time fun."

I laughed until he got a palm full of soap and washed between his legs where I'd come all over him. It was so dirty sexy. I could've beat on my chest and howled from the primal triumph. I'd claimed my man...and I wanted him again.

"Finish up," he said. "I'm not done with you."

You bet your ass. I grinned.

He got out of the shower, and I rushed through washing the essentials before stepping out, too. A strange intimate feeling flowed through me while watching him dry off. I could be here, was expected to be right here, as he did that. It was a perfectly normal, boring task, but it felt special to me.

He gave me a towel, hung his up on a rack, and then used a wide-toothed comb on his hair. He used the same anti-frizz hair product I had at home, but he needed way more of it. While my hair was just fat curls that would corkscrew if I let them, his was that wild mane of dense waves and sort of kinked up curls. Soft, though. I knew his hair was amazingly soft. It was a really cool, intimate detail I was allowed to have now.

We got into his bed, facing each other on our sides. Being like this, naked and just relaxing, was so perfect. No worries and— Well, I guess I had one worry and maybe now was a good time to talk about it. He'd answer and not think I was stupid or anything for not knowing this. I was pretty sure, anyway.

"Wes?"

"Hmm?" He watched one of my curls wind around his finger.

"Can we... Can we talk about... You know, um..." I licked my lips, and then forced out, "What we just did?"

He frowned a bit. "What did we just do?"

I sighed. "In the shower?"

"Oh. Intercrural sex."

"What?"

He chuckled. "Sex between the thighs."

I blinked a few times. "It's got a name?"

"And can be traced back to the Ancient Greeks." He waggled his eyebrows at me. "A favorite past time of the boys at those old British boarding schools, too."

Mouth open and brows furrowed, I stared at him. I needed to learn about gay sex research going back thousands of years? And boarding schools? "I... Well, okay."

He tucked his fingers up into the curls at the base of my neck, gently flexing and petting me. "Did you like it?"

"Oh, *yeah*." I grinned even as my cheeks heated.

"Me, too. It's like anal in a lot of ways, but you don't have to worry about all the prep." He pecked a kiss on my lips. "Feels amazing from both sides, so if you want me to do you, just say the word."

I wasn't frowning now, but my mouth hung open again. I might have a stroke from the blushing. Well, that was... Okay, maybe that was a good way to sort of try the whole anal thing without actually doing it. Especially if there was some kind of awful prep to worry about with anal.

Wes's expression was only a little teasing when he said, "Do you have any idea what I'm talking about?"

"Um..." I gulped, but answered honestly. "No, not really."

"That's okay. How about this? Ever play back here?" His fingers slid down my spine and right into the crack of my ass. "Teased this when you're getting yourself off?"

I shook my head, a little mesmerized by the tickle of his fingertip finding my hole. "Not there, exactly. In front of...there. You know? It kind of feels—" I gasped when he pulled a bit and a shiver skittered up my back.

"Your perineum? Get a good rub going there and it's almost like pegging your prostate."

Okay, I didn't know that smooth patch of skin behind my balls had a name, but I recognized the other name. Mostly because of a cancer screening thing on Twitter once, but I'd looked it up and knew what it was all about. Biologically speaking, anyway. I'd never tried to...peg it.

Wes's finger pushed into me just a little, and I squeezed on it as I gasped. His face was wicked delight while he just left his fingertip in me. I kind of wanted to make him move but not get out, while at the same time I wasn't sure I wanted him to know I wanted that. I made myself unclench. He wiggled, and I tightened up and gasped all over again.

He leaned in and spoke between kisses to my nose and cheeks. "If you're curious, baby, I'll show you anything you want to know."

"Oh…" I was breathless and my eyes kept fluttering shut without permission as his finger now stroked and teased, little circles and nudges. "Okay. I… Okay."

"You can touch me, too."

That got my eyes popping open. He wanted me to… Well, alright. I couldn't look at his face while I did, though. I stared at the hair between his pecs while I glided my hand down his back like he had done. *Hell.* This was completely awkward. Like a weird medical exam or something. *And this would be the furrow of no return that leads to our puckered friend the anus.* I gulped and sort of left my finger there, like maybe it would know what to do.

Wes snort-chuckled. I looked up to see his eyes half-lidded while he bit his lip and totally failed to hide looking like he was about to laugh his…ass off. I rolled my eyes and took my damn finger back. He let his laughter out and grabbed me up, wrapping his arms around me and rolling onto his back, me flopping on top of him.

"Shut up," I grumbled.

He rolled so we were side-by-side again and tapered down to another snort before pecking my nose. He was so adorable sometimes. I grinned despite myself.

"You know," he said, "it is more than just the physical that I like. Don't get me wrong, that's fantastic, but I love being wrapped around my partner. Being held and holding." He gave me a squeeze. "Even when it gets crazy hot and all I can concentrate on is coming so hard, I'm still right there and tangled up with someone I care about."

That took my breath away again. "I-I wanna do that."

"Cool." He massaged the back of my neck. "Don't worry, Mal. We'll do whatever whenever. On our time."

I took a breath and sighed it out. "Thank you."

He nodded, and then nuzzled my cheek on the way to my neck.

It felt like a good time for me to say, "I love you, Wes."

He whispered, "Say it again."

"I love you, Wes."

He leaned back a little and... Oh, that smile. It was all mine.

Chapter Thirteen

Pornification

Going from the sanctuary of Wes's bedroom to the sterility of my parents' house for dinner was becoming more and more depressing. I lost my smile when I came through the front door and my father gave me that bland look over the edge of his newspaper. And for the first time, I recognized the loss of happiness and an increase of...caution. I watched my father to figure out his mood so I'd know how to behave around him. I knew him reading the paper before dinner meant he would react to the stories he read and his mood could be anything. I realized right then that I was worried about which way he could go.

Was I able to see this now because it wasn't like this with the Kinneys? I might've been nervous over there the other night, but I hadn't felt guarded, like I waited for someone to snap. Here? Depending on what my father read in the paper, the whole night could go in any number of directions. He could come to the table pissed off about something he'd read, rant about it, and I'd be quiet and not interrupt so he wouldn't aim his anger at me. And...well, my mother did the same thing, didn't she? Neither of us wanted his attention when he got like that.

I walked into the kitchen to wash my hands and only then remembered how I might look right now, after the fight, when my mother turned around. The bruises were stark on my pale skin and Wes had replaced the butterfly bandage on my forehead when it bled a tiny bit. My mother's brown eyes widened as she exclaimed, "Malcolm!"

"I'm fine." But it was nice to see her sudden concern.

"Did your father see you yet?"

Oh. Not concerned for *me.*

"Sort of."

She sighed, her eyes cataloguing me. As I stared at her, I couldn't help comparing her to Mrs. Kinney. They couldn't have been more different. Mrs. Kinney smiled a lot and seemed to enjoy everything. My mother frowned a lot and seemed to be waiting for a problem to pop up.

I was, again, the problem.

She sighed, but it didn't ease anything about her. "Go wash up and try not to—" She cut herself off, her gaze on the space behind me.

I tensed right along with her as I turned around. My father stood there. He didn't have anything in common with Mr. Kinney either. And though I looked a lot like my father, I was determined not to have those permanent frown lines all over my face. I had a photo in my room of my father smiling, so I knew he could do it, but he didn't very often. Definitely not right now.

"Another incident at that garage?" he said with a glare.

"Um, no." My face burned, but was it in shame or anger? "I was attacked."

He shook his head and sighed. "If you can't avoid these conflicts, Malcolm, take a self-defense class. I'm sick of having to explain to people why you're constantly injured." His squinted eyes raked over me. "You're eighteen now. Stop getting into scrapes with boys and start acting like a man."

I clenched my jaw and avoided looking at him. Definitely anger. Damn him.

He walked out. "Hurry up with dinner."

The microwave dinged, and my mother flew into action. I didn't give a damn about the possible condition of my hands anymore and got things out to set the table.

Start acting like a man. My father had been saying that to me since my birthday in January. The crazy part was that he had never once offered any advice on how to do that. What did he even mean? And I couldn't ask. I already knew that much. I'd tried observing other men—teachers, other fathers, random men on the street—but there didn't seem to be any specific things they did that I could start doing.

That was, I'd never seen one of them stand up to bullies. Until Wes. He'd done that brilliantly. Could I maybe learn to be a man from him? My father would lose his mind if he knew I was going to pattern myself after a gay man. I'd heard plenty of my father's rants about what the homosexual agenda was doing to ruin America.

I dropped a spoon, the clang of it hitting a knife echoing. I couldn't ever be like Wes. Not in this family. I'd known I couldn't ever tell my parents I was gay, but suddenly it really hit me. My father would freak. I'd be one of those kids who got kicked out of the house. And because I was eighteen, there wouldn't be any kind of child services thing to help me. I'd be completely on my own.

Well, no, not really. I picked up the spoon and straightened it out before continuing on with setting the table. Now that I was with Wes, I wouldn't be alone. He'd help me. Maybe even his parents would help me. Wes had an apartment once, so maybe he would get another one and I could go with him. I'd lose my parents, but really, that wasn't much of a loss—they didn't seem to like me much anymore.

Except... What if I lost Wes?

I put a hand over my suddenly racing heart and tried to take a deep breath. Oh, my God, that would be horrible. I'd have nothing. No one. If my parents found out about me and if Wes ever dumped me, I'd be ruined in every possible way. How could I ever survive that? And it could totally happen. One slip up with my father or... Well, how did people lose boyfriends? I'd never cheat on or steal from Wes or anything like that. I wasn't an arguer and I didn't start fights. He'd have to get tired of me being with me. I gasped and turned a chair around so I could sit and drop my head between my knees.

Getting tired of me probably wouldn't take that long. I mean, we'd been together for, like, a few days and I'd already seriously disappointed him by being a wuss. And then I'd let him know just how completely inexperienced I was in everything sex-related. Wes couldn't possibly want to be with someone who was afraid of everything and didn't know anything.

I sat up and smacked my shoulder on the edge of the table as I did. But that was okay. It was like a punch of encouragement. A painful one, but it gave me an idea: I'd just have to improve myself. I'd start doing things that made me afraid, but I'd push through the fear and be tough. I'd watch more porn and learn whatever it was gay guys could do with each other so I could know things. Then it could be me telling Wes about some sex thing that would make his eyes bug and his dick spring up.

Yeah. I'm gonna do that.

I stood up, ready to go to my room and get started, but my mother came in with the first bowl of food and recruited me to fetch the rest. So my plan to become a gay sex expert would have to wait a while.

Sitting through dinner got harder—literally—when Wes started texting me and my phone kept vibrating in my pocket. I knew it was him; Wes was the only person who had my number aside from the parents. I'd put my phone in my front pocket, so the three vibrations with every text was nice and close to all the parts of me still humming from earlier in the day. By the time the fourth text came through, my dick was straining against my fly and I could barely eat. Amazingly, I still had plenty of blood available to push up a blush, too.

I hoped Wes wasn't expecting a reply right away, like something urgent had happened, because there was no way I was going to interrupt my father's speech on Democrats in Congress wasting everyone's tax money on...something. Immigration? Then he said, "That El Camino across the street is the perfect example. Just look at those people moving into our neighborhood, bold as you please. Like they have the right."

Good grief, did my father think the Kinneys were illegals from Mexico because of Wes's car? My father's shame in not being the whitest he could be was getting crazy if he was accusing other white people of being Mexican now. And maybe the Kinneys had all kinds of ethnicities going on in their blood, but it just made them gorgeous people. Carter and Katie were going to be hot when they grew up, no doubt about that, and I already knew everything about Wes was incendiary. Who cared what races resulted in that?

"Can I be excused?"

Only when I was met by sudden silence did I realize I'd just interrupted my father. At the dinner table. In the middle of a rant. My mother looked at me like I'd lost my mind, and my father was clearly shocked.

Well, I'd wanted to be fearless. And that definitely got rid of my boner. I gulped, but looked over at my father. Maybe this was a man thing to do because he blinked, frowned, and then waved his arm and sent a green bean bit sailing across the room. "Fine. Go to your room. No dessert."

For a second, I only stared. Act like a man, but get punished like a child? I resisted rolling my eyes as I stood up and walked toward the stairs. I supposed this was still a success since I'd been bold and now had what I wanted. And if I could stand up this little bit to my father, maybe more of doing that with other people wouldn't be so bad.

I closed my bedroom door behind me and took my phone out of my pocket. Heat pooled in my groin as I thought of Wes holding and kissing me before I'd left his room. I wanted to be back there. When I called up his texts, I sighed all dreamy.

Close my eyes and feel you here.

Sigh and wish you were, my friend.

Love you still and deeply.

Come to me again.

Poetry. Wes had written me poetry! I read the words over and over again, standing there in my bedroom, and feeling all gooey inside. Oh, that third line was like an arrow to my heart. A sappy, squishy, pink-feathered arrow. *Jeez.*

I sat down on my bed and wrote back the only two words I could think of since that last line sounded like he wanted me to meet up with him again.

When? Where?

Probably tomorrow. Maybe we'd go work on Ted some more. What if I suggested a movie? Like a date. We hadn't done that. Well, maybe going to the garage and ice cream afterward was kind of our dates. And sex in his room. Wouldn't mind repeating that part of our dates. A lot.

My phone vibrated, making me twitch. I'd set it on my fly. Wow, I was turning into a pervert unconsciously or something. But I smiled, reading his replies as they arrived.

I want you under the trees, under the stars.

Laid bare before me, mine to take, to love.

Come to me in darkness, as we tick into tomorrow.

I want you under the trees, under the stars.

How was that for a super pretty way of asking for sex outdoors? I snickered. The words were lovely, still poetry and kind of like song lyrics actually. But this was Wes asking me to meet him at midnight outside somewhere and then get naked.

Could I do that?

Okay, yes, this was another chance to push boundaries and not be scared, but really? Sex outside? That was kind of serious. People got arrested for that.

Kind of exciting, though. I bit my bottom lip and shrugged at myself. I could *try*. I'd give myself points for... *Oh*. Sneaking out. *Hell*. I'd have to sneak out because no way was my father going to be fine with me going out like someone normal would. Even if I told him I had a date, that would just open up the door for a whole barrage of questions and, possibly, a demand to meet *her*. So no, I'd have to sneak out.

My hands shook as I texted Wes that I would do it, meet him outside at midnight. He sent me back a brightly smiling face and wrote, *Come to the park. I'll be waiting*.

I reached down and rubbed at my dick because it was about the only part of me totally on board with any of this. Apparently the conviction to improve myself and actually doing it were very different things. I sighed and sent Wes an OK before setting my phone aside. Maybe the thing to do now was focus on my other objective, the porn as education one. Might as well use Mal Junior's current enthusiasm. Then tonight I could make some wickedly sexy move and rock Wes's world.

I'd never really watched porn before. I'd accidentally stumbled across a site now and then while looking for other things, but I'd never stayed. It was embarrassing. I didn't know why. It wasn't like I was peeping into people's bedrooms; they knew this stuff was on here, if they hadn't actually uploaded it themselves. I needed to know these things, though, so I pushed through the embarrassment and toggled some choices to say I was male and interested in men.

"Whoa," I whispered, and then covered my mouth as my eyes went wide. An ad—not even a video but an advertisement—showed a guy getting his mouth pounded by a big cock and then it was up his ass and still slamming into him. His eyes were watering for one, and then his whole face was scrunched up for the other. Was that...normal? I couldn't stop watching, but my erection was fading fast.

Okay, maybe there were levels to this sort of thing. Like skills or maybe, um, preferences? And that wasn't for me. I grabbed some sticky notes and covered up that continuously replaying ad. Then a few more, too. I needed, like, the beginner videos. Intro to Gay Sex. There had to be a few of those somewhere. I gripped the mouse like a lifeline and forced my eyes to look around the page.

A search box. *All right.* I clicked on it and it opened up with what were possibly categories or popular searches. I didn't know what some of them meant—Bears, FTM, DP—but there was one called Barely Legal. I figured that meant my age and so maybe that's where the newbie vids were. I clicked on it.

Through the sticky notes, I could see a whole new crop of flashy ads, but I ignored them. At least my concealing efforts were holding true.

So, okay. Tiny still shots of the videos, titles, dates, star ratings, and weird usernames covered the page. Most of the guys did look about my age. Which to choose? *Oh, wait.* That one said "virgin" in the title. I hesitated, took a fortifying breath, and clicked on it.

Well, at least it didn't start playing right away. I had to move the sticky notes around, though, because there was a whole line of ads across the top now with— Was that *two dicks* plunging in and out of— *Nope, I don't want to know.* I slapped notes up until I'd practically framed the monitor. I was *not* ready for the advanced class. *My God.*

Except... Okay, the whole title of this one was "Breeding my virgin ass." I whined behind my hand and closed my eyes for a moment. I could guess what that meant, but did they—we—really call it that? Breeding? That seemed sort of insensitive or maybe misogynistic. But the guy bent over looked the same as the photo on the side of the user who'd uploaded this video, so maybe it was fine since he was okay with calling it that. I certainly wasn't going to, though. *No way.*

I read the brief description written by someone who wasn't fond of using vowels for some reason. Looked like this was going to be his first time getting fucked. Did I like that word? Not really. I'd only ever heard it used as a curse or a threat. Why couldn't I just call it sex? Well, all of it was sex, wasn't it, so... Oh, Wes had called it anal. Yeah, that was direct, but kind of clinical. *I shall now insert my penis into your anal passage. Ew. Very no.*

So, fine. I sighed. Fucked. I was going to watch this guy get fucked.

I clicked the play button. At least the virgin seemed happy about this.

The volume blasted. I flinched and nearly tossed the mouse as I scrambled to turn the volume down. I paused the video and went searching for my earbuds. That was safer. I got up and locked my bedroom door. Much safer.

Ready again, I clicked play. Even with my earbuds in and the volume adjusted, I couldn't understand them. *And that would be because they're not speaking English, Malcolm.* I rolled my eyes at myself. Did it matter what language they spoke? I doubted either of them was going to talk through this, giving instructions. It was probably dirty talk. I could do without that.

I jumped when the one guy slapped the other's butt. They laughed, so maybe that was like what athletes did. Or it was some kind of Russian version of a pre-fuck greeting. I tried to focus. I was actually nervous, the skittery jumpy feeling making me twitch involuntarily. Good thing Wes hadn't suggested we watch porn together. At least, I was pretty sure couples might watch porn sometimes. I'd seen them do that on TV once, before my father blocked all the premium movie channels.

At the end of the guys' opening conversation, the one guy bent over, bracing himself on the arm of a plain brown couch. Since he was the one who'd uploaded the video, I figured he was Sergei. I decided to call the other one Ivan just because he needed a name. Ivan gave Sergei a couple butt cheek squeezes while saying something that made Sergei nod. Must have been asking if he was ready, because then Ivan picked up a bottle and squirted out some clear gel. That was lube. I knew that because someone had thought it would be funny to put three bottles of it in my gym locker once and— *Stop*. No thinking of that crap. Not now.

I cleared my throat when the video suddenly showed a really— really—close up shot of Ivan sticking his glistening finger into Sergei's asshole. There was some moaning. Ivan's finger went in and out a few times and then it looked like Sergei was moving his ass back and forth. That probably meant it felt good. He liked it and wanted more? *All right*. I put my chin in my hand and leaned my elbow on the desk when Ivan pushed another finger in with the first one. Sergei flinched. Must not like two so much. Or had to get used to more? Oh, maybe this was the prep Wes mentioned. Assholes were tight, right? Maybe this was all about loosening it up. That made sense.

By the time Ivan was sailing four greased fingers in and out of Sergei's red asshole, I was squirming a little in my chair. Was this hot? No, not to me. The squelching sound Ivan's fingers made going in and out of Sergei's ass was not exactly a turn-on either. Now the camera moved around—making me realize there had to be another person in the room holding that camera—and though Sergei was a pretty good-looking guy he was skinny and had awful teeth. Ivan was hotter for having more muscles and somewhat better teeth, but *meh*. Wes was way hotter than either of them.

Oh, here we go. Ivan took his fingers out and— Okay, that was a weird view of Sergei's open asshole kind of pulsing. Was that good? If it was Wes's ass doing that, would it be good? I shook my head. No idea. It looked like a butt that had had something big shoved— And there went Ivan's big-headed, wetly shiny cock poking right into Sergei's red and puffy-looking hole. I gulped as somebody let loose a long, low moan. A shiver slithered down my spine. That was

115

a good sound.

But more sucking, wet sounds as Ivan started moving were not so good. It kind of sounded gross. I didn't want to turn the volume down any more because I'd finally found something that turned me on in their moaning. Or maybe it was just Sergei moaning since Ivan was biting his lip now as he thrust his hips faster and faster. The slap of his groin hitting Sergei's ass cheeks wasn't bad, but now they were doing that pounding thing. Sergei's face was all tightened up like he might not be happy about this part.

Well, he couldn't be too unhappy about it with his cock all stiff under him like that. It and his balls bobbed and swayed with every plunge of Ivan's dick. Not a bad visual there. And then Sergei was obviously pushing back, meeting Ivan's thrusts, so it couldn't be that painful. Okay, why another butt slap? Good God, it looked like Ivan was telling Sergei to giddy-up. Seriously? I sat back, frowning, and crossed my arms.

This wasn't working for me. I had some interest going on in my pants, but it wasn't because of what I was seeing. And since the whole point was to see what was going on and learn from it, this just couldn't be the right video for me.

Sighing, I debated seeing it through to the end—was not watching all of it recorded somehow and the stats given to Sergei? I didn't want him to feel bad. It wasn't his fault there was something wrong with my gayness or whatever.

I let them finish. It was messy. Cum flew all over the couch thanks to Sergei's fist flying over his cock. Then it got weird for me again when Ivan came in Sergei's ass, pulled out to shoot a couple times all over Sergei's back, and then plunged back into his ass again. No condoms. Maybe that was the reason for the "breeding" in the title. It just made me more uncomfortable to know Sergei was taking a health risk like that.

I clicked back to the lineup of video choices. With a groan, I rearranged the sticky notes again. I did *not* want to know why there was a horse in one of them.

My gaze flicked over the preview images and titles, took note of the number of stars, and I sighed. Did I really want to keep doing this? All I'd learned was what I didn't like. Well, I guessed that was something anyway.

Then I happened to see one titled, "My boyfriend loves me." That sounded...sweet. I huffed a breath. I supposed that was more my speed. It didn't mention either of them being a virgin, but maybe it was something nicer than what Sergei'd gotten. Love was good, right?

The still image from the video showed two black guys lying together on a baby blue bedspread. While I re-stuck sticky notes, I read the description and smiled a little. Mitchell—the guy with the dreadlocks—was crazy in love with his boyfriend, Andre. Okay, I liked that. Apparently, I would hear Andre call Mitchell "honey boy" a few times and, though it embarrassed Mitchell, he loved it anyway. I couldn't really understand why either of them would want to put this out here publicly, but I'd take advantage of it since they had.

The video started with someone adjusting the camera onto Mitchell on the bed. He was on his back, smiling and running his palm up and down his abs. Already half-hard, he had that leanly muscular build of, like, runners or cyclists. Way better looking than the Russians. Where was Andre? Oh, he'd been the one adjusting the camera and now he was climbing on top of Mitchell. They smiled at each other, hands already roaming, and started kissing.

This was better. Not the greatest angle and the lighting could've been brighter, but I saw the love and I liked this. These weren't strangers. Andre was doing something very deliberate to Mitchell's neck and totally getting Mitchell hot based on the way he held onto Andre tighter, wiggled around, and started moaning. Andre knew exactly what to do to get Mitchell worked up.

Me, too, actually. Andre was kissing his way slowly down Mitchell's chest, and my hand was hovering over my fly. Should I? I could learn and play at the same time. Wasn't like they'd mind, and my parents wouldn't bother me without a crash or something to get their attention.

I opened my pants, dropped them to my ankles, and brought my dick and balls out. I liked the pressure of my underwear waistband pressing under my sac and digging into my cheeks, so I didn't take my briefs off. I gently fingered my foreskin against my cock while cradling my nuts in my palm, sighed at the pleasure, and then refocused on Mitchell and Andre.

Mitchell had his eyes closed, hands resting on the pillow beside his head. He moaned and pushed his chest up, while Andre sucked at Mitchell's nipple. It made my breath quicken to see how Andre was staring up Mitchell's body at him. Andre watched Mitchell's every reaction, totally concentrated. When something Andre did made Mitchell gasp, Andre did it again. When Mitchell spread his legs wider and rocked his hips against Andre's chest, Andre surged up to kiss Mitchell, and I heard the first "honey boy" whispered in Andre's deep voice.

They were *beautiful*. Not just their bodies, so dark and toned, but because they so clearly loved each other. I almost wanted to stop and leave them in privacy, but I also couldn't quit looking. I had to see what Andre did next and how Mitchell would react. I needed to hear their sexy sounds. I wanted to know what would get Andre to say Mitchell's adorable nickname again.

When Andre tapered off the kiss, Mitchell whined and tried to hold onto Andre a little longer. But Andre smiled, white teeth flashing, and backed up again. I stopped touching myself when Andre lifted Mitchell's legs up and out before burying his face lower than Mitchell's balls. I tried to look around Mitchell's leg to see just what Andre was doing, but of course that didn't work. Was he rubbing his nose into Mitchell's nuts? Well, okay, if that was their thing. But wait. Was that flash of pink there Andre's tongue? Mitchell was making all kinds of moaning noises, and then he grabbed his legs behind his knees and hauled on them to lift his butt up off the bed and— *Whoa*. Andre was *licking* Mitchell's *asshole*.

That should have been gross. Honestly, *eew*. Except... Mitchell really liked it, and since Andre was humping the bed a bit, I had to assume he liked doing the licking. When Wes had rubbed me there, it had felt...interesting. A tongue on my cockhead was mind-blowing, so maybe one on my asshole would be, too. I rolled my balls in my fingers and went back to stroking. There were some possibilities with ass-licking. Needed a better name, but there it was.

Mitchell's moaning dropped down way deeper when Andre got up on his elbows and started sucking Mitchell's balls. They were big as eggs and shaved, all of him was, and Andre did the watching-Mitchell thing again. *Okay, that's just hot.* I'd liked seeing what Wes did to me, so I'd have to remember to watch Wes while I did things to him in case he'd like that, too.

See? Learning stuff.

Andre sat up between Mitchell's legs and reached for a bottle of lube. Oh, hey—Andre was uncut. Nice to see. And Mitchell seemed to like seeing Andre slick himself up with the lube since he started begging. "C'mon, Dre, fuck me. Oh, baby, *please*." He was writhing on the bed now, like he tried to entice Andre to hurry up. Andre was grinning triumphantly.

I bit my lip when I realized there was no condom again. But I could see their love, the care, so maybe they'd gotten to a trusting place with each other. Then, I knew, it was okay to stop using condoms if a couple wanted. So, okay. Andre and Mitchell were there.

"My sweet honey boy," Andre said as he placed Mitchell's ankles on his shoulders. I smiled and matched my hand's stroke on my dick to the one Andre used on Mitchell's hard cock. God, it felt good. I almost felt like we were all connected.

Something was going on between them that I couldn't see, and then Mitchell threw his head back and cried out. Was Andre pushing into him? They hadn't done the fingers thing. Was that optional? Maybe taking a cock was something you got used to eventually. They'd probably been doing this for a while now.

I reached down and rubbed at my peri-whatever behind my balls and felt my ass clench. Wes had said something about my prostate being inside somewhere in there, so I stroked myself and pushed on where it felt best with every thrust of Andre's hips. *Oh, damn.* I felt that. And if I could feel it on the outside, was Andre pegging Mitchell's on the inside? Was that why Mitchell was moving all over the place and sounding like he might come any second? He clutched at the sheets, rocked up to meet every one of Andre's thrusts. And Andre was panting and groaning, too. Still staring. Yeah, that was hot.

Oh, my God.

I grunted and lost sight of the screen while I shot cum all over my shirt. I might end up with a bruise on my peri-thing from rubbing it so hard, but goddamn, it felt fantastic. Orgasmic. I chuckled at myself and just lightly stroked my cock now.

Mitchell was coming, Andre's hand flying on his dick like he was tugging it out of him. White sprayed all over Mitchell's taut, dark abs and he wailed so loud and good it made me shiver. Then Andre grunted and thrust his cock into Mitchell a couple more times before he went still. He hardly made a sound, but his whole body was tense, muscles standing out, and he threw his head back. Total triumph. God, they were beautiful men and what they'd just done was the best thing I'd ever seen.

Second best. Watching Wes would forever be number one.

"Thanks, guys," I whispered as Andre lay down on Mitchell and got cuddled. "That was awesomely educational."

I grinned happily and slumped in my seat. Yep, I was going to rock Wes's world.

Chapter Fourteen

Rendezvous Revelations

Maybe it was the intensity of my last couple orgasms thanks to my new porn education. The possible danger in sneaking out of the house after my parents went to bed probably contributed. Or maybe it was both and the fact I was about to hook up with Wes in a park late at night were the reasons my hands shook, heart pounded, and everything looked brighter and sounded louder. It was awesome and epic and, if I didn't die from the amazing before I found him, it was definitely going to get even better.

As I came within sight of the pond, I didn't care about anything except the man sitting on top of a stone picnic table. He wore no shirt and was leaning back on his hands, staring up at the sky. The light had been broken in this area, so only the half-moon illuminated the scene. Bathed in silver, he looked even more beautiful.

And he was *mine*.

He turned to look when he heard me trot closer. I was eager now to touch him, kiss him. My heart beat hard in my chest as he smiled at me, sat up, and held out a hand. I got up on the table, first on my knees and then sitting on his thighs, before he gathered me in and kissed me. I didn't care if anyone else was nearby, if someone might see us. I just wanted to be with him in every way I could.

"You changed," he mumbled against my mouth.

I nodded as he trailed his hands over my back and down to my ass. After coming all over my original shirt thanks to Mitchell and Andre, I'd changed. Twice. Finally, I'd settled on those jeans that were a little too big and a blue T-shirt that was a little too tight. The pants had a reason that I was definitely stoked about Wes discovering.

Oh. That was probably another reason I was all worked up about tonight.

"I like it," he said. "I feel like I'm corrupting a very studious, very good boy."

I chuckled. "You are."

He smiled and lay back on the tabletop, taking me with him. "Should I have dressed up, too?" he asked, stroking my hair.

Leaning against him, I shook my head. I brushed my lips over his as I said, "You did. Bad boys always wear jeans and cowboy boots and no shirts. You're perfect."

He hummed and angled his head for a deep kiss, sliding his hand up under my shirt now, caressing my back as his tongue toyed with mine. I shivered when his fingers delved under the gaping waistband of my jeans and reached lower. He paused in kissing me and his whole body went still. I smiled against his lips. I wasn't wearing any underwear.

I stared down at his surprised face and waggled my eyebrows. "Now who's the bad boy?"

His chuckle was wicked as his middle finger went right down to slide over my asshole. I gasped a breath while realizing Wes had complete access to all of me right now. Memories of Mitchell writhing on Andre's tongue made me so unbelievably horny I tipped my ass up to rub on Wes's finger. His grin was crooked as he looked up at me, eyelids lowering, and breath coming faster.

"You want it so bad," he whispered.

Oh, I did. I really did. He explored with that fingertip, and I opened up for everything.

"Malcolm Small?"

Huh? It took me a few seconds to realize someone else was here and they knew me. In the time it took for Wes to remove his hand from my pants, I looked over and gasped so big I thought I'd die. But not just because Todd Casey stood there watching me get groped. It was the fact one of my tormentors stood beside me while he was *holding hands with another guy.*

That... That didn't make sense. Why was Todd holding some guy's hand? Why was he staring at me all surprised instead of making fun of me? Todd was more bark than bite, but he wasn't doing anything now. This should've been when he lit into me for everything I was just doing to prove I was as gay as they'd all said I was. Todd just stood there.

"Mal," Wes said and sat up, his arms coming around me. "You okay?"

I looked at him. "I don't understand."

"Don't be afraid. He's the queer one."

"Afraid? Queer?"

I looked back at Todd, frowning. "Why are you holding..." I flinched as it finally clicked. "Are you *gay?*"

Todd grimaced and swallowed just before he nodded.

He nodded.

Something else, something red and throbbing, clicked inside me now. I lunged toward him, but Wes stopped me from reaching Todd. He stepped back fast, and I liked the sudden fear on his face. I wanted him to be scared of me.

"You son of a bitch!" I pushed at Wes's hands on my hips, but my eyes were on Todd. "All that time, and *you're* the gay one? Every word you said, everything you did... You horrible fucking bastard!"

I struggled out of Wes's hold, pulling against the edge of the table, kicking. Todd kept backing up and his friend with him. I was going to tear them apart. I lurched off the table, aiming for them. He deserved it. He deserved to bleed and cry and—

Arms around my waist stopped me. "Let me *go*," I snapped at Wes and clawed at his forearms. "Wesley!"

"No, Mal. Calm down."

"Fuck you! Let. Me. Go."

He spun me around, and I nearly fell over. Wes's hands bit into my upper arms and he shook me. "Knock it *off.*"

Faced with Wes looking angry—at me—another something

clicked inside me. This time it was trembling and horrified. *What have I done?* I cried out, shaking. *Oh, my God.*

Wes gathered me in, his arms nearly crushing me, but I needed it. I was shattered, just broken from the inside out. And I didn't understand why. What just happened? That wasn't me. I didn't fight and hurt and oh, sweet Jesus, had I hit Wes?

"I'm sorry! I'm *so sorry*."

"It's okay, baby. Everything's fine."

I huddled inside Wes's embrace, my face hidden in his throat. I couldn't get over what I'd nearly done. What if I'd hit Todd? What if I'd really hurt him? I hadn't even been *thinking*. I would've been no different than—

"What the hell did you *do* to that guy?"

I sniffed and turned just enough to see Todd's friend looking between us like we were all crazy. When Todd reached for him, the guy slapped Todd's hands away and stepped back.

"I'm sorry," Todd said to him, and then looked at me. "I'm sorry, okay?"

I flipped him off and leaned into Wes again. I might've been horrified at my reaction to learning someone who'd bullied me for being gay was gay himself, but I wasn't about to accept some lame-ass non-apology.

"I was *scared*," Todd said. "I thought if everyone thought you were gay, they'd never think I was."

"You threw him under the bus?" That was Todd's friend again. He sounded disgusted. *Good.*

"What was I supposed to do?"

Wes said, "You're no different than Rick, and you know where he is right now? County lockup. Ask me how he got there."

I'd never heard Wes sound so deadly. It was strangely comforting to see him staring over at Todd with challenge bright in his green eyes. Part of me wanted to— *No.* No more fighting.

"Go away, Todd," I said without turning around. "And you keep your distance from me or I swear to God..." I left it up to Todd's imagination what my near-attack and Wes's threat might result in if he didn't listen now.

Wes's hand rubbed up and down my back in time to the deep

breaths I was taking. I could hear the shuffle of feet on a path and low voices, one harsh and the other whining. I hoped that guy dumped Todd and told everyone they knew what Todd had done to me. I hoped Todd regretted every word he'd ever said to or about me for the rest of his life. I wanted him to remember me forever.

And I wanted to forget him completely. Everything they'd done still hurt *so much*.

"Why'd they have to do that to me?" I whispered into Wes's shirt. "Why couldn't they have left me alone? I wasn't hurting anybody. I was just *shy*."

"Aw, Mal."

I sniffed as tears threatened. "I could be an entirely different person right now, if it wasn't for them. You know?"

"Honey—"

"I could be strong and brave and—"

"Mal, stop." He held my face in his hands and made me look at him. "Baby, you *are* strong and brave and you're getting stronger and braver all the time. Just look back at what you've done *today*, Mal."

I blinked back tears and stared up at him.

"You helped rebuild a car, stood up against a bully and sent him to jail, gave a spectacular blowjob, took care of me..." His eyes got glassier and he smiled. "And you told me you love me. I think that's a *damn good day*."

He was right. I tried to smile. "Yes," I whispered and wiped up his tears as he dabbed at mine. "I'd be happy to repeat...almost all of it."

He huffed a laugh, gave me a quick kiss, and then cuddled me back up again.

Eventually, we moved to the picnic table. Wes sat on the top again and spread his thighs for me to sit between them. I sat mostly sideways so I could lean into him, and he draped one leg over my lap and held me, too. I was protected and safe. Time passed easily in comfortable silence.

I sighed when I caught sight of my watch face. It was after one-thirty now. I twisted and wrapped my arms around his shoulders.

"What?" he whispered.

"It's really late and I should go, but..." I pressed my too-hot eyes into the cool skin of his neck. "I don't want to be alone."

His fingers massaged the back of my head. "You can stay the night at mine."

Could I? Yes, he'd let me, and his family probably wouldn't mind finding me there in the morning. But what about *my* parents? They'd get up for work around six; would they notice I wasn't in my bed? I'd taken a nap on it for a couple of hours earlier, but I hadn't made any kind of effort to disguise its emptiness. Did they ever check on me?

"You could sneak back in before they woke up," Wes said like he was reading my mind. Of course, it probably wasn't that hard to know what I was thinking.

"What if one of them is up early? What if they catch me coming in?" Because I really didn't know what to do about that. I'd never been this reckless.

"You can tell them you took up jogging. I'll make sure you're sweaty and put you in some shorts and a tank."

I leaned back and laughed. It made my blood buzz to imagine how he'd get me good and sweaty first thing in the morning. And I loved his crazy creative mind. It might actually work.

"Okay," I said. "Take me home with you."

Chapter Fifteen

Out for Breakfast

I was watching Andre use his tongue all over Mitchell's ass again. Except I felt it, too. But Andre was over there, and Mitchell was moaning with him, so how was something happening to *my* ass? *What's going on?*

I opened my eyes and realized right away that I was in bed. A dream? But it felt so real. Actually, it *still* felt really real. I looked over my shoulder and gasped.

Wes had his face buried between my ass cheeks. His tongue was... It was... Oh, my God. He was licking my asshole. Licking and wiggling and, like, flicking at it, too. And moaning. Wes was moaning while he did all that. Like he liked doing it to me. And then he was looking at me, and I could see in his eyes how turned on he was to be *there* and doing *that*.

He did something, a poking something, with his tongue, and I almost choked on a moan. Oh, that felt good. I'd never known a good like that. I had to spread my thighs more and lift my ass up. I didn't really think about it, just moved up and back so Wes wouldn't stop doing this glorious thing to me.

One rub of my erection against the bed had me thrusting again and again, humping the bed and Wes's tongue, too. I dropped my head onto the pillow and moaned, pulling at my own hair for no reason except that I couldn't stop moving around. I stuck a hand under my chest and pinched my nipple in time with the thrusting wiggles of Wes's tongue into my ass.

He stopped.

"No, don't," I whined and looked back at him. "Wes, please."

Grinning at me, naked and with his cock red and stiff, he moved over me on his hands and knees. I pushed my ass up and realized…he could fuck me. He could, right now, and I'd let him. My hole was pulsing and wet. I needed something in there. I was empty.

Wes eased his lower half down, wedging his cock between my cheeks. I gasped and dug my knees into the bed to press us tighter together. He was so hot and ready. "Please. Yes," I said and tried to grab his hand to get him to do something, *anything*, so these amazing sensations wouldn't end.

He nuzzled into my neck and moaned quietly while rocking his hips against me. He humped my ass, his full dick sliding on his saliva between my cheeks and right across my hole. I fell back down against the pillow and thrust my cock on the bed and my ass up on him. It was almost like fucking. *So close.* This was what we'd do. Just like this. When he finally fucked me, we'd do it like this.

I groaned before biting the pillow.

"You like this, Mal? Huh?" His voice was deep, breathless.

"Yes. *Yes.*" I lifted my head and moved my hips faster, pounding up and down.

"So good. Aw, baby."

Wes's groan vibrated all down my back as he pushed against me harder. We weren't so much sliding now as pressing on each other, but it was enough. I was going to come with him almost fucking me into the mattress. He was going to come on me.

I gasped when he did and felt liquid spurting onto my skin from my ass up my back. I *liked* it. I liked it so much, it pushed me over the edge, too. Clenching muscles, a wash of heat, and I soaked the sheets beneath me. I could barely breathe as I collapsed and twitched with Wes still on top of me. I had cum all over me, like Sergei last night. I'd thought it was gross, hadn't liked it at all, but I loved Wes's cum on me. It was filthy and so fucking hot.

Was that normal? I'd thought Andre and Mitchell's sexy love-making was better than Sergei's dirty fucking, but now... Maybe they were both good. Maybe that was normal...for me. For Wes and me.

Wes sighed heavily. "Fuck, Mal."

"Yeah." I gulped and huffed a laugh. *You almost* did *fuck me.* I reached back, smoothing my hands down his hips to the tops of his thighs. He shivered against me, and I smiled.

"Oh, sorry." He pushed up off of me.

"No, it's fine. I like the feel of you on top of me." I blushed. Was that a silly thing to say out loud, or a really suggestive thing?

"Well, okay, then." He squashed me back into the mattress.

He pushed an *oof* out of me before I laughed. Wes did, too, but then he rolled off to lie beside me. I turned onto my side to face him. After wiggling closer, I kissed him. *Oh, hey...* There was a new taste to his lips and tongue. Not bad, just weird because I knew where it came from. I moved back, blinking at him.

He grinned like he knew what I was thinking. "Yep, that's what ass tastes like."

"Oh, my *God.*" I hid in the pillow.

Wes laughed. "Specifically, what *your* ass tastes like."

I moaned. That was just too freaky.

"Don't worry, Mal," he whispered near my ear. "I loved it and I'll do it again any time you want."

I peeked at him.

"Really," he said.

I smiled at him, feeling strangely shy. "Does it—what you did—have a name?"

"Rimming. Rimjob." He stuck out his tongue and swirled it in a circle.

I laughed as my blush grew hotter. I had to ask, "Do you like getting...rimmed, too?"

"I do." He petted the back of my hand and looked a little shy himself. "You can do anything you want with me. I love you."

I leaned in and kissed him again. I didn't care what that sort of salty taste came from if he didn't. I could happily wake up every morning to—

Morning!

I twisted around to see the clock. It was twelve after nine.

"Wes! Oh, my God."

"Aw, crap, Mal. I'm sorry. I totally forgot about setting an alarm."

No chance of trying that fake jogging idea—though I *was* good and sweaty—since my parents left for work hours ago. I grabbed up my phone and…

No missed calls. No messages. Had neither of them noticed I wasn't home? A little part of me ached to realize that.

"Anything?" Wes asked.

"No. I guess it's okay. Nothing to worry about."

"I am sorry about the alarm. I—"

"Don't be." I kissed him before I got up. I was about to say more, but I could suddenly feel his cum slowly dribbling down my back. My ass was all wet between my cheeks, too. It didn't feel so hot anymore.

He chuckled at me, probably from the shocked expression that was, no doubt, on my face. "Come on, hot stuff," Wes said as he got up. "We'll shower, and then let's go out for breakfast. My treat."

"Yeah, okay."

I gasped when he wiped something down my back, and then up my crack. I spun around to see him tossing his T-shirt from yesterday into a laundry hamper. Well, at least I didn't have to worry about leaving a trail into his bathroom. *Yech.*

When I picked up and shook out my clothes, Wes put a hand on my arm. "Would you do something for me?" he asked.

"I guess so. What?"

He grinned and went over to his dresser. Did he want me to wear something? He held up a pair of navy blue track pants and bit his bottom lip. *Look at him be all bashful and hesitant.* Confident as he was, I hadn't thought he could feel that way.

I took the pants. Only when he waggled his eyebrows at me while walking by and into his bathroom did I realize I didn't have any underwear to put on. And he knew that. So… I looked down at my dick hanging there all happy and covered in spooge. Wes was looking forward to seeing me free-balling it in a pair of his pants. I snorted and dropped them on yesterday's T-shirt. *Oh, my God.*

It turned out Wes decided to wear gray sweatpants that showed off his non-underwear state, too. It felt pornographic. Sweatpants porn. *Who knew?* He also had on black flip-flops that made his feet actually look sexy, and a black tank that let the world see how toned his shoulders were. He kept eying *me*, though, like I was the hot one. And he didn't make fun of me when I wiggled involuntarily every time it felt like my dick was way too obvious against his much too silky track pants.

Man, if I'd gotten a boner, *everyone* would have seen it right then. And since Wes looked hot enough to melt my brain and kept checking me out, it would definitely happen. Like now. *Damn it.* At least we were in the car for the moment.

It was while I was trying *not* to look at him as he drove that I found myself cataloging our differences. Like the fact I had skinny arms and bony shoulders, while he looked like he knew his way around a weight room. He wasn't bulky, but he was athletic-looking, and I was...slender. All the other gay couples I'd seen so far—and, yes, they were from last night's pornification experience—were more alike than different. Sergei and what's his name were lean, Andre and Mitchell were muscular... But here I was all girly compared to Wes's masculinity.

"Am I the girl?"

Oh, good God. Did I actually say that out loud?

His laugh sounded like a honk. "The girl?" But then he looked at me, saw me blushing and nibbling my bottom lip. "Hey, no. It's not like that." He held my hand as he divided his attention between the road and me. "You're all man, honey. Just the way I want you."

I nodded, threading our fingers together. So I was smaller and not as...manly-man as him. Didn't make me a girl—which, come to think of it, was maybe a little insulting to girls. And it wasn't like he ignored my dick or anything, so I wasn't a substitute. So what was bothering me here?

"Have I done something, Mal? Like... Like when I call you pretty?" He pulled the car into the lot beside a Bob Evans restaurant, concern on his face. "Or when I call you baby and stuff?"

Did it bother me? "No," I said, turning to face him more fully. "I like it. That you think I'm pretty and all that, I mean." Sure, pretty wasn't really a boy-associated word, but he said it with love. "And I like the names, too." They made me feel special.

He unbuckled and scooted across the seat to kiss me. "You're beautiful to me, Mal, and you're everything I want because you're a man. Your cock makes my mouth water."

I chuckled, stole a kiss, and then shoved at him. "Ditto. Now get out before we do something illegal." Because, damn him, I'd just gotten my boner under control.

He grinned but said, "There's no roles or expectations, okay? You just be yourself."

We got out of the car, and I thought about that, about being myself. Who was I really? Could I still be figuring that out? I mean, I'd just realized my sexuality. Maybe there was more for me to understand about myself. How I wanted to be with Wes—what I liked, how I acted—might work itself out in me the longer we were together. Everyone grew and changed as they got older, right? So I probably wasn't done. That was kind of…exciting.

What really wasn't a good feeling was the one that hit me when we walked into the restaurant. I tensed, flicking glances at the people around us. I knew about safe spaces now, I wanted to stand up for my rights—*oh, my God*—but what was I supposed to do here? How should I act? If I had to go into every public situation and assess the danger before letting down my guard, I'd lose my mind in no time.

It felt way too much like coming home and having to analyze my father's mood before I could relax, if I did. That kind of caution and reaction wasn't good enough for me anymore.

With Wes right there beside me, I tried following his lead. He stood near me, but didn't really do anything that might define us as a couple. We were together, but so were the three girls ahead of us and the four older men in front of them. I needed to be casual, that was the thing. Maybe with the whole growing into myself stuff, I'd become more comfortable with letting strangers know exactly what kind of relationship Wes and I had. For now, I could handle acting like we were friends since we were.

We got a table and ordered, eventually eating omelets while chatting about Ted, how we felt from our injuries—mostly fine, though my bruises were more pronounced today—and what we wanted to do after breakfast. I'd settled in, relaxed, until I happened to notice two boys join that group of girls at their table across the room from us. None of them looked older than maybe high school sophomores, and the boys were holding hands before they sat down.

I couldn't stop staring at them. I knew I was staring and tried not to, but my eyes kept wandering back over to them again and again. They were being casual, too, but it was obvious they were a couple. It was the physical stuff. An arm over the back of a chair, one's little touch to the back of the other's hand to get his attention, leaning together when they laughed, and one resting his head on the other's shoulder afterward. Maybe other people didn't see it, but I knew they were way more than friends.

I tried to look around at the other tables without being obvious about it. Those four older men were looking at something on the table between them. A family with little kids was totally oblivious to anything but the kids. The guys at the counter weren't turning around. Seriously, no one noticed the gay boys at all.

"Mal?"

"Huh? What?"

Wes smiled a little bit, and then I watched his eyes cut over to the boys and back to me. "You okay?"

"Um… Well, yeah. I'm fine. It's just…" I had to glance at them one more time. "Nobody seems to be noticing them."

He shrugged. "Well, they're not really being overt about it."

"They're doing more than we are."

"I'll be as out with you as you want to be, honey. I'm letting it be your decision."

I stared at him for a moment. "But you don't want to hide. You said that even before we got together."

"Right, but I'm willing to let you lead because you're the one still getting used to all this. I'll go at your pace."

I smiled and blushed, but it was with happiness. That was really nice of him. "Thanks." And then I took a chance. I reached across the table, covering his hand with mine.

He looked so pleased, I was glad to take a risk. He turned his hand over and we rested that way, palm to palm, until the waitress came to refill his coffee. He used that hand to wave her off, but I was pretty sure she saw. I smiled at her when she didn't say anything before walking away. That was, maybe, quiet acceptance. I was a lot more relaxed after that, but it was still strange.

"Really, why isn't anyone noticing? I've seen those *20/20* episodes or whatever where they set people up to see how they'll react to gay people. We might not be making out, but there's *two* gay couples here, just in this section, and no one's reacting at all." I looked around again, confirming that not one person was staring.

"Most people don't look for signs of someone's sexuality; they just assume everyone's straight." He sipped at his coffee. He probably hadn't wanted a refill because he'd put so much cream and sugar in it, it was practically white.

"Well... Okay, so someone would have to see something...overt."

"Right."

"But then how did you know about me? Because I didn't do anything but sit there." And I'd been wearing a heck of a lot more clothes at the time, too.

He chuckled. "At first, I just hoped. Please God, let me catch that pretty boy next door."

I snorted a laugh, but reached for his hand again. He teased my palm with his fingertips.

"And then over the next few weeks, while getting to know you, I saw your interest or curiosity building, and..." He shrugged. "I was just waiting for you, then."

"Sorry I made you wait so long." I caught two of his fingers and held onto them.

"I already told you, Mal, you're worth the wait."

If I could've done it without landing in our dishes, I might have leaned over and kissed him right then. I puckered my lips while staring him in the eyes and, when he winked back, I knew he knew he'd just gotten kissed anyway.

One more glance at the boys and I had to wonder something else. "Am I a late bloomer for figuring it out at eighteen?"

He finished a sip of his coffee and shook his head. "Nah. Everybody's different. Ben, at the garage? He was twenty-six when it clicked for him."

The paint guy was gay? I'd had no idea. He looked so— *Oh*. None of that. Gay didn't have a look.

I fiddled with my napkin. "So, um, what about you? How old were you when you figured it out?"

"I was fourteen. Summer camp." He waggled his eyebrows at me.

I grinned. "Did you discover a new extracurricular activity?"

He laughed. "Boy, did I."

"What happened? I mean, if you want to tell me."

"I want to share everything with you, Mal." While the warm fuzzies of that skipped around inside me, he said, "All the beds were bunk beds, and that made each set into a team right off. Carl had the top bunk, and he would get up at least three times a night to go to the restroom in the next building. He was a shy kid, but friendly and did his work. We got along, but we weren't best buddies or anything."

His grin was a little bittersweet. "I followed him one night, wanting to see what he was doing because I couldn't believe he had to pee so much. I found him standing in the shower area crying. I got him to talk to me, and he confessed to never having been away from home before. I hugged him because he was just so sad, missing his huge family and all his siblings. I think he had, like, eight brothers and sisters or something."

Of course Wes wouldn't be able to let someone feel alone. He was a good friend.

"One thing led to another, and Carl kissed me."

"He kissed you?"

"Yep. And that was the other reason he cried so much. He was afraid I couldn't possibly feel the same way about him."

"Aw. That's so cute."

He chuckled. "I credit Carl with waking me up. That was my best summer camp ever."

"No one caught on?" All those kids and camp counselors watching…

"We figured out pretty quickly that the free time we were all given in the afternoons to mess around in the woods could actually be spent messing around in the woods."

"Well, damn." I laughed. "Maybe all I needed was summer

camp."

He smiled, but it didn't reach his eyes, and it occurred to me... "You like being my first."

"Yes."

"You want me all to yourself."

"Yes."

I licked my lips, enjoying how his eyes followed my tongue. "I'm all yours, Wes."

He gave me a very possessive and smoldering look. I hadn't, until then, known you could have sex with just your eyes, but damn, that's what this felt like.

"A friend of mine," he said, holding my gaze, "invited me over to his house on the Portage Lakes for the Fourth."

I sighed. "Okay."

Secretly, I'd been looking forward to doing what normal people did over the Fourth of July. Like hanging out with Wes, eating hotdogs, and watching fireworks. My parents didn't do anything much for any holiday. It had always been too intimidating to go do something on my own—even going downtown to watch the fireworks display was too much. So, without Wes, I'd be in my room watching fireworks online. Again.

"Want to come with me?"

I blinked, my heart suddenly thumping. "Go with you?"

He leaned over the table on his elbows. "Take a vacation with me, Mal. We'll play in the lake. Make out on the dock and in the boat." He smiled so sweetly. "We'll sleep together every night, no worries about anybody."

I shivered, imagining that, and leaned closer, too. "Your friends won't mind?"

"Hell, no." His knee rubbed into mine under the table. "They'll love you."

Really? I grinned. "And we can be, you know, out around them?"

"There'll be another gay couple, Brian and Jean-Louis, and it's their house. And I think Roger's going to be there, so there'll be five of us and some other people, mostly couples."

"Oh. Okay."

He grinned big. "Say yes, Mal."

"Yes," I said on a laugh.

"Good boy."

"Yeah, not so much right now." I chuckled and squirmed in my seat. "Better take me home."

He grinned, grabbed the check, and sauntered over to pay. I got up, realizing I'd follow this man just about anywhere for one of those smiles. He gave me a great one and took my hand as we walked out into the sun.

Chapter Sixteen

Wherein I am Epic

A couple weeks later, I lied to my parents and told them I was going to an overnight orientation thing on campus in one of the dorms. Amazingly enough, they totally bought it. My father even managed to tell me it showed good initiative—if he only knew.

Wes very patiently waited for me around the corner and drove the El Camino down to the Portage Lakes area. Our first vacation together... I was completely psyched for it.

I'd never been to the Portage Lakes before and wasn't sure what to expect. I thought maybe it was expensive to live there just because the houses would be right by the water. But when Wes started driving into residential areas, the houses didn't look like much at all. No porches, just garage doors taking up most of the front, hardly any landscaping either... The planned and sterile design of my neighborhood was ugly, but not this bad. Did they not care about their homes at all?

Wes grinned at me. "This is just the back. Don't judge it yet."

"I wasn't." I tried for a more neutral expression.

He shook his head as he slowed the car and turned into a pinkish-beige tiled driveway. It was another boring house with gray siding and white trim, the garage doors being the biggest "feature" to the whole thing. Did they open the doors to show off their cars later in the day? Was that the point? It was just weird.

Getting out of the car, my stomach cramped and a cold sweat washed over me. Heart rate skyrocketing, I tried breathing through this latest bout of anxiety—there had been a lot of them since I'd said yes to our vacation—but my hands shook and my shoulders and back muscles tensed up. Meeting Wes's friends was going to be the death of me.

I kept flicking glances at the door, waiting for people to burst out and surround us. Nobody came. "You sure this is the right house?"

"It's the right one." Wes set my suitcase on the driveway. He looked around and shrugged. "Might be they're out on the boat. I can't see the dock from here."

So a temporary reprieve. That was kind of good. Maybe. I could at least get comfortable with the house so that, if my nerves got to the really gross stage, I'd know exactly where the bathroom was. And I'd find all the corners I could lurk in without being seen.

I took a deep breath, held it, and then slowly let it out. I picked up my suitcase, trying for some calm and positivity. I wasn't going to panic. I wouldn't hide.

I refused to freak out and embarrass Wes.

He led the way inside through that boring front door. I looked around at the nice, grown up furniture and had to remind myself that Brian and Jean-Louis had been living together for three years now and were actual adults with real jobs. Brian was Wes's age and getting his Master's in something, but Jean-Louis was almost thirty and taught French at a university somewhere. Despite the party Wes said there would be for the Fourth, this wasn't a college frat movie set at all. They had things that looked like antiques.

"This floor," Wes said, "is the sitting area there and the bedrooms. Upstairs is storage and a bedroom that has three single beds for anybody who shouldn't drive home or whatever."

The sitting room was sunny, all pale blue and white. It seemed like a quiet place to have breakfast or read a book—though I doubted book-reading was something partiers would do. I was so out of my element.

We walked down the hallway. A few doors on either side were open to show bedrooms that seemed to have themes, or maybe just specific color schemes. Wes stopped outside a cream one with lots of wood and lace.

"This is ours." He smiled and stood back to let me go in first.

The room had dark wood furniture and lace everywhere. Doilies on the dressers, a thick comforter on the bed with lacy accents, and lace curtains on the one window. There was a print over the bed that looked Victorian. It screamed fussy old lady's room. I turned and eyed Wes.

He chuckled. "I know, it's kind of awful."

"Kind of?"

"Just tell Jean-Louis you love it. He's into decorating and this was his froufrou dandy phase."

"Fitting words." I looked back at the bed. I hoped it was new and not an antique from the Victorian era or I'd never be able to have sex with Wes in it. We would've been hanged back then.

Wes set down his suitcase. "This is the good part." He opened another door and gestured for me to have a look.

"Oh, nice." The bathroom was modern with a big, built in tub and a shower that had a green glass door. White tiles were on the floor and up the walls to about waist high, then pale green paint went up to the ceiling. The tub looked like it could fit more than one person. "Very nice."

"Brian does the bathrooms."

"I'll thank him for that." I turned back to the bedroom. "I don't even want to consider what they used back in the nineteenth century."

Wes's chuckle faded into the background as I stood beside the bed again. Part of me wanted to lie down and try to relax before the others got back or arrived. Before the swarm of introductions started and I had to cough up the lines I'd memorized should someone ask me to tell them about myself. *Actually, maybe I should study my notes one more time.*

Wes wrapped his arms around me from behind. Beside my ear and in his rumbly voice he asked, "Wanna try out the bed?"

"Yes," I said, thinking of my nap idea. His hands slid down to my belly and up to my chest. My navel and nipple got a tease. "Oh. That kind of— What if they come back?"

His fingers went lower and gently massaged me through my fly. I leaned back against him, losing the battle as usual. I should have been glad he wasn't doing this on the dock, wherever that was. I'd probably be helpless to resist him there, too.

"Well, I'll lock the door and they can wait." He nibbled at my neck. "Could open the window so they know we're busy."

I rolled my eyes. "I don't want them listening." But there was a weird little flutter in my chest at the possibility of being overheard. I wanted others to know about me being with Wes. That he chose me. I reached down and massaged my dick with him.

He nipped my earlobe, and then moved away. "Get naked, baby," he said with a pat to my butt.

I lifted my T-shirt over my head and saw him lock the door. While I got my pants open, he really did go over and open the window. I bit my lip, dropped my shorts, and didn't protest. What would we sound like? Would it be obvious we were having sex?

Why did that kinda thrill me?

"Relax, Mal," Wes said kindly. "It's just you and me."

The heat and need for sex was already making my dick push against my underwear. I watched Wes lick his lips and undress, his green eyes roaming over my body. When he looked at me like that, I was like the hottest guy on the planet. So I teased him, trailing my hands down my chest and stomach. When I fondled myself through my briefs, his mouth popped open. When I squeezed and made a little wet spot in the red cotton, he groaned.

But when he took off his T-shirt, he winced.

"What's the matter?"

He shrugged. "Stiff shoulders from driving. It's fine."

"How about a massage?" It popped out of my mouth without me really thinking, but then I did think about it and I liked what I thought. Wes on his belly, naked and relaxed, with me on top of him and running my hands all over his muscular body. It'd be way more like foreplay than therapy, but did either of us really care?

His grin said nope.

Naked, he climbed onto the bed and lay down on his stomach. Head turned and arms on the pillow, he watched me step out of my briefs. I got on the bed, straddling his lower back, and sighed a shaky breath when I settled my every throbbing bit onto his warm skin. I wanted to rub on him like he'd done to me a few times now. Being under him and feeling him ride me into the bed was ecstatic. What would it feel like to do the same back to him?

But I had a job to do—or at least to fake—before we got to the sex part of this. If he was in any kind of discomfort, I wanted to make that go away first. I leaned forward and pressed my fingers into the meat of his shoulders. I had no idea how to actually massage someone, but his moan seemed to indicate I was doing just fine. And it was good for me, too, since I was practically laying on him and squeezing his muscles.

I worked my way down from his shoulders to his back, using my thumbs to rub out from his spine. I could almost feel the way— *Oh, damn.* I looked down and realized I'd moved back and he'd tipped up and my cock was now wedged into his ass crack. To hell with best intentions, I rolled my hips and made my dick slide on him right there, foreskin catching and feeling so good.

"You're an ass man."

"What?" I sat up and looked at his smirking face. "Am not."

"You so are. Can't get enough of the butt. Yours or mine."

"Oh. Well…" That didn't sound like a bad thing. "Guess not."

"It's cool, Mal. I feel the same way."

And he reached back to grip his cheeks and pull them apart. My heart skipped a beat when I saw his asshole tighten and release. That should not have been so fucking sexy. Fucking… Oh, dear God, I wanted to fuck him. I gasped when he released his cheeks and they clamped my dick between them.

"You wanna, baby?" he asked and his voice was all growly. "Wanna make me take that long, uncut cock of yours? Sink it into me? Ride my ass?"

I clutched at my chest where my heart just stopped beating. Well, no, it was thundering in there so I wasn't having a heart attack. But… "Oh, my God, Wes."

"Get the lube. You can have me right here and now."

Never had a mission been more urgent, but I could barely think. Where was the lube? Not on the bed. This wasn't Wes's bed. Where were we? Vacation. Suitcase! I threw myself off the bed and hauled my bag— No, I didn't have any. Wes's suitcase. He'd have some. He was always prepared. I was going to fuck a boy scout. Oh, holy shit. No, not shit. Don't think about *that*.

I looked up when I realized Wes was laughing. Like honking goose laughing. I also realized I was maybe a little bit overeager and kinda crazy-looking while straddling my suitcase and pawing through his. A madman desperately seeking lube. "Shut up," I told him and very calmly found the lube in with his hair products and toothpaste.

He couldn't answer because of the laughing. I threw the lube at his head, and he fended it off from hitting his face. At least it seemed to bring him down a level or two until his chuckles stopped altogether. He gave me a look that made me think love and want and please. I bent over him and kissed his grinning lips, taking the lube back. We were going to do this so good.

"I need some prep." Wes spread his legs. "If you don't want to do it, I can myself."

I looked at my hand. "Fingers? For stretching?"

"That's right." He looked amused. "It's been a long time since I did this, but I can tell you when I'm ready."

"Ready for my…" I gulped.

"Your gorgeous cock."

I didn't know why that made me laugh breathlessly. But then I turned toward his bag again. "Should I put a condom on now?"

When he didn't say anything, I turned back around. He still lay on his stomach, head pillowed on his arm, but his expression was so serious. He'd changed his mind. *Oh, dammit. What'd I do wrong?*

"What if we didn't use one?" he said.

"What?"

He sat up on his elbows. "You're a virgin, and I've always been careful. The risk here is mostly mine, but there's no risk because you can't have anything."

"Well, I could." His eyes went wide, and I backtracked. "I mean, I *don't*, but I did some research and people can be born with HIV and stuff. I'm fine, though. Completely. I just mean, you know, assumptions and stuff."

This was killing the mood. It was necessary and important—I

knew that—but my erection was fading fast.

"It's your choice, Mal." He lay back down and smiled softly at me. "I'll be happy with either."

I honestly didn't know what to do. It would probably feel better to be bare inside him—maybe for both of us—since even a thin condom was still a barrier. I wasn't worried about diseases because I trusted Wes and I knew the risk was more his than mine, like he said. But... Well, that. I was going to stick my dick up his butt. Was he...clean up there? I rubbed at my forehead. Was I supposed to ask?

"Mal, honey. If you're changing your mind, it's okay."

I shook my head. "I'm not." *Huh. I'm actually not.* "I just..."

"You have questions?"

I nodded, fiddling with the lube.

"Ask me. There's nothing bad about questions. No stupid ones and all that."

I couldn't look at him. I took a deep breath. "Cleanliness."

"Oh, sure. I didn't douche or anything, but it's all available."

I peeked at him. He raised his eyebrows like maybe he wondered if he needed to explain that availability, but I got it.

"Then no condom, I guess," I said and got back up on the bed with the lube clutched in my fist. At first, I straddled his calf, but then I moved in between his legs.

"Hey," he said, looking over his shoulder. "C'mere."

I set the lube down beside us and leaned over his back. Feeling his warm skin against mine had me pressing down on top of him again. I sighed and rested on him so my head was on his bicep and we could see each other.

"This is a big step, Mal," he said quietly. "It's important and good that we do it knowing everything is safe and what we both want."

"I understand."

"Okay." He kissed me quick. "So if you're into this still, c'mon and gimme what you got, hot stuff."

I chuckled, and then moved in to really kiss him. I adored his soft, smiling lips and the scratch of his afternoon whiskers. His tongue teased mine into his mouth, and the plunge and retreat revved me up for doing that same thing with other parts. It was good we'd talked, but now I wanted to *do*.

And though Sergei's performance came to my mind first, I did not smack Wes's ass.

I focused instead on getting lube on my fingers without getting it everywhere else, too. It was clear and smooth in its slickness. Wes widened his thighs, and I didn't look at his face as I used one hand to spread his cheeks. There it was, a puckered dark pink place both of us wanted me to visit. My hand shook as I aimed a slick finger at it.

When I pressed the tip of my finger inside him, his sigh made me look at his face. I paused, concerned I'd messed something up already. But his eyes were closed and his expression seemed pleased. His…asshole held onto my finger, warm and strong. *Warm and strong…* I looked at my finger inside him and shivered. Pushing in deeper, watching his body open up around mine, I discovered the heat and that it was soft in there. Soft but firm, definitely a muscle gripping me.

I wanted in there.

Shifting closer, focused, I eased my finger in and out. Wes hummed a happy sound. Encouraged, I thrust repeatedly. When Wes lifted up, like he wanted to meet each push, my breath caught. I swallowed hard and added another finger. Wes moaned. A good moan, though, because he lifted his hips higher. I twisted my fingers while plunging into him, and he hollered. I snatched my hand away.

"Oh, my God. Are you okay? What happened?"

He chuckled breathlessly. "Prostate. Found it."

"Oh. That's a good thing."

"Fuck, yes." He dug his knees into the mattress and stuck his ass up more. "You're awesome. Don't stop."

I looked at my fingers. They looked wet but so ordinary despite what they'd just been doing. Should I keep using them?

"C'mon, baby. Gimme some more."

I used more lube, assuming that would be better than not enough. With my own cock standing up tall, pulsing with my heart beat, I poked three fingers into Wes this time.

His grunt turned into a long groan and his ass clamped tight on my fingers. I bit my bottom lip, but then had to let it go to gasp a big breath. I wanted in there. Fingers were great—*yay, fingers*—but feeling all that slick, firm heat wrapped around my entire dick? Yeah, I wanted in there *now*. Especially when Wes started fucking himself on my damn hand. He was going to come if he kept— *Oh, hell, no.*

I took my fingers back and spread the lube all over myself.

"Mal!"

"You can't— I need— *Wait a minute.*"

Wes frowned back at me, but then he caught on to what I was doing when I added more lube to my cock. I was panting from touching myself. I had to hold on long enough to get in him. After that, well, hopefully he'd understand.

"Yeah, Mal. Do me, baby." He got up on his hands and knees, dipping his back to thrust out his ass.

I didn't think. I knew where I wanted to be, knew how to get there, and in I went. He had a clenching, throbbing hold on me, all hot and smooth, but so strong. I gripped his ass cheek and his hip and slowly pushed deeper. Sweat broke out all over me while I watched his body stretch and swallow my cock until I was snug up to him, fully inside him.

I was *inside* Wes. I swear I felt his heart beating from the inside.

Of course, that's when I had to go and have some kind of twitchy seizure thing because oh, my God, I was inside another *person*. It was so real. And right there. And I was supposed to do something. What the fuck was I supposed to—

Oh.

I pulled partway out, moaned with Wes for how good that felt, and thrust back in again. Talk about mindless. I let it all go and my hips took over, no problem. This was, like...freedom. Just movement and sensations and letting everything happen. It was glorious and I reveled in it.

Until Wes smacked my thigh and said, "Up."

I paused. "What?"

"Lemme get up."

Even though I was teetering on the edge, I managed to grasp the fact he wanted me to stop and back up. Something might be wrong. Feeling super clumsy, I still managed to move away. I couldn't stop the whining sound that left me when my cock left him. "Wes, I—

What's—"

He rolled over quick and pulled his legs back. His whole groin was exposed to me. Cock hard, balls tight, and his ass right there, open and wet. I practically dove between his thighs.

"Yeah, baby, get back in me. I wanna see you fuck me, Mal. C'mon."

I fit my cock to his hole and pushed while watching his face. Oh, this was *better*. His eyes rolled back and closed and a moan rolled out of him as he reached down to stroke himself. I sank all the way into him, mesmerized by his fist flying over his swollen, red cock. He needed to come. He was going to come while I fucked him. I wrapped my arms around each of his legs and let my hips thrust fast. I was going to make Wes come.

"Yeah, yeah, yeah," I couldn't stop repeating. The grip, the slide, the heat of him wrapped all around me, and he'd clench tight, groan, while he jerked his dick and twitched from the pleasure. I sank lower on my knees and angled up with each thrust, trying to find that spot that would make him—

Wes howled and arched up, his body strung tight, his ass squeezing the hell out of my cock. Streamers of white shot out of his dick, splatting onto his chest and coating his fingers. I couldn't breathe as I slammed deep into him one more time and came, too. Gasping a breath, I groaned it out and my head swam from the pounding release and knowing I'd just filled his ass with my cum.

He was so mine. All mine.

I leaned against his legs, and he relaxed them against me, the opposite pressures the only thing keeping me upright. But then he spread his thighs wider, and I fell over onto him. I couldn't get my arms to work, to push me up, but he didn't seem to mind. We panted hard against each other. He hugged me, one hand covering the back of my head. I was almost folded in half, he was splayed under me, and it shouldn't have been comfortable at all, but it was so right and exactly where I needed to be.

The warm togetherness feeling washed through me again, and I almost got teary over it. The fucking had been filthy perfection, and here was the sweet glory of loving him. I hadn't realized sex could be so dirty and beautiful at the same time. It was dizzying. There was cum and sweat all over us, but I didn't want to move away from my Wes, the man I loved.

"Spoiled for life," he whispered.

"Hmm?"

"You've spoiled me for life." He pet my hair and gave me a squeeze. "It's never been so good. That it was you and bare inside me... Aw, God, baby, I've never done that before and I'm so glad it was with you. It was just... Sensational. *Epic*. No one'll ever top this."

Never had I ever made such a significant mark on someone else's life. His words choked me up all over again as I stared at the wall and blinked back tears. I didn't have anything to compare this to, but that Wes thought it was better than anything else he'd done, that it was more because of me and our trust, it *was* epic, and I finally knew what that meant.

I swallowed hard so my voice wouldn't crack. "I love you, Wes."

"Mmm, yeah, Mal. So much."

Chapter Seventeen

Friends and Misunderstandings

After that spectacular start to our vacation, I would've thought I'd be way too chill to freak about anything. But no. Once we'd cleaned up and left the bedroom, my nerves came roaring back with shaking hands, rebellious belly, and nervous sweat. This weekend was going to kill me.

I knew—I really did—that all I had to do was keep it together through some introductions, and then stick to Wes. I'd be just fine. Nothing would happen because these were his friends, most of them were gay or accepting, and they didn't know me at all. Hadn't that been one of the things that had sold me on first approaching Wes?

But, oh, the crazy quaking inside me wouldn't be convinced that this would be easy and survivable.

The setup of the house distracted me for a minute or two as I followed Wes down a spiral staircase. The floor with the bedrooms was nice, but this lower level was where the real living happened. Wes got to the bottom of the stairs and started greeting his friends, but I took a moment to appreciate the huge kitchen that flowed into a comfy sitting area positioned in front of a wall of windows overlooking the lake.

Brian and Jean-Louis were loaded. That was the only way they could afford such an amazing house. I wanted to go outside and look back at the house from there because I bet that was the impressive scenery I'd been looking for when we got here.

"Mal." Wes held up his hand for me.

Everyone was staring at me expectantly.

I needed a full breath from my lungs, but only managed a tiny gasp. I reached for Wes and the pressure of his hand holding mine got me down the last few steps. He put his arm around my back, holding my hip, and walked us over to a tall, muscular blond.

"Mal, this is Brian," Wes said.

I stuck my hand out to shake Brian's and pushed out, "Hi."

He grinned and his blue eyes flicked down to my hand and back up. *Oh, shit.* Did people not shake hands? Was I being a dork or something? I got a grip on the back of Wes's shirt.

Finally, Brian took my hand and shook it. "Nice to meet you, Mal. This is my partner, Jean-Louis."

I let go of Brian's hand to shake Jean-Louis', but he came right on into my space, put a hand on my shoulder, and pressed his cheek to mine on both sides. I didn't really do anything back except drop my hand and blink a few times. I'd never had anyone do that before, but I guessed I should've expected something like it from the French guy.

Jean-Louis smiled at me and shook his head before saying, "He's adorable," in French.

"I prefer handsome," I said back and was surprised at the snap to my tone.

His black eyebrows jumped up, brown eyes wide, grinning. "You speak French."

"Yes, I do." I cleared my throat.

"Your accent is very good."

"My teacher was Parisian."

"Ah! Excellent. Too often you Americans sound like Canadians."

Brian stage whispered to Wes, "You think they're going to do this all weekend?"

Wes chuckled and squeezed me, and I blushed.

Jean-Louis rolled his eyes. "My lover," he continued in French, "he only learns enough to be dangerous."

"Dangerous?" I asked.

"What's dangerous?" Brian asked in English. "Are you talking about me?"

Jean-Louis cupped Brian's jaw and kissed him. "You are dangerous," he said in English. "Mangling my language and making me not care because you only do it when you are naked."

Brian blushed, which made me snicker. And, suddenly, I realized this was okay. I'd made a good impression with my French and kind of gotten included in a little friendly teasing. Definitely okay stuff.

When a short redheaded girl, a tall skinny guy, and an Asian guy with a faux-hawk came over, I held tight to my realization and smiled at them. I could do this.

"Pumpkin Saunders," Wes said as he indicated the girl. "Her boyfriend there is Alan, and this is the irrepressible Roger Kwan."

Roger stepped up and kind of curtsied while holding his hand out to me like I was supposed to kiss it. I chuckled and reached for it, but he snorted a laugh and came in for a quick hug.

"It's fab to have you here, man," Roger said. "You need anything, you come see me." He winked before walking off to join Brian and Jean-Louis in unpacking grocery bags on a big island table in the center of the kitchen area.

"Count your underwear before you leave," the girl said. "And don't give him too much sugar."

I just blinked at her. She was so deadpan, but that had to be teasing, right? Then she smirked and stuck out her hand. I took it.

"It's nice to meet you, um…" Was I really supposed to call her Pumpkin?

"Yes, it's my real name," she said and let my hand go. "Parents." She shrugged. "I take comfort from the fact it isn't Carrot."

"Oh, wow. Yeah," I said, nodding. "It's a…cute name."

She snorted, and then looked up at the skinny guy partially behind her. She cocked her head at me while looking at him.

"Hi, Alan," I said, but didn't offer my hand since he stuffed his hands into his pockets.

Alan nodded at me, a tiny smile lifting his lips, and his prominent Adam's apple bobbing as he swallowed. He was kind of hunched, like a sunflower with a heavy bloom. *Oh, my God.* He was shy. Shier than *me*. I had an urge to hug him, but resisted for both our sakes. I'd make an effort to sit with him, though. He probably wouldn't make me do the small-talk thing.

Pumpkin giggled and patted Alan's chest before looping her arm through his. "Come on outside, guys. It's a gorgeous afternoon."

I quickly realized, the back of the house was the real selling point. *Here* was the awesome. The house had a redwood deck that had plateaus all the way down the hill to the water, the last level being a dock with a pretty impressive boat tied to it. Gorgeous landscaping of flowers and ferns, rocks and benches, followed the deck on both sides. Tall and broad maple trees provided some shade, and one thick branch held a tire swing.

If I'd grown up here, I never would've been bored.

Turning back, I got a good look at the house, specifically how the upper floor stuck out to make a roof over a huge sitting area. There was a fire pit covered now by a coffee table, a long couch and a couple of smaller ones, three chairs and an ottoman. It even had lamps, pillows, and knickknacks, like it was just another room of the house.

I was instantly in love with the whole place. Happily, I toured the grounds with Wes, holding hands and investigating everything. The boat was really cool since it had a top deck for driving, a big area on the back for sitting around, and a cabin inside with an eat-in kitchen and a bedroom. Wes said Brian and Jean-Louis sometimes took it out for a weekend and slept onboard.

A few hours later, at dinner, I sat at one the corner of the table, with Wes on the end, and Alan beside me. Though Alan and I didn't say much, it was still great because Wes, Pumpkin, and Brian—who were across from me—told stories on each other and had all of us laughing. Even when Pumpkin asked about Juan the El Camino, and Wes told the story about the car being how they met, it was a sad story I was glad to know.

"See, my dad was diagnosed with leukemia and we needed cash in the worst way. Then this hot guy," Pumpkin said and grinned at Wes, "comes sauntering down the driveway to ask about the beat up old clunker abandoned in the front yard." She paused and looked across the table at me. "Certified redneck." She hooked her thumb at herself.

I said absolutely nothing, just smiled. I wasn't my snotty father, but didn't know if congratulations were appropriate either.

Wes exaggerated a pout. "That poor car just needed some TLC."

"Uh-huh. It was rust and yellow paint chips." Pumpkin rolled her eyes. "There was *a tree* growing through the back of it."

I laughed at the image.

"Just a little sapling," Wes insisted.

Pumpkin snorted. "And the car *called* to you."

"It was screaming," Wes said seriously. "That was a rescue mission."

She practically hooted. "I still can't believe you paid eight grand for that heap of scrap."

Wes smiled. "I still can't believe you wouldn't take it back once I'd fixed it up."

"Nope." She shrugged, her blue eyes sort of twinkling. "Dad wouldn't have wanted that. Ol' Juan is your special baby."

A little pluck reverberated in my chest to know her dad hadn't lived. Pumpkin and Wes held hands for a second. There was probably more to the story, how they got closer, no doubt Wes being an excellent friend, but Pumpkin changed the subject.

"Alan's fixed up the Buick, Wes. Did I tell you?"

Though Alan fidgeted and stammered through it, Wes managed to coax out a few details about the job of restoring another car from the Saunders front yard. Apparently, Alan's shyness manifested in or was because of a stutter. My heart went out to him, but it was genuinely nice to see no one got impatient with him or made him feel any worse. He was a sweet guy. I actually wanted to be his friend, too. I found myself trying to project my own calmness so it might help him and it felt good to maybe understand him a little and be another person on his side.

After dinner, we headed back outside. I was glad to see Roger had a can of bug spray and hurried over to him. I was a magnet to buzzy little bugs and mosquito bites on me swelled up to gross proportions. My weekend would not be ruined by giant itchiness, thanks.

By the time I got to him, Roger had created a cloud of bug spray and was twirling around inside it like a music box ballerina. Thankfully, the wind was on my side and swept the cloud out over the water. Roger stepped toward me and opened his eyes before exhaling.

"I hate this stuff," he said, "but oh, my God, I am *not* a buffet."
He winked. "Not for mosquitos anyway." He pointed the bug spray
at me.

I chuckled and held my arms out. "Same here." I held my breath
while he sprayed all over the front of me, and then spun so he could
get my back, too.

"You want it in your hair?"

"Just a spritz." Mostly to myself, I added, "I'll just take another
shower before bed."

"Another, huh?" There was a leer to his voice. "Did you already
get dirty once today?"

A blush exploded across my face, but I turned back around and
grinned as I shrugged at him. A kinda not small part of me was
proud as hell for how I'd gotten dirty by fucking my boyfriend like
a boss. Roger laughed before looping his arm around my neck.

"I know we just got all anti-buggy, but come help me get some
beers, huh?"

I shrugged and smiled, and we went back inside. Brian and Jean-
Louis were putting leftovers away, so Roger and I waited by the table
for them to finish with the refrigerator. Was I about to have my first
beer? What would that be like? The whole set up was like a
summertime beer commercial. Kicking back with friends near some
water, good food, laughter... I'd just have one beer, see how that
went.

"So," Roger said conspiratorially beside me. "I know Wes does,
but do you play?"

"Play what?"

"With others."

I blushed, clueless and hating that I'd have to say so. "Um, I don't
understand."

He cocked his head and frowned. "Like... Swing? Invite a third?"

"Oh." Did he mean a threesome? He couldn't mean that.

But then he smiled and stepped closer, his fingers caressing up
my bare arm and making me shiver. "You wanna fuck, sweetie?" he
asked.

I gulped, staring. This wasn't just getting flirted with or even hit on. Roger wanted to have sex with me and Wes. Both of us. He'd even said— "What do you mean, Wes does?"

Roger shrugged. "He's brought other guys around, and we've had some fun." He stopped touching me. "It's no big deal."

No big deal? It was huge! I'd said I wouldn't share Wes. He'd agreed. I remembered that clearly. So what was this? No sharing with strangers, but it was okay with friends? *Oh, shit*. Was that expected? Was that what they did on these weekends? *Oh, my God*.

"Mal?" Roger reached for me, but I jerked back and jostled the table hard enough to send something glass crashing onto the floor.

Brian rushed over. "Shit, Mal, don't move."

I looked down and realized there were little shards of blue glass all around my bare feet. My heart pounding rapidly, urging me to flee, and I was stuck right here with Roger and the possibility I was some kind of sex party door prize. Had Wes let me fuck him so I'd know how? Or was my virgin ass for sale this weekend?

Tears burned at my eyes and my nose started to run as I stood there and sniffed, trying not to move while Brian swept and Roger held the dust pan. The last thing I needed was to cut my foot and faint from the blood.

"What happened?" There came Wes, striding in from outside. He reached for me, and I batted his hand away. "Mal?"

"It was me," Roger said from his position crouched at my feet.

Wes frowned. "You broke the whatever-it-was?"

"No, I screwed up. I thought Mal might—"

"Shut up," I snapped at him. "And stand up. I don't want you down there." Because he was practically kneeling and looking up at me and it was too much like maybe getting a blowjob and I didn't want to think of him like—

"Mal, what the hell hap—"

"Stop," Brian said and stood up. "Just hold on a goddamn minute. Mal, can you hop up onto the table? The glass is tiny and it went fucking everywhere."

I lifted my hands, arms shaking, and made to hop onto the table, but Wes was suddenly there and lifting me up under my arms. It was way too easy for him to do that and, this time, I didn't like it.

Our chests collided as he backed away from the area and pulled me into his body. He tried to wrap his arms around me, so I raised a knee and pushed at his shoulders. I didn't want to be held. "Don't manhandle me. Let me go."

"What the hell?" he said when I got free and shoved at him.

I didn't know where to go now that I could walk away without cutting my feet. But then Wes grabbed my arm and hauled me over near the stairs.

"I swear to God, Mal, what the hell is going on?"

"I'm not fucking Roger and neither are you." I poked him in the chest to punctuate my words and instantly felt like a child for doing it. "We said *no sharing* and I am *not* here for that. I don't care if you thought you could, it's—"

"You're damn right there's no sharing." He glared down at me. "Why the hell would you think otherwise?"

"Roger told me." I stepped closer and matched his glare. "He said you shared before. Brought guys up here and 'played.'" I made air quotes right in his face.

Wes's eyes widened and his mouth dropped open. What, did Roger ruin the surprise? A moment later, and Wes was back to frowning anger as he pointed a finger in my face.

"What happened before has nothing to do with you. It's not the same." He turned and went over to shove at Roger's shoulder, nearly toppling him over Brian who was still sweeping up glass.

I charged out the door and all the way down to the last landing before the water. For a crazy second, I wanted to jump in and scream until I went under. But I couldn't swim and I sure as hell wasn't going to die because Wes was an asshole.

His past didn't have anything to do with me? That didn't make sense. Couples shared that stuff; I knew they did. So what the hell did he mean? And what wasn't the same as what? The sharing, the place, me? *Oh, great.* Was I not good enough to share?

Well, that gave me pause and I sat down on the wooden deck. I didn't want to be shared, so I couldn't get upset if there was some qualification I didn't meet. I didn't *want* to meet it. Fuck them and their kinky sex weekend, or whatever the hell this was. I wouldn't participate. If that ruined all the "fun" and "play," well, too bad for them. My dumbass boyfriend who supposedly loved me should've asked first.

I huddled over my bent knees. Did Wes not mean it when he said he loved me? Was there some kind of love that meant it but also meant he wanted to have sex with other people? While I did, too? I was still getting used to *one* person, I couldn't possibly let another in. Sure, all the guys here were hot and interesting in their own way, but to just jump into sex with one of them—or more—was craziness. I couldn't do it. Had Wes thought I could?

Didn't he know me at all?

"I'm sorry."

I looked up at Roger. He stood slightly hunched over and grimacing, one arm across his stomach and gripping his other arm.

"It's fine," I told him and stared back out at the sunset-spangled water. *Go away.*

"No, it isn't." He came closer and sat down, wrapping his arms around his bent legs like me. "I didn't mean to fuck with you and Wes." He sighed. "I mean, with your *heads*. To cause trouble? You guys are new, so I didn't think it was that serious yet. But I guess everyone else saw it, except me. So I'm sorry."

I shrugged. "It is fine. It wasn't really your fault." I rubbed at my eye, and then rested my cheek on my knee to look at him. "We'd kind of talked about it, but not really. He never said he'd done that stuff before. And it never occurred to me, so... I just freaked." I cleared my throat. "I sometimes do that."

"I guess it could be shocking at first."

"Is it..." I hesitated to pry, but he did start all this. "Is it something you do a lot?"

Roger grinned. "What exactly?"

Damn my blushing. "The, uh, three people swinging thing."

He made a little hiccup sound, and I rolled my eyes. My innocence was screaming out at him, no doubt. At least he was making an effort not to laugh too much. I concentrated on the water again and let him get hold of himself enough to answer.

"Um, well, sometimes," he said. "If the guy's hot, if the couple's willing. It's just sex, you know? Feeling good with like-minded guys." He cleared his throat. "But I don't mess with monogamy and commitments. I get that that's different. It'd maybe be nice to have that someday."

He sounded a little wistful there. I didn't have any experience with sex just being sex, but it was probably possible. I could understand seeking out what I had when Wes and I made love. Maybe it helped people feel not so alone, even if just for a little while. Was Roger lonely?

"I'm sorry I freaked."

"It's okay. I'm sorry I came on too strong."

I flashed him a smile and nodded. He didn't seem like a threat anymore. And neither did his ideas. I still didn't understand Wes, but at least this wasn't the kinkfest I'd thought it was.

Roger mimicked my tucked up position. "You get that you've got nothing to worry about, right? I've known Wes a long time, and I've never seen him like this with someone. He means it, Mal."

I sighed. "Then how come there's this sharing thing?"

"Some people share. There's nothing wrong with that."

"I don't like it."

"Then don't do it."

"Well, I'm not."

"And neither is Wes."

"Uh-huh." I'd believe that when Wes told me.

Roger huffed an annoyed breath and pointed up at the house. "He was just in there yelling at me for even suggesting it to you. And when he was done, the rest of them jumped in."

"Oh. I didn't hear—"

"And I just said they all saw how much he loves you." He wrapped his arm around his knees. "I'm sorry I missed seeing it myself because we could've avoided all this."

They all saw how Wes loved me? I sighed and closed my eyes for a second. "I love him, too."

"So how come you're out here alone, and he's inside packing?"

I sat up. "Packing?"

Roger sat up, too, and stretched out his legs. "Yep."

"Son of a bitch." I stood. "He's not leaving me here."

I stalked up the walkway toward the house.

Everyone paused in the kitchen, their conversations going silent, and watched me. I didn't stop, heading right up the spiral staircase to the top. I did, unfortunately, have to take a moment to regain my equilibrium after that fast spin. But then I was off down the hall to our room.

Wes was tossing things into his bag on end of the bed. I stood in the doorway and said, "You are *not* leaving me here."

"No, I'm not," he said without looking up. "Grab your shit."

"What?"

He finally looked at me, frowning. "We're leaving, Mal."

"Why?"

He dropped the shirts in his hands and stepped toward me. "*Why?* Because my friend just hit on you, scared the hell out of you, pissed me off, and now I don't…know what to do." He'd gone from angry to lost by the end of that. Quietly, he asked, "What do you want to do?"

That was easy. "I wanna know why you shared other guys."

"I didn't love them."

That was it? *That* was the difference? *Oh, hell, I'm an idiot.* I closed my eyes and covered them with my hand as I sighed.

"I love you, Mal." But he sounded scared saying it now.

I opened my eyes, and he still looked so lost. I was finally finding my way, but I needed a little more direction. "Why did you say your past has nothing to do with me?"

"Because it's not the same with you." He touched his belly and grimaced. "The thought of someone else touching you makes me feel sick."

I rubbed at my eyes. That's what he'd meant.

"Mal, did… Did you want to? With Roger? With—"

"No. Not at all."

My quick answer seemed to relieve him since he gulped and put a hand over his heart.

"And I don't want you to either," I said and stepped closer to him. "That thing we said about not sharing? At the garage? It's a…condition. A requirement. We're never doing that."

"Never, Mal. I swear."

"Okay. Me, too."

I reached for him, and he was there in a heartbeat. We hugged so close and tight, his shiver skated through both of us. When he straightened up, lifting me off my feet, this time I hugged his hips with my knees. He turned and got on the bed, laying down on top of me and hiding his face in my neck.

I got it now. He'd been scared, packing to run away with me. Had he thought I'd wanted to be with Roger? So while I'd felt betrayed, he'd felt worried. It'd be sweet, if we weren't such morons.

"I got upset," I whispered, "because I thought you hadn't yet told me the weekend was, like, some big boyfriend-swapping sex party."

He snorted against my throat before lifting his head. "Jesus, Mal, I'd never have brought you to something like that." He kissed my cheek. "I wouldn't ever ambush you with something like that. Not *you*."

He did know me well.

I hugged him with arms and legs. "I'm sorry I made assumptions and spazzed out on you."

He nodded. "I'm just sorry."

"Yeah, me, too."

He cleared his throat and lifted his head. "Baby, I love you, but you stink."

"Stink? Oh, the bug spray."

We got off the bed, and I wasn't sure if I should shower and spend the rest of the evening right here. No, I couldn't do that. We might as well keep packing and leave, if we weren't going to spend time with the rest of them. And Wes was looking at me with an expression that asked what I was going to do next.

I took Wes's hand and led him from the room. He slowed us down in the hallway.

"You should know…" Wes said quietly. "Roger will probably end up in someone's bed tonight. It's friendship and affection and no big deal for him, but he only goes where he's wanted like that."

I nodded. "Yeah, he told me about that."

"And Brian and Jean-Louis will sometimes do it with Roger or with someone else. Their relationship's completely solid, but they just…open it up sometimes. It's only meant to be for fun and has to be someone they're both into."

I shook my head. "I just don't understand that."

"That's fine. You don't have to. Just try not to judge them for—"

"Oh, no, I wouldn't judge."

"Okay."

"Okay." I smiled back at him, took a deep breath, and headed down the staircase into the kitchen.

Everyone was out on the deck, the sun just peeking over the trees across the lake now. Long shadows thrust across the water like fingers pointing. Roger still sat on the last dock down by the water while everyone else was in the sitting area under the overhang of the house.

Wes sat down beside Brian on the couch, and there were a few murmurs about if everything was okay, but I was focused on Roger. I knew what it felt like to be outcast and I didn't want him feeling like he should do it to himself or that the rest of them were allowed to keep him out. He'd made a mistake, but all was forgiven now.

I went down and took Roger's hand, leading him back up and into the group. We sat on the ottoman together in the middle of everyone like a pair of citronella candles. Wes's smile made me feel good inside, and Roger giving me a little hug let me know I had a new friend.

Chapter Eighteen

Accidentally on Purpose

On the Fourth, it seemed like every house around the lake was set up with a game of some kind and a table of drinks or snacks to encourage neighbors to wander from yard to yard. Brian and Jean-Louis had put down a Twister mat, and Roger was trying to entice every muscle-bound jock who sauntered by to come play with him. Wes, Pumpkin, Alan, and I sat on the deck one level up from Roger's, laughing at his over-the-top attempts.

It had been a great day. Not one ounce of nervousness or bout of miscommunication. I was feeling very good, totally relaxed. I had spent part of the day alone in town with Wes and the rest of the day here. We'd even gone around the lake in the boat, Wes showing off his skill at driving it. Honestly, I couldn't remember ever having had a better day.

Watching the sun slip lower, only just peeking over the trees now, I was getting excited for the fireworks. People were on their boats or in their yards, settling in for the display as the time ticked closer. I couldn't seem to sit still, and Wes kept chuckling at me.

Earlier, he had refused to let me get a beer or even a fruity little wine cooler. But I'd discovered I could kiss him after he took a drink of his beer and taste it by running my tongue all over the inside of his mouth. I wasn't a giant fan of the taste of beer, but when he switched to an alcoholic apple cider, I loved it. He hadn't caught on to what I was doing, but I knew he was enjoying my attentions from the smoldering looks he kept giving me.

Last night, after everything, we'd gone to bed and kissed and held each other. It had been comforting. Tonight, I was going to get good and laid. I wanted all kinds of explosions.

Wes took another swig from the bottle. I waited for him to swallow, and then leaned in for another kiss. As I slid my tongue over his and the roof of his mouth, he moaned into me. I licked around a little more, before giving his lips a peck.

"You little shit." He grinned. "I just figured out what you're doing."

"What?" I tried for innocence, failing since I blushed.

"You're drinking through me." He laughed, and so did Pumpkin and Alan. "You kiss me like a nympho after every drink I take."

"Do not," I muttered, blushing hotter. A nympho? Good grief.

He nuzzled my neck, biting me softly. "Kiss me like that again, and I might have to take you inside before the fireworks."

I nibbled my bottom lip. Tempting as that suggestion was, I wanted my first Fourth of July party complete with fireworks just a little bit more. He took another drink, staring me in the eyes, and laughed at me when I didn't kiss him this time. But he did pull me tight to his side.

I was lost in the warmth and scent of bonfires, greenness, and Wes for a while, just listening to the conversations around me and watching the sun dip below the tree line. Roger finally attracted two guys to play with him, and I smiled as they laughed at something Roger said. Right then, I envied him. He wasn't afraid at all to speak up, gain attention, and get what he wanted. So not me. I'd managed to get to know everyone staying in the house well enough, but…Wes was always there. Dammit, but I didn't want to use him like a crutch. I wanted to be able to do things on my own. I really did.

My gaze strayed over to the neighbors' yard. They were an older couple named… Crap, I couldn't remember. It was something old-fashioned like Elmer and Mavis. But they adored Brian and Jean-Louis like a local set of grandkids, and they'd set up a table covered in different bottled drinks. Wes had gotten his cider from there, but

I hadn't been thirsty. Right now, there was a swarm of people between me and the table. I wanted to walk over there with my head up, smile at people, and get a drink, just like any normal person would.

Gulping, but suddenly determined, I sat up and uncrossed my legs. Wes raised his eyebrows at me in silent question. "I'm going to get a drink," I said.

He grinned. "Something non—"

"Non-alcoholic, I know." I stood. "I'll be a good boy."

"Part of why I love you."

Oh, yeah, that kind of thing helped. Feeling lifted, I headed up the grassy hill to the table.

The encouragement faded as I had to excuse my way closer to my target. There didn't seem to be any good way of interrupting people as I wove through bodies. When I stepped on a woman's foot and then stumbled back into a guy, I nearly gave up and ran back to Wes. General attention freaked me out enough; having hostility aimed at me was going to break me fast. But I persevered that final two feet and made it to the table.

I had to take a moment to stand there and breathe, hand over my galloping heart, before I could focus on the options. Was there really nothing soda-based? My God, I could barely see. I closed my eyes and tried for deep breaths. After three of them, I was suddenly worried people might notice me panicking and opened my eyes. I surreptitiously looked around, but only the woman I'd stepped on was glaring at me. I'd have to give her a wide berth on the way back.

And no, there didn't seem to be anything non-alcoholic on the table.

"If you find a Bud Light, send up a flare."

I startled to find a girl standing beside me. She smiled at me, teeth dazzling white and blue eyes bright. I tried to smile back. She made me think of that blonde actress who played ditzes in those spoof movies but who was actually smart in real life. Her little summer dress was pale yellow with tiny pink flowers. She was cute.

"Um, same thing if you see a Coke," I said and was impressed with myself for managing it.

She held up a finger and ducked under the table. When she came back up, she handed a sixteen-ounce bottle to me.

"Hey, thanks." I took it from her. "Shoot, it's warm."

We both looked back at the overburdened table—no ice in sight.

"Yeah," she said with a little laugh, "good luck with that."

I laughed with her, suddenly realizing I was doing it. I was interacting and talking and not screwing it up at all. *Yay me!*

"I'm Tanya." She gave me her hand.

"Mal."

She had soft skin and pink fingernail polish. Her thumb rubbed the back of my hand before she let go.

"Do you live around here?" she asked, her face open and curious.

I shook my head. "Just here for the Fourth."

"Yeah, me, too. What school do you go to?"

"Well, I don't yet, but I'll be at Akron U this fall."

"Yeah?" Her face lit up. "Me, too! I'm finally a sophomore."

"Finally?"

She rolled her eyes. "I thought it was in the bag at the end of spring. But then I discovered I wasn't doing so well in this horrible trig class." She shrugged.

"Oops." Hadn't she kept track of her progress?

"Yeah, but that's what summer sessions are for." She winked at me.

I smiled because I thought I was supposed to. "Well, um, at least you know your way around campus. I haven't seen it yet." Which made my stomach cramp all of a sudden. Maybe Wes would take me there soon, like a trial run. That would probably—

Tanya stepped closer, her breast grazing my arm. "It's a great school. You'll find your groove and love it. And hey," she said with a grin as she touched my upper arm, "now you've already got a friend on campus."

I blinked at her because… Oh, my God, was she *flirting* with me? That didn't make any sense. Nobody had ever flirted with me before. I was pretty sure anyway. This didn't look the same as the long-distance version Wes had explained ages ago at the ice cream shop.

She moved closer still, and that was a definite boob-graze to my arm. "Do you know what you're going to study?" She had to know she was poking me with her chest, but she was doing a great job of looking innocent.

"Oh, um. Computer science," I said, but only because I didn't think running away would be polite. And, knowing me, I'd probably take down ten people during my sprint.

"Cool. I know a few people in that field." She winked at me again. Definitely flirty. "You don't look like a computer geek, though."

I actually looked down at myself. A red T-shirt with the white stripes and stars of a flag hugged my chest a little tighter than I was used to, but Wes had said it looked good when he bought it for me that morning. Cargo shorts that somehow managed to make my legs look a little less skinny. Bare feet. Yeah, I guess I wasn't geeked out at the moment. When I looked back up, she giggled at me and sort of cuddled into my side. I held my breath and felt my eyes go wide.

"Are you here with anyone, Mal?"

I nodded. *Oh, hey.* That was how I could end this insanity. "My boyfriend, actually."

She jerked back. "What?"

"I'm here with my boyfriend."

As I watched her upper lip curl and eyes narrow, I realized that I'd just outed myself and that she was disgusted by this new information about me. I gulped and stepped back, bringing my Coke bottle up in front of me like a shield.

"You're a fag?" she practically shouted.

Trepidation vanished and I glared at her. "No, I'm gay."

"Whatever." She brushed at her dress like she was cleaning it off. "I can't believe you *touched* me."

What the hell? "I didn't touch you. *You* were practically humping me."

When her mouth dropped open and her face flushed red, fists clenched at her sides, I realized it was time to go. Quickly. I didn't run exactly, but I didn't waste time either. I arrived back on the deck with Wes much faster than I'd left and only somewhat sure I hadn't knocked anyone over on the way.

"You okay?"

I looked down at Wes staring up at me. "Um. Maybe."

I looked back toward the table, but couldn't see her. No one else seemed to care either. Feeling sudden relief, I dropped down to sit on the deck. My fingers ached when I loosened my grip on my Coke.

"Mal?" Wes reached over and held my hand.

I smiled at him. "I just came out to a homophobe."

His green eyes went wide. "Uh... Why?"

"She was hitting on me." I blew out a breath and put a hand over my heart. "I thought flirting was supposed to be subtle. That was like using a mallet to open a peanut shell."

Wes snorted and grinned. "So a girl was flirting with you, and you came out to make her stop?"

"Seriously, Wes, she was..." I peeked at Pumpkin and Alan, but they weren't paying attention. "She was *rubbing* on me. Like, her boob on my arm. It was kinda freaking me out." I shivered and it wasn't for effect.

He bit his lips together, but it didn't stop him from smiling at all. I shoved at his shoulder, and he laughed out loud. Now, afterward, it was a little funny, so I let myself chuckle, too.

"C'mere," he said and spread his arms and legs open, patting the space between his thighs. Since I could use a cuddle, I moved around until I could sit with my back to his front. I sighed as I leaned against him, his arms tight around me.

He nuzzled into my neck to drop a kiss and sigh against my skin. I smiled, tilting my head to let him in, and rested my hands on his knees to tickle my palms with the hairs there. He gave me another kiss, and then both of us jumped when a huge red, white, and blue explosion lit up the sky over the water.

"Beautiful," Wes whispered.

I nodded because it was. Everything was.

Chapter Nineteen

You're the One

Lying in bed with Wes in the morning, just cuddled up and lazy, was one of my most favorite things in the world now. We talked and laughed, kissed, and sometimes made plans. So it felt perfectly natural to broach a subject I'd been mulling over. It was our last day at the lake before we'd have to go back to the real world and that's what put this idea in my head.

"Since we're going to the same school in a few weeks," I said, toying with his hair, "what do you think about maybe living together?"

He blinked at me and looked...uncomfortable.

I blushed, my heart thudding hard. "Oh. Um, that's a bad idea, then?"

He rolled onto his back and stared up at the ceiling, sighing.

Shit. I closed my eyes, not wanting to see when he said he loved me but not *that* much. Maybe this weekend of being together all the time hadn't been as amazing for him as it had for me? I could've sworn he'd had a great time—after the mess with Roger got cleared up, of course. Was that still an issue somehow?

"When I was your age," Wes said quietly, "I was all over the place. Meeting new people, dating all kinds of guys. Then I met—" He cut himself off and shook his head like he didn't want to go there.

"Things started to change a couple years ago. I stopped wanting to just have fun."

He sighed again and turned his head toward me. I got the feeling he didn't want to say whatever it was, but felt like he had to. I braced myself for something awful.

"I want to be in a long-term, committed relationship, Mal."

I frowned and blinked at him. And? What did that— Oh, damn him. He was expecting me to say that wasn't what I wanted. Because I was younger? Fresh out of the closet? Seriously?

He huffed a breath and looked away, pinching over his eyes with his fingers. "I know. I shouldn't expect that from someone your age—"

"Asshole."

He flinched and stared, his eyes wide.

"I'm eighteen, so I couldn't possibly know what I want? Well, what if I do know?"

I didn't. Not entirely. I knew I wanted him, but other than that I didn't have a fucking clue what I wanted. I wasn't going to lie there and let him assume I'd run for the hills because he'd said he wanted a commitment, though. Yes, sweet holy hell, Wes Kinney was saying he wanted me and nobody but me. That right there was reason enough to pass out. And maybe because I thought that was awesome, that meant commitment was what I wanted, too.

"What are you saying?" Wes asked.

"I'm saying, love me and live with me and all that stuff." I cleared my throat and relaxed because I sounded angry. I tried again, softer this time. "Really, Wes, I may not have known a lot of love in my life, but I know what I feel for you, and I don't want to lose that."

"What about that girl?"

"What girl?"

"The one you came out to last night. Mal, that's going to happen a lot."

I squinted at him. "Are you saying all this because you think I won't be able to handle people hating me? Being bullied?" I snorted at him. "Have you forgotten who you're talking to?"

He didn't say anything, but he did reach over and thread his fingers into the hair at my temple and rest his palm on my cheek. I stared into his eyes, feeling like this was more important than I really understood. What was he trying to say? What was I?

"If you hadn't come out to her," he said quietly, "you might've been able to see what it was like to date a girl."

"But I'm gay."

"Maybe you're bi."

I frowned at him. "What?"

He took his hand back and curled his arms near his chest. He looked…vulnerable.

"You've said you never had a chance to explore who you really are," he said. "Maybe you're bisexual. Maybe I've—" He sighed heavily and looked away. "Maybe I've taken advantage of you."

"That's insane. You seriously think I'd let you manipulate me or something?" I poked his temple to make him look at me again. "I love the sex we have, Wes. I love being with you, period."

He gave me a small, sad smile. "I do, too. But I don't want to be what's holding you back."

"Holding me back?" I sat up. "Are you kidding me? Like I'd want the chance to fuck anyone I saw as some kind of experiment or something?" I ran one hand up into my hair and gripped hard as he looked at me guiltily. "Oh, come on."

"I'm not the best catch in the world," he said and there was such defeat in his voice. "You're supposed to come out and play the field and see who and what you like best."

I didn't know what else to say. How was it possible he didn't believe he was good enough for me? How could he think I wouldn't choose him? That this amazing man didn't have the confidence to believe I'd pick him over someone—everyone—else just didn't make sense to me. Couldn't he see how wonderful he was?

I leaned over him, nearly nose to nose. "You're not holding me back, Wes. You've set me free."

I watched his eyes turn glassy as he swallowed hard. He wanted to believe.

"I don't want to find a better man," I whispered down to him. "There's no one better than you. And I don't care if some other label might fit me more someday, because I'm in love with you right now."

Maybe the time for words was over. I rolled over onto him and kissed him, all tongue and lips and delving deep inside him. He made a small sound that seemed a little sad and a lot needy as his hands slid over my back and those strong arms held me tight. *Poor Wes.* I couldn't let him think he wasn't absolutely wanted.

I gentled my kiss, wanting to show him I loved him, not just that I desired him. The difference between want and need, I guessed. Maybe, too, it was important right then to show him that I didn't hesitate to love the fact that he was very definitely male.

He sighed as I started kissing my way down his body. I gripped his biceps, feeling their strength, and nuzzled into the hair on his chest. Smiling up at him watching me, I made sure to lick and rub my face on him so he'd know I was happy with his maleness there. He gave me a small grunt and a little grin.

I devoted myself to his nipples, flicking them with the tip of my tongue to get them all pointy before I sucked them bright red. He was humming by then, so I nipped to get a groan. I did love his sounds.

I wiggled down farther, pressed my chest against his erection, and sucked at his abs. I think he tensed them up so I could properly appreciate every ridge and valley with my tongue and lips. I'd never done it before, but I managed to suck up a mark just south of his navel, where his skin was soft and smooth. It felt like I'd signed my name.

He was biting his bottom lip when I looked up at him, hunger all over his handsome face.

I chuckled when his cock poked my chin. I didn't have any scratchy stubble to torment him with, but it sounded like my baby-smooth cheek did the trick anyway. I rubbed and licked, hoping he'd see this for the happiness it was. His dick was just about the best toy I could ever have to play with. There wasn't a single thing I didn't love about it. The soft skin on my tongue, the salty taste—*suck, suck*—that musky male scent trapped in the hairs at its base—*tug, nibble*—and the way it made my mouth open wide to take it all the way in—*swallow.*

"Ugh, Mal!"

I pushed up on my hands, bobbing my head, only to discover that he could thrust up and do it himself. I stayed put, sucking as he pulled back, and let him fuck my mouth. *See, Wes, see? Look what I let you do to me. I wouldn't if I didn't love you.* I stared up at him, hoping he could read all of that in my expression.

When he pressed up into my mouth and came, I held still and tried hard not to follow him over the edge. I did manage to gentle my sucking and relax a bit as I swallowed every spurt he gave me. When he groaned, I lifted off and crawled close on my knees. Grasping my did, I pulled only three times before I was coming all over him, painting him with stripes of white. I was kinda proud that one of them hit his chin as he watched me.

I kind of collapsed over him, catching myself on one hand. I took a deep breath, savoring the scent of sex, and slid my hand through the mess I'd made. Looking him right in those shining and hugely dilated green eyes, I swirled a bit of cum into the plum mark I'd made on him.

"My Wes," I said, hearing the rasping depth of my voice and enjoying the shiver that shot through him.

He nodded at me, still sucking in deep lungfuls of air. *Well, yay, he gets it. Good boy.* I chuckled at myself and flopped down onto my side next to him.

He turned and kissed my forehead. "I do want to."

"Hmm?"

"Live with you at school. We can get an apartment."

I smiled, feeling the heat of happiness blossom inside me. "An apartment would be great. My parents are paying for everything for me, and they said that was an option."

He didn't need to say it. I could see it in his eyes.

"I haven't told them anything about us," I said, "and I'm not going to. But only they won't know. I want to be out with you everywhere else in every other situation."

He smiled his sweet smile. "I can live with that. And if you ever want to tell them, I'll be right there with you, if you want."

"Thank you," I said, though I doubted that would happen anytime soon.

He rolled onto his side, apparently fine with being sticky. I could hear the excitement in his voice as he said, "It's going to be so amazing, Mal. So free. We'll meet new people, have fun, and spend every night together."

"Like being here."

He nodded and gave me a little kiss before he made an amused sound. "And study really hard," he said as though remembering the purpose of the whole thing.

I chuckled. "Every now and then."

Chapter Twenty

Apartments and Driving Lessons

"What do you think?"

I shrugged at Wes. He knew more than I did about apartment hunting. That was obvious the instant he'd asked the property manager about amenities, what was and wasn't included in the rent, and how they handled security. I let him take over that stuff and only really cared when we got to the cost. It was higher than my parents were willing to pay—since they still thought I'd be living alone and I wasn't going to correct them on that—but splitting the rent amount with Wes made continuing to dupe my parents totally doable.

What would it be like to make this place my home? Well, *our* home, but to be in charge of it all. Wes would get his things out of storage, and we would make a home here. Together. I felt impossibly grown-up and, as exciting as that was, I was also…frightened.

"Mal?"

I sighed. "I don't know. It's nice, I guess." I looked around again at the boring white walls and beige carpeting. "I can't see it with stuff in it, but it seems…big and…fine."

He shook his head, grinning. "How about the neighborhood then?

"That I like."

It was called Highland Square and was kind of like it's own little village inside the city. You could stand on the sidewalk, look East, and there was downtown Akron—and the campus—but this place felt like a fun spot with nightclubs, bars, cute shops, and even a grocery store. Tons of trees, a little library, and everything around it was just a short drive away.

Plus, apparently, this was *the* place to be if you were a gay college student in Akron. I figured that had to be a great benefit.

With the property manager back down in her office and waiting for us there, I walked over to Wes and leaned into his chest. "I've missed waking up with you," I quietly admitted. Because as scary big as this move was, I did desperately want to be with Wes. It had been a week since our vacation at the lake together and I ached without him.

He put his arms around me and kissed my cheek and the corner of my mouth. "We could get bikes and ride to school when it's warm. There's a bus stop right out front, too." He paused, and then smiled at me. "You can drive my car whenever you need to, though."

That seemed really significant, but... "I don't know how to drive."

He blinked, one eyebrow going up. "Huh. Well, then, I'll teach you."

"Really?"

"Sure." He smirked. "I hear people learn better when there's a rewards system in place. I suddenly have a lot of ideas for that."

A sparkle of sexual desire went through me as I grinned up at him. "Can I have a demonstration? Just to know if this is the right program for me. I mean, there's always Triple-A."

He snorted. "Starting the car," he said and kissed me briefly.

I made a "meh" noise and shrugged a little.

"Adjusting the mirrors." A kiss with tongue that made me cling to him.

Breathlessly, I said, "Mirrors are so important."

"Mm-hmm." He slid a hand down my back. "Putting it in reverse." A quick grope to my ass.

I gasped and tipped up in case he wanted to do that again.

He kissed at my neck and bent his knees so he could stand up again while sliding his hard body against me. "Easing...down the driveway."

Dear God, what would merging into traffic get me? I was already erect and aching. *Oh, man...* I'd get a boner during every driving lesson now. That should make the eventual driving test with a cop beside me really interesting.

"Wes, I think—"

But he bit at my neck and rumbled, "Parallel parking." His finger firmly and rhythmically pressed the seam of my pants into my crack.

And I was *there*. Not thinking of parking at all, but that feeling of spreading myself open and letting him have me, giving everything up to him, burst to the surface and left me moaning in his ear. "I wanna," I begged.

"Yeah?" He rubbed into my ass harder, but said, "Maybe we'll find a nice, quiet lot for you to practice in on the way home."

I shuddered and whined his name because he wasn't hearing me.

But he chuckled, the sound like sin, and dropped to his knees. I gasped and stared while his big hand pressed on my belly, pushing me against the wall behind me. I flattened myself against it, cock straining at my fly. He nuzzled into my groin and moaned as my dick rolled a little bit back and forth. I thrust my fingers into his hair and got a grip on his shirt collar, already panting too much to beg him not to stop.

He did that wicked chuckle again, but he tugged open my pants, too. Actually, he got them open, and then he surprised me by pushing them and my briefs down to my ankles. I gulped at the feeling of vulnerable exposure and looked around even though I knew the door was closed and we were completely alone. My erection didn't fade at all, though. That flutter of wanting others to know Wes wanted me—wanted me so much he couldn't wait, didn't care where we were—made me groan and pull him closer.

"Mmm, yes," I said, my voice huskier, as he eased my cock into the heat and wetness of his perfect mouth. His lazy slurping made me grin and relax against the wall, closing my eyes.

The hand he'd had pressed to my belly petted a little, and then slid down to fondle my balls. I massaged his scalp and the back of his neck because I wanted to let him know I loved this. Not just for what he did, but that he wanted to do at all. I couldn't get over that fact. But I was distracted by...

Huh. He had his finger in his mouth beside my cock. That looked and felt kinda weird, but his green eyes blinking up at me and sort of twinkling mischievously made me chuckle. He took his finger out and amped up the suck and bob of his mouth on me. I moved with him, just a little, and let the heat of desire build and build. No rush, but oh how good this felt.

Wes eased my thighs farther apart, and I complied, smiling. Braced against the wall, knees bent and spread, I rocked my hips with the bob of his head. Then his wet finger touched me very close to my asshole.

I gasped and stilled. He stared up at me while I stared down at him. *What is he...* His slippery finger pushed into me, and I realized *he knew.* Wes knew I wanted him to fuck me. More than the fantastic feeling of the stretching invasion of him inside me, I suddenly came so hard right then from knowing he wanted to fuck me, too.

My mind reeled for the way my ass clenched and released on his finger while he sucked the cum out of my cock. Did it do that because he was in there? Did it always do that and I'd never noticed? I remembered the feel of his ass spasming all around me the only time I'd fucked him. I wanted to give him that feeling. I wanted his cock inside me.

He pulled off and sat back on his heels. I panted and blinked, trying to focus, and realized he had his cock poking out through the fly of his pants. His fist sped over it, tugging the orgasm out of himself. A shiver snaked through me as I watched him beat off. He was so rough, demanding. His narrowed eyes raked over me, and then he arched and shot onto the floor by my foot, spattering white cum on the entryway linoleum as it jetted out of his cock.

And I needed that.

With a whine, I dropped down to the floor. Shivering when my bare ass met the cool wall, I slurped Wes's fat, hot cock into my mouth and sucked greedily. He groaned and gripped at my hair. "Oh, fuck," he said. "That's hot. Jesus, baby."

I knew he was too sensitive to keep going, but the salty taste of him on my tongue was all I'd wanted. I pulled back and licked my lips, blinking in a weird daze at him now. My smile felt crooked on my face.

When he grabbed me up and kissed me all sloppy tongues and moaning breaths, I collapsed against him like somebody'd cut my strings. I felt so…open. Was that the feeling? Maybe. I'd have given him anything right then. He chose to cradle me in his arms and trace the contours of my face with a fingertip.

"Think this counts," he asked, "as a housewarming party?"

I huffed a laugh.

"My parents are having an actual party for theirs this weekend. Mom finally unpacked the last box and, apparently, that's reason enough for a party. It's an open house sort of thing for new neighbors and old friends—their work friends, too." He kissed me. "And you, of course."

"Okay."

He nuzzled into my neck. "It's possible you might have to spend the night."

I just hummed, basking.

"Let's go sign the lease on our new home, baby."

Whatever he wanted.

Chapter Twenty-One

Too Many Secrets

"Sure I can't convince you to stay?" Wes asked.

I smiled and cuddled closer against him here in the little foyer of the Kinney's house. "You know I would, if it wasn't for that call."

He grumbled and sighed, but he didn't argue.

I'd walked out the door of my house a few hours earlier, merging with other neighbors going to the Kinney's open house party. My parents had known where I was going, having refused to "engage" with such a "ridiculous" crowd—my father's words. Neither of them had liked my decision, but that was just too bad. Now, though, a terse and angry call from my father had demanded I come home.

Despite all my newfound strengths, I couldn't quite ignore that.

"Thanks for coming," Wes said and winked before he kissed me.

I rolled my eyes and nipped at his bottom lip. He laughed quietly. Wes opened the door. "Come again."

"Oh, shut up," I said on a chuckle and walked out onto the porch.

We waved at each other as I crossed the street, but then Wes closed the door and I knew I needed to get my game face on. God forbid I walk into my house too happy, carrying around any sort of delight over having fraternized with the enemy while my father could see me.

Yeah, part of me wanted to rebel. I mean, for crying out loud, I'd gone off on a vacation with Wes not that long ago. In my father's eyes that should've been a whole lot "worse" than eating a few hors d'oeuvres and sipping sparkling cider right across the street. This party was miles tamer than what we'd done that weekend—not that my father knew or ever would know that.

What was the big deal?

I opened the front door and found my parents sitting in the living room. My mother fidgeted with the pleats of her skirt and didn't look up. Sitting with his legs crossed and looking like a king ready to have me executed, my father frowned at me and waved for me to take a seat on the couch.

Apparently, I was actually in trouble. I sat down, more curious to see what he'd do than anything else. I'd never been punished before. Not really. I was always the victim of the bad things other people did.

"You've been spending entirely too much time with those people," he said.

I frowned back at him. "There's nothing wrong with them. I'm even pretty sure Mr. Kinney is a Republican." A total lie, but maybe it would help.

"I don't care about the parents. It's that boy."

That boy. He said it like Wes was some kind of… *Oh, shit.* Could my father tell Wes was gay? Had he seen the rainbow bumper sticker on Juan?

Did my father think I was gay?

Do you care?

That was a scary thought. Mostly. Sort of? I'd planned not to tell them, afraid of what they might say, how intolerant they were. Did I really care what they said? If he yelled? If they were disappointed in or disgusted with me?

Not really.

"Well?" my father snapped. "Why do you spend so much time over there? Why do you go gallivanting off with that boy?" He glared at me. "He's a bad influence, Malcolm. Obviously, since this defiance is unlike you."

"He's not a bad influence." I matched his glare. "Wes has been a great friend. I've learned so much from him this summer."

"Like what?" my father dared. "What have you learned?"

I gulped. How was I supposed to say— What could I— *Oh*. "I've learned how to be a man."

My father snorted derisively. "That boy's no man. He acts more like—" He cut himself off and his eyes flicked all around. *Oh, shit.* Was he making connections? Did he know?

"Malcolm," he said with a frightening sort of calm. "Malcolm, you answer me honestly. Do you hear me?"

I nodded, mesmerized and terrified.

"Is that boy homosexual?"

I couldn't take a breath for the longest time. This was it. I hadn't ever wanted them to find out, but my father had guessed. Well, suspected about Wes anyway. Same difference, really. I glanced at my mother; she shook her head frantically, her eyes wide and glassy.

"Malcolm," my father barked, making me flinch.

"He is," I whispered. Even though I shook and felt like I might cry, I still said, "And so am I."

I heard my mother gasp, but my gaze was glued to my father's face as he morphed into someone I could barely recognize. Flushed and snarling at me, he said, "I *knew* it."

I'd never heard my father sound so enraged before in my life. He stared at me with dark eyes full of...hate. Oh, my God, my father *hated* me. I'd known they'd be disappointed and angry, but this? I couldn't breathe again.

"I should've sent you to that military school when I had the chance," he said as I sat there stunned to my bones. "But I listened to *you*." He jabbed a finger at my mother as he stood up. "You thought he'd be fine in a public school. Well, what do you think now, Margaret?" He sneered her name and actually bared his teeth like some kind of rabid dog.

What's happening?

"Harold, please," she said, tears falling across her cheeks, her face pale and scrunched up in grief. "This isn't anyone's fault."

"Bullshit!"

I wasn't prepared for him to rush at me.

My father never touched me. No hugs, pats on the back, squeezes to my arm or shoulder. Nothing. I was completely shocked when he grabbed a fistful of my hair and latched onto my upper arm. I just gasped. Then he used his grips to haul me up onto my feet.

"Stop! What're you—"

He stomped toward the front door, dragging me with him.

"Dad!"

I tripped, and we suddenly slammed into the door. I hit with half my face and cried out at the impact. The rest of my breath left me in a whoosh as he crashed into me and stayed there. He kept me pinned to the door. I was gasping for breath, unable to think of a single thing to do. What was I supposed to do?

"I wanted my son to be a real man," he said with such a vicious snarl his spittle hit my face. "Instead I got a faggot who lets some hippy punk turn him into *a weak little girl.*"

"What? No," I said, my own anger rising. "I'm *not.*"

I grabbed his bony wrist and tried to make him to let go of my hair. The pull of that brought tears to my eyes and that made me even madder. I did *not* want to look like I was crying. He wouldn't let go and even tightened his grip, tearing a painful sound from me.

I was shocked all over again when he hit me. He'd let my arm go, and then plowed his fist into my side. I couldn't breathe as a dull pain grew and grew into searing agony.

"Real men don't let other men fuck them."

He hit me again. I found my voice that time, managed a gasp and screamed it out. The pain was so sharp. Wet heat spread across my groin, down my thigh. Oh, God, I'd pissed myself.

"Real men are strong and powerful."

I saw him pull his arm back to punch a third time, but something in me kicked in then to stop him. Some instinct for survival I hadn't even experienced when Rick Lockhart and his abusive buddies had come after me suddenly snapped into place now. Fight or flight. I had to get away before my father killed me right here against the front door.

Planting my hands on the wood, I pushed and managed to shove him off me. He punched the door instead of me and howled. Causing him pain shot courage through me. I thrust back an elbow. He twisted to avoid it, tearing my hair out and making my neck wrench back as he pulled. But he was off me for long enough to yank the door open.

I yelled in frustrated anger when he was suddenly back on me. But this time, he tore the door open so hard it hit the wall while grabbing the back of my shirt and choking me.

I fought with my tie, my collar, as he held me up and forced me out onto the porch. He wasn't that much taller than me, but it was enough to make breathing next to impossible. When he let go of my shirt, I had just a second to gasp a breath before he pushed hard at my lower back. I went stumbling down the porch steps.

Hitting the walkway on my knees, I pitched forward and just managed to get my hands in front of me to stop my face from smearing across the concrete. Gasping and blinking through tears, my whole body throbbing and shaking, I looked up and back.

Where was he? Was he coming after me again?

Standing on the porch, hands on his hips and panting with the effort of tossing me here, he glared and snarled down at me. "Real men fight against the abomination inside them and turn away from it. They don't give in like you. They don't *embrace* it." He pointed that accusing finger at me. "Don't you *ever* come back here, you disgusting little faggot. You're nothing to me now."

He turned back to the door, shoved my crying mother out of his way, and went inside.

For a moment, she and I stared at each other. I realized in that moment that I didn't want anything from her. She wasn't safety and comfort. My mother was a silent witness to a brutal attack. No different than countless others who'd watched someone hurt me and done, said nothing.

I pushed myself up, waited until the world settled, then started a slow shuffle across the street. I just needed to get to Wes. I'd be fine, everything would be okay, if I could get to him. He'd know what to do.

Dear God, my side hurt with every step. Had he bruised a rib? Was that my kidney? I started shaking more. Would I need surgery? *Jesus, not that.* I couldn't stop my teeth from chattering.

Once I got to their porch steps, I looked up as I reached for the railing. In the window, I saw Katie and a flash of regret went through me when she turned and hollered something I couldn't quite make out. She and Carter shouldn't have to see me like this or know what had happened. It would scar them and it wasn't right that my father should hurt them, too.

The door opened, light spilling out, and I recoiled a little. It was Wes, though, and I needed him more than I could worry about bruising anybody's innocence.

"Jesus, Mal," he said a second before he reached me. "What happened? Oh, my God."

He didn't seem to know where to touch me, maybe wasn't sure he could without hurting me more. I grabbed at his shoulder and pulled. Like it usually did, the move got him wrapping his arms around me, even if it was more gently than I wanted just now.

"F-f-f-father," I managed to say. "Told him. You and me."

"No," he said like a moan. "Oh, God, baby."

I stumbled as I tried to get closer to him. The world spun around again, but this time it was because he scooped me off my feet. I tried to relax in his arms while he carried me inside, but the shaking was too violent. What was wrong with me? Hopefully, it wasn't my nervous system shutting down or something. "*Ugh.* M-make it stop."

"What, Mal? Talk to me. Tell me what's wrong."

"Shaking... I can't-t-t-t..."

"Just adrenaline. You're okay," he said and turned sideways to get us through the door. "Hey! I need help here."

Mr. and Mrs. Kinney ran into the room, immediately guiding Wes and asking questions. I let him answer and heard their horror and anger at what my father had done to me.

Again, I didn't want the kids to see me, to witness this, but they stood on the fringes anyway. Carter was crying quietly, and Katie kept standing on her toes like she wanted to see more. "I'm...s-s-s-sorry. Sorry, C-Carter," I whispered.

Mr. Kinney went over and actually picked Carter up, talking quietly to him. Katie used the opportunity to come over and hold my hand. Weird kid. Weird, compassionate little girl. I tried to smile at her.

"Mal," Mrs. Kinney said, "try and take deep breaths in through your nose and out through your mouth." She got a thick, fleece blanket from somewhere and wrapped me up in bright red softness. Wes cradled me on his lap on the couch.

I didn't know why, but it actually took some thinking to make myself breathe like that. Which was probably the point. My shaking started to subside and I wondered if this was some kind of meditation thing. But when Wes whispered, "Everything's okay, baby," I remembered what my father had said.

He'd kicked me out. I couldn't go home. Where was I supposed to live? How would I take care of myself? No home, no job, and school... Oh, God, what about school?

"Mal, honey," Mrs. Kinney said, "deep breaths. Slow down."

"I don't— He kicked me out." I clutched at Wes. "What'll I do? I can't—"

"You'll stay here."

I looked over at Mr. Kinney with Carter sniffling in his arms. He'd said that. *My* father kicked me out, but *Wes's* wanted me to live here?

"What?" I asked.

Mr. Kinney nodded even as he frowned. "You'll stay with us."

"For now," Wes added.

I stared at his face, my eyes wide open right along with my mouth. A time limit? Wes was giving me a deadline?

"Baby, take it easy. We just signed a lease, remember?" Wes smiled kindly at me. "We'll move in there together like we planned to. You'll just stay here in the meantime."

It's okay. Oh, God. Tears gathered in my eyes and my bottom lip trembled as I managed a few desperate gasps of air. Burrowing into Wes's neck, I held onto him and let myself cry. Everything really would be okay; Wes *did* know what to do. And his parents? This was the best family in the whole world.

Chapter Twenty-Two

My Message

At one-fifteen in the morning, with Wes sleeping in his—our—bedroom, I went downstairs to fetch another ice pack. There were four of them in various sizes, so as one warmed up, I could swap it out for another. Since the cold helped my various bruises feel better, I'd been watching the clock and diligently adhering to the twenty-on/twenty-off bruise aftercare procedure.

And thinking. Dammit, but I couldn't stop *thinking*.

Which was probably why, when I saw the Kinney family computer in the kitchen, I went over and turned it on. I had so many questions and I wanted answers. This was far enough away from everyone that what I was about to do shouldn't bother them. I had a moment's doubt that this was the right thing to do, but pushed it aside. I needed this.

I got online, turned on the web cam, and logged into my Google account. From there, I hit YouTube and figured out where my channel was. After a few minutes of jumping through hoops, I was ready to load a video. I switched over to the video software on the desktop and clicked record. Then I started talking.

"I've heard about the *It Gets Better* project. A lot of videos from people about how everything'll be okay. Maybe not now, but someday."

I gulped, sniffed, and said what I couldn't stop thinking about.

"How does that happen, though? And when? When will getting beat up by your own father get better?"

I looked up, making sure the camera could see my bruised and swollen face. Going for it all, I stood and showed it the purple fist marks on my side. I sat down, stared at the keyboard, and continued.

"I told him I'm gay a few hours ago. I didn't mean to. I know he's a hater." I shook my head at myself. "Didn't know it would be this bad, of course. But he's always telling me I should stand up to bullies, you know? Be a man. Take control. Don't let people push you around."

I laughed at the irony.

"I finally found the courage to tell him who I am. I'm gay and I'm not sorry and I'm not weak."

A tear slipped out. I wiped it away and sniffed.

"He kicked me out. Literally tossed me onto the front walk like a bag of garbage." I looked at the camera, seeing my own confused face on the screen, too. "How can someone do that? How can a parent throw away their kid? And I'm eighteen, so he can do it, right? I mean, I've heard of kids who get kicked out when they're younger—which should be illegal—but I'm an adult now. Nobody gives a damn about me. How will *that* get better?"

I sighed and rubbed at my eyes. I wasn't even sure where this was going. I just had to say it, had to send it out there. The internet had helped answer other questions, I needed it to do the same thing now.

Then I realized I'd said something wrong.

"No, that's not right. People *do* give a damn about me." I managed a smile. "I'm sitting in my boyfriend's kitchen right now because his parents said I can live here—with them, with him—until we can get into our new apartment. *They* care. Even with his little brother and sister just broken because of what they saw me go through tonight, this family's taken me in." I sniffed again and wiped at my nose.

"So maybe that's one way things get better, huh? I've figured out who really loves me. I don't have anything else—" and I trembled to realize it "—but I have love. *Real* love. I have no idea at all what I'll do to get the things I need or how I'll manage to go to college anymore or afford that apartment, but I'm not alone."

I got choked up on more tears, but pushed through. "It doesn't seem like enough, though, you know? It's great I have love—miraculous—but I can't live off that. I'm a burden now. Relying on the kindness of others. I mean, I literally have no money for anything. If my parents won't let me have any of my stuff—which they bought, so it's their stuff, right?—I won't have any clothes. *Clothes*," I said again because, dear God, that was so basic and I couldn't manage it. "I'll have to ask my boyfriend for help. I'm totally dependent on him now."

I almost called myself useless right then, but I didn't because I wasn't. "I'm not useless or worthless. I'm a great person. Sure, I'm shy and awkward sometimes, and I've been beat down more times than I can count by people who hate me for being me. But that makes them the garbage. *I'm good.*"

The tears fell and I stared into the camera. "I don't deserve this just because I fell in love with a boy. He's amazing in every way, and I need him *so much*. This has to get better, so tell me how, okay? Somebody just tell me how."

I clicked the stop button, uploaded the video for the world to see, and then leaned over the keyboard with my face in my hands and cried.

I awoke in the morning to Wes smoothing his fingertip along my eyebrow. Immediately, I smiled at him.

"Hi," he whispered.

"Hi," I whispered back.

He tried to smile, I saw his lips lift, but then he grimaced and scooted closer to me. I let him arrange me so I had my arms tucked up between us and his leg over my thighs. He was hurt, too, maybe realizing how bad it could've been or going right back to when Rick had ambushed me. Wes had blamed himself for not being there to help.

"It's not your fault," I mumbled into his shoulder.

"I should've been there when you told him."

I shrugged a little. "I don't think it would've changed much."

"I never would have let him touch you," he said with such angry conviction.

Reaching up just a bit, I petted his collarbone. "You were exactly where I really needed you to be, Wes."

If only's didn't make sense. I mean, maybe they had once upon a time, maybe they'd helped me, but not anymore. Wishing I'd never said anything, or that I'd had Wes beside me, wasn't helpful now. I couldn't change the past. This enveloping hug, though, that meant everything to me.

"And you're here, too," I told him and leaned my head back to see his face. "I love you, Wes."

He sighed, and then kissed me gently. "Love you. Let's get you up and see how you're doing."

Wes untangled us, and I rolled over only to discover an ice pack all squishy blue and warm under my butt. "Should I keep doing ice?" I asked and lifted my T-shirt so he could see.

He grimaced but shook his head. "I don't know. Is it the first twelve or twenty-four hours that you're supposed to ice bruises like that?"

I stood up, definitely feeling the ache. "Your mom'll know."

He shuffled me into the bathroom first, but then he lingered.

"I think I can handle this," I said, standing in front of the toilet.

He nibbled his bottom lip before saying, "You need to check for…discoloration."

I frowned. "Uh, I'm definitely bruised."

"No, I mean…" He sighed. "Just aim and piss, and I'll look to see if there's any blood in your urine."

A shiver snaked through me and my eyes felt really big as I gasped. But he was right. I'd even thought about it last night. Kidney punches could have me bleeding internally. Right now. Blood oozing through my abdomen and—

"Hey-hey-hey," he said softly as he walked over and wrapped his arms around me from behind. "If things were really bad, I have to believe you'd have way more symptoms, right?" He caressed my belly.

"Okay. Sure." I took a deep breath. "But I really don't want you to watch me pee. That's just weird."

He chuckled and kissed my ear. "The things we do for love…"

So I peed. I stood there, holding my dick, looking up at the ceiling, and—after a few minutes of supreme awkwardness because, good grief, Wes was holding me while I held my penis and it wasn't meant to be anything sexy—my stream finally flowed into the toilet bowl.

"Nice aim," Wes commented. "Good, strong stream."

I snorted. "Don't grade it."

"But I was gonna give it a ten."

I laughed and finished. "Just tell me what color it is."

"Taxi cab yellow." He patted my ass. "You need to drink more water."

I tucked myself away and looked down. "Oh. So I'm good?"

"Awesome. Now scoot." He fished his dick out of his sweatpants.

My first instinct was to leave the room and give him privacy, but I ignored that. Fair's fair, right? He chuckled, but then let fly, and I watched. Which was weirder by the second since I really liked his penis, even doing this. Really weird. There went my blushing, as I moved away to look in the mirror like the condition of my hair was very important just then. But he knew anyway that I was kinda creepily turned-on because he laughed again as he finished and flushed.

"You're adorable," he said and kissed my cheek. The one that wasn't bruised from slamming into my parents' front door. Seeing it in the mirror sobered us both up. "Everything'll be okay, Mal."

While he gently hugged me, I considered telling him about the video I'd made and published to the world. But I didn't say anything. Maybe no one would watch it. Maybe only jerks and bullies would comment. It felt like a journal entry, a way to purge something from my head and get rid of it. I didn't feel like looking at it again.

I definitely didn't want Wes to watch it. He'd seen me freak out and cry and worry enough. Now was the time to buck up, move on, and make my life what I wanted it to be.

Chapter Twenty-Three

It Ain't Over

Living with the Kinneys was strange. I'd known they were a whole different kind of people from my parents for a while, but seeing them so up close like this really brought that difference into focus. Catching Wes's parents in the kitchen making out first thing in the morning had been surreal, especially since the twins sat there at the breakfast bar. Yeah, they'd been rolling their eyes and making gagging noises, but their parents just laughed into their kisses. And then Mrs. Kinney had made everyone pancakes, while Mr. Kinney went through a whole bag of oranges so he could try out his new juicer.

Watching the Kinneys, being right in the thick of their family, kind of broke my heart. What was wrong with my own parents? Why didn't they express love like this? Did they not love each other?

Had they ever loved me?

At the same time, though, I got to be a part of a family that didn't hold back on squeezing hugs, kisses on my cheeks, or asking how they could make me feel more included. But it was like I'd been adopted, so I didn't need anything more. They made me feel like Malcolm Kinney.

It shouldn't have surprised me when Wes asked, "Want to go get all our books this afternoon?"

"For school?" At his nod, I said, "Yeah, I guess we better. We've got... What? Three weeks?"

"Yep." He grinned at me. "I bet you've already activated your school email."

I shrugged, blushing. I'd jumped on setting up anything and everything the second the university sent it out to me. School had been my escape plan. Now it was...just a regular plan.

"So get your class list," Wes said and waved a piece of paper at me. "It'll have all the books you'll need, too."

For a moment, it hit me that I'd already printed out that information, but it was being held hostage by my father along with all my other things. I could've called up the info on my cell phone since the school had an app, but no, I couldn't do that either because my phone was in my old bedroom, too. How long would it take for me to afford... Afford...

"Oh, God," I whispered and dove for the family computer in the kitchen. "Please, please," I kept repeating as I opened a browser and made my way into my school email site. "Please, don't."

"Mal?" Wes came over and put his hand on my shoulder. "What's going on?"

And there it was, an email from the school with a subject line confirming my sudden fear. I opened the message and read that my parents had gone through their bank to stop payment on the check they'd written for my tuition. The university had been forced to refund every last penny to them...and now expected me to pay the bill. I had until the first day of classes, three weeks away, to come up with my first semester fees.

Five thousand dollars.

My vision focused in on that money and that deadline. Distantly, I heard Wes talking, but I couldn't respond. How? It wasn't possible. How could I ever come up with five grand in three weeks? There was no way. Absolutely none.

I blinked as the world twirled around me. Was I fainting? Oh, no, it was Wes swinging the chair I sat in so now I faced him crouching in front of me. He brushed at my cheeks with his thumbs, his green eyes tear-bright.

"It's okay," he whispered. "There are ways to pay it."

I shook my head slightly between his hands. "I have nothing."

He stood up and went around me to snag a chair from the dining room. "Here," he said as he sat and pointed at the email. "We'll just go to the Financial Aid office like they say. They'll help."

He held my face again, making me look at him. I was so numb.

"They'll do whatever they can," he said, "to get you in their school, right? They want your money like any big company. So we'll talk to them about…about grants and scholarships. Loans, if we have to. But, honey, I've got plenty. From selling the cars? We can do this together, I promise."

My shocked numbness vanished in a hot wash of desperate sadness and utter gratefulness. I leaned into his arms and let the tears that had been falling already keep right on going. *Saved by Wes. Again.* For a panicked moment, I clung to him and wondered just how many times he'd be willing to rescue me. When would he get tired of being my knight?

"Don't think of it like that," he said and made me look at him again. I must've said my thoughts out loud.

"I'm sorry."

"No, don't do that either. I *want* to help, Mal. Need to." He kissed me for a moment. "I love you. This… It's just what you do."

I swallowed hard and whispered, "Help the one you love."

"Yes."

Nodding, I leaned back into him. His heavy arms held me tightly.

Would there come a day when I could help him back? I was such a burden right now. I knew he would tell me I wasn't at all, but I really was. I had to wear *Wes's* clothes, for Pete's sake. That's how much nothing I had. And when I went shopping for clothes that would actually fit—because eventually someone was going to mention I should, regardless of how much I didn't want to be a *financial* burden, too—I'd have to let Wes pay for everything.

Backpack, cell phone, shoes, food, books… I couldn't provide anything for myself. I'd been sheltered and trained to rely on my parents to get me anything I needed or wanted, and now they'd abandoned me to fend for myself. And I had no idea how to do that, except—

"I'll get a job," I mumbled into Wes's neck. "You can have everything I earn."

Wes sighed. "I'm not keeping a running log of your expenses, Mal. I don't care if you want to think of it all as a loan, but I'm not going to."

I squeezed my eyes closed. "Nobody's ever..." I gasped a breath. "I feel like... Like I *matter*."

"Ah, Jesus, baby." Wes held me tighter and said into my hair, "Of course you matter."

But did I? Did I really? It was such a difficult thing to believe. I could barely grasp my own self-worth, but here was a perfectly wonderful man saying I was worth his time and money and energy? I was worthy of *him?* It just didn't seem possible. And even more so, what if it didn't last?

"I don't know what I'd do, if I didn't have you." I gulped and squeezed him. "What if it gets to be too much? What if I stop being worth it, and you dump me?"

"Mal." He held the back of my head. "I can't promise we'll always be together forever, but I also can't imagine not being your friend. I'd stick by you because of that." He swallowed hard and his voice got croaky. "You were my friend first, right? And you always will be."

I lost the battle not to cry just knowing he fought it, too. We held so tightly to each other, sniffing and trembling. I wanted to believe him, and I guess part of me did believe we'd always be friends. I knew our chances of being a forever-love were slim—stuff like that was fairytales, really—but I wanted to be worth keeping. I had to get my life back together.

Wes dipped his head and planted a kiss on my cheekbone. I saw him lick his lip, no doubt tasting the salt of my tears. He cupped my cheek while I leaned back and wiped at my eyes.

He sighed. "I can't stand seeing you so sad."

"I'm sor—"

"No, not like I wish you'd stop it. Like I want to make you happy." He smiled just a little bit and ran his thumb, gently and slowly, across my bottom lip.

"Oh," I breathed out like a sigh and closed my eyes, tilting my head back. He did know how to make me blissfully happy, and I really could use some of that feeling right now.

He quietly grunted a laugh before leaning in and kissing me deeply. A brilliant, beautiful distraction. This kiss—right here and now—meant so much. It sealed our promises to each other, and helped ease my mind. I didn't need to worry, shouldn't have doubted him, not Wes. We were just entering the tough stuff, but he was here, and nothing had changed in the way he kissed me.

"Ugh," groaned a young voice. "Not you guys, too. Does *everybody* have to suck face in the kitchen today?"

Wes and I chuckled at Carter's complaint and stomping feet as he left the kitchen. When Wes waggled his eyebrows at me, grinning with suggestion, and cocked his head at the stairs... *Ah, hell.* All my trepidation about sex while people were home flew right out the window. I was the one who dragged Wes back up to his bedroom.

Since we'd still had on our pajamas, it was quick and easy to lose T-shirts and lounge pants in a couple swoops of cotton either up or down. Naked, we tumbled back onto his bed. Right away, I knew this felt different.

We'd been getting really good at winding each other up to a needy frenzy. But this was...deeper. We clung to each other, and I realized it was almost as if we were afraid we'd be ripped away at any moment. I'd scared him. Or made him worry about the future, too. There was just something in this love-making that felt desperate.

"I love you, Wes. So much," I said when he moved to sucking at my neck.

He lifted his head, panting in my face, and stared into my eyes. It was almost uncomfortable, that intense scrutiny, but I held his green gaze. What was he looking for?

"I know you do, Mal," he finally said. "And I know you can't hardly believe it, but I've been looking for you for a long time. I'm in this, honey. I'm where I want to be."

I gulped back a burst of emotion. He always knew just what to say. All I could do was nod and pull his head back down to reclaim his lips.

He notched us together, tangling our tongues and legs, and

started rocking his hips against mine. I moaned, moving with him as best I could. We were so tight together, him on top and pressing me hard into the bed. I could barely move at all, but it didn't seem to matter. The heat of desire built and built as we undulated and kissed, tongues mimicking what bodies had no room to do. This was so simple, so basic, but it felt as intimate and connected as staring into his eyes. In fact, as we came, we stopped kissing and watched each other instead.

He was so beautiful right then. If it was the same for him as for me, he came not because of overwhelming physical sensation, but because of undeniable emotion. That was love. Right there in the flush of his cheeks and the flutter of his eyelashes, I couldn't see anything but how much Wes loved me.

Chapter Twenty-Four

The Kindness of Strangers

"You have some really nice stuff," I said as I surveyed our apartment's main room.

We'd spent about four hours directing the movers between picking everything up from Wes's storage unit to delivering it to the apartment. After seeing how many big, heavy pieces of furniture Wes had, I was very glad we didn't have to move it ourselves. I could've moved the lamps and that was about it.

"Thanks," Wes said, "so do you." He pinched my ass on his way to flopping down on the couch.

I flinched and snorted at him. "Furniture, Wesley. Furniture."

"Oh," he drew out and winked at me.

Since he took out his phone, popped in an earbud, and started scrolling through something, I accepted that it was break time and sat down in one of the leather club chairs. I was pretty sure this was going to become "my chair."

I hadn't asked what kind of stuff Wes had in storage before we got to the unit. I supposed, I might've been expecting hand-me-down furniture—stuff that didn't match, was obviously used, and definitely from a different decade. Wes's things were, well, they were kind of like that, but in a really cool industrial chic kinda way. He had things that looked like they'd been repurposed from factories and libraries, given new life with fun paint colors like turquoise and dark, supple leathers.

His furniture added a new layer to the already amazing man.

Wes had encouraged me to think of things I wanted, and we'd get them in order to put my mark on this place, too. Sitting here now and looking around me, I couldn't see what might be missing, but I also hesitated to find something. Already he'd bought me clothes and other necessities. This afternoon or tomorrow, we were going to get me a new phone and, if I caved to his insistence, a new laptop, too. Did I really need to say I wanted a different coffee table? Besides, his coffee table had wagon wheels and doubled as a handcart; there was no improving on that kind of antique awesomeness.

I was having a really hard time letting him spend money on me. I knew it went back to the whole burden discussion. Should I get over it? Was I—

When Wes sniffed, I was startled to see he was crying. Before I could say anything, he held up his phone and plucked the earbud from his ear. "Why didn't you tell me?" he asked.

There, on the little screen, was a paused view of me from my video the night my father kicked me out. I couldn't believe it.

"How did you find that?"

"Mal."

"What?"

"Why didn't you tell me?"

I leaned forward on my knees. "Because I just wanted... It was like a journal entry, you know? I wanted to express myself, what I was feeling. But I wanted to send it out there and... Well, I had questions and I thought maybe someone out there could answer them. Like, you've never been through it—" I raised a hand when he made to speak. "And I know you love me and you're here, and I'm so in love with you right back, Wes. But people should know, too. They should see what it means to be so unacceptable by your own parents that they'll beat you and abandon you." I gulped to a stop, tears burning at my eyes.

He wiped at his face and nodded. "People have seen it, honey." He sniffed and did something on his phone before holding it out to me.

I came over and sat beside him, discovering the screen now had an article on it. Just the title made me gasp.

Viewers Determined to Prove It Does Get Better
for Beaten and Disowned Gay Teen
Support Fund Reaches $30,000—But Who Is MS619?

"They... They've..." I looked at Wes, hardly daring to understand.

He nodded again, smiling this time while tears spiked his eyelashes and made his green eyes sparkle. "Complete strangers put together a fund and filled it with thirty-thousand dollars just so you can know it really does get better."

A sob tore out of me and I cried so suddenly that I couldn't see the article. Wes took his phone back and read it to me, every word, and he was right. Hundreds of strangers wanted to make sure I was okay. The author had been so moved by my video that he'd gone and set up a place where people could donate money to help me. Some of the donors left encouraging notes. A few related "I've been there" stories of their own and how they felt like they were paying back those who'd helped them by now helping me.

I honestly couldn't believe it. I'd hoped for a response of some kind, but not this. Never *this*. I'd put it out of my mind to even check my email or the video's page for fear of a negative response. Positive? Helpful? *Giving?* I'd never considered that.

I sniffed hard and tried to get it together once Wes stopped reading. "What should I do?" I asked, because the last line of the article had asked me to make contact.

"Let's start with your email." He got up and reached for my hand. "The author said he messaged you through YouTube, so let's see what happened when he did that."

I stood and took his hand, needing him to guide me back to the bedroom, where I'd set up his computer on the desk. Sitting there, I was at a loss all of a sudden as to how to get going.

"C'mon, baby," Wes whispered in my ear as he reached over my shoulder to rub my chest.

I cleared my throat and reached for the mouse, waking the computer up. My focus slowly returned with the familiar steps of opening a browser window, logging-in with my new account, and getting into my email.

There were hundreds of unread messages. "Oh, crap," I whispered.

"Uh-uh," Wes said. "Don't look at all of them. Just look for one from the author, Harlan Urban." He pointed at the screen. "There. Down there. See?"

I saw and clicked. Harlan pretty much said a lot of the same things he had in the article. He said he didn't need me to come forward publicly in order to claim the money from the fund he'd set up, but he believed people would want to see some kind of follow-up from me. To know I was all right and discover what I'd do next in my new life would be a sort of return on their investment.

"You say as much as you want," Wes said and rested his hands on my shoulders. The warmth and solidarity reassured me.

"But should I accept the money?"

He hesitated. "Well, what if you did, and then used only what you truly needed? You decide what that is and, afterward, you donate what's left."

My thoughts whirled trying to grasp that concept. Truly needed? Shit, I'd been grappling with that since Wes offered to buy me new underwear. How would I know where to draw the line? What was necessity and what was indulgence?

Wes kissed the top of my head. "How about this? Just reply with your thanks and let the guy know you're out here and doing okay. You can tell him you need some time to think about the rest."

I nodded. "Yeah. Okay."

Briefly, I replied to Harlan, trying to let him know I was grateful without gushing or rambling or showing how completely overwhelmed I actually was. Didn't type OMG once. I read it over a few times, and then made myself hit send. I'd signed it Malcolm Small, committing to whatever would come next.

Faced again with all those unread messages, I gulped and stared.

"Want me to go through them?" Wes asked gently. "I can weed out the negative ones, any you should consider replying to... That kind of thing."

"No. No, I think I just need some time there, too." I logged-out and closed the browser. I could breathe a little easier then. "I'll look at everything. Just later."

With a few mouse clicks, Wes sent the computer back to sleep. He took my hand again and guided me back into the living room. In seconds, he had us back to front on the couch, the sun warming our legs, and his arms tight around me. I relaxed back against his chest and closed my eyes. His right hand rucked up my T-shirt, and then smoothed up and down my belly in the most soothing way.

"Why MS619?" Wes asked, referencing my username. "I get the MS is your initials, but what's the number?"

I smiled. "June nineteenth. The day I met you."

Chapter Twenty-Five

Not The Only One

It was on the fifth day of living with Wes in our apartment that it really sank in that we lived together. I opened my eyes in the morning, and there he was. Again. Because that was where he and I were supposed to be. It was the first time I didn't wake up with worries on my mind. I just smiled and watched Wes sleep until I had to wake him up so I could love on him for a while.

I was part of a couple. We lived together. With those truths, life couldn't be *that* bad, right? Sure, there were tons of things to figure out—and that negative self-worth would blip in my mind now and then—but Wes was here with me, and he chose this and us, so I was going to do the same. I could make this work.

After I completely caved and let Wes buy me a new phone and a laptop, he decided to go grocery shopping. Since he knew way more about how to cook things that didn't go in the microwave, I kissed him and sent him on his way. I suppose part of it was also that I didn't want him to see me totally geek out over my new tech while I set everything up just the way I wanted it.

As I sat in my chair and typed in all the contacts Wes had written out for me, I realized I had friends now, too. Yeah, my belly cramped at the thought of calling any of them, but I could technically do it because they were friends of ours. Sitting there staring at the entry for Roger Kwan, I suddenly had a desperate need to hit call.

When it started ringing, I realized what I'd done and nearly fumbled the phone onto the floor while trying to get it up to my ear. I took a breath and tried to calm down, wondering if he'd answer an unknown number, and what I'd say if I had to leave a message. I didn't even know—

"Hello, there," he said in a saucy voice. "I don't know you, but I bet I'd like to. How about you give me a reason?"

I snorted a laugh. "It's Mal, Wes's—"

"Sweetie! Hi! Is this your new number at the apartment no one's invited me to see yet?"

I laughed again. If nothing else, he was making me happy.

"Actually, it's my new cell phone."

"New? What happened to the old one? Because I've been texting you."

Ah, crap. "Wes didn't... He didn't tell you?"

"Tell me what?"

I closed my eyes and gulped. I'd known Wes had talked to Brian a few times about everything and must have assumed Brian would tell everyone else. Unless Wes had asked him not to?

"Mal? What's going on?" Roger sounded worried.

"I came out to my parents, my dad beat me up, disowned me, and kicked me out." I cleared my throat in an attempt to dislodge the sudden lump in it.

"Oh, *honey.*"

I nodded to myself because there was so much in just those two words and his sympathetic tone. "But it's okay," I said, "because I stayed with Wes's family until the apartment was ready and...some other stuff's happened, too. I'm doing all right."

And it sunk in that I really was doing okay. It honestly had gotten better than that night, even if my life wasn't completely set. But should I tell Roger about my video and the response to it? Actually, it might be nice to get another perspective on what to do there. I'd added my email to my phone and found another response from Harlan Urban, the journalist. He respected my decision to think on things first, but also said that if I didn't want or need the money, he'd donate it directly to an LGBT youth charity. I still couldn't decide what I thought of all that.

Roger asked, "Are you at the apartment now?"

"Yeah."

"I'm coming over."

"Oh. All right. Um, do you know which number we are? Roger?" My phone beeped at me, helping me realize he'd already hung up.

So, okay, he was coming over.

I cleaned up all the boxes and papers, and then thought about whether we had anything to eat or drink that I could offer him. But, honestly, I probably only needed to make sure there was a fresh box of tissues nearby. I sincerely doubted I'd be able to get through telling my awful tale without crying over it. I hadn't managed to so far.

Roger arrived quickly, making me realize I didn't know exactly where he lived.

"I just love this neighborhood, don't you?" he said as he raised his sunglasses to sit on top of his head. "Such good memories." He nudged my side. "And some I can't remember that must be spectacular."

I chuckled and brought him in, feeling a tad underdressed in simple jeans and a T-shirt. He looked like he was on his way to a party or something in very short shorts and a silky top that had a neck big enough to slip off one shoulder. Around his wrist was a strap attached to a case holding his phone and his shoes were sandals I just knew hadn't come from the men's side of the store. He looked so gay and completely sure of himself. I didn't want to mimic his look, but for a minute there, I envied him.

After a quick tour of the apartment, we settled at the kitchen table with glasses of lemonade.

"So," he said, "did Wes ever tell you how we met?"

I shook my head. "How?"

Roger sipped his drink. "My mother came to pick me up after school one day and saw me kiss a boy." He smiled and rolled his eyes. "We'd thought we were so great at sneaking around, but, like, everyone knew we were together by then."

Fearing the worst, I said anyway, "What'd she do?"

"She took me home and told me to go to my room." He shook

his head and quirked his mouth like it was all so stupid now. "When my father got home, I hear them talking, but not really what they're saying. Then my dad comes and gets me, and the two of them give me an ultimatum: Either I stop being gay immediately, or I can't live with them anymore."

"Can't live with *them?* Like you'd have to live with someone else?"

"Sort of." He waved his hand dismissively. "I get all rude and angry, telling them I am who I am and they can't stop me. Just spouting off all over the place. And they get me in the car and drive off, and I'm all about not letting them see me afraid and it doesn't matter where they take me, I'll show them." He sounded like he had a thing or two he could've told his younger self now.

"Oh, Roger. What'd they do?" I bit my lip.

"They took me to a homeless shelter."

I gasped. "No."

"Yep. And my dad had to drag me out of the car because I'd totally lost it and wouldn't get out. Then they just drove away." Elbow on the table, he flipped his hand palm-up and shrugged. "Just left me there."

I slumped in my seat. "That's so much worse. I mean, how old were you?"

"Fourteen."

"Oh, my God! That's horrible." I pressed a hand over my heart. "They abandoned you *in the city*. All alone. At least I only had to walk across the street to Wes. Oh." I perked up a bit when it occurred to me... "You called Wes? Is that how you met?"

He grinned. "Well, we'd met months earlier...and had been secretly dating for about a week by then. But, yes, I called—"

I gasped. "You were *dating?*"

"Easy does it, sweetie." He patted my hand. "It got obvious fast that we made better friends, so don't go all loopy because we're exes. That's so not it."

"Okay." I settled back into my seat. "Yeah, okay." *No big deal.* "So, um, you stayed with the Kinneys, too?"

Roger nodded. "For eight months."

"Did your parents change their minds? Let you come home?"

"Ha! Not at all. No, my older brother got discharged from the

Army. He got a job with this awesome tech company, set up an apartment, and was finally granted custody of me."

"Your brother?" I smiled. "He didn't agree with your parents?"

"Nope. Turned out he's gay, too."

My jaw dropped open. "Seriously?"

"I know, right? Could've knocked me over with a feather boa." We both laughed, me because I could so see Roger wearing one and working it, too. "But there it is," he said soberly, "the twenty-year-old raised his baby brother up right and, as far as I'm concerned, everything turned out okay in the last ten years." He shrugged and smiled fondly. "George is married to a great guy and they have a little girl, Abby. She's adorable. And I'm totally embracing my hottie years and slutting it up the best I can." He fluffed pretend hair at his shoulder and winked at me.

I chuckled, but then found myself leaning over and hugging him tightly. He made a little cooing noise and hugged me back. Whatever issues I'd had with him earlier were gone now. This guy was my friend.

As I let him go, I asked, "Do you ever talk to your parents now?"

He shook his head. "No. For a while, I tried to get them to hear me, but they refused. I still don't understand how they could cut us out of their lives like they have, but I'm not waiting for them to change their minds and I'm not nearly as angry at them as I used to be. It is what it is."

I couldn't quite tell if he was genuinely that over it or not.

He patted my knee and smiled. "Someday, in your own way, you'll make peace with them. Maybe they'll learn to change, maybe they won't, but it's not about them anymore, you know?"

Nodding, I said, "I have to live my life for me."

"Exactly! Look at you being all wise and shit."

I smiled, but took the opportunity to segue into my video and the article. "Well, I didn't get to that on my own."

"I'm sure Wes helped. And his truly amazing parents. Love those two."

"Oh, yes, definitely, but also..." I cleared my throat. "Um, have you heard of a video from a guy calling himself MS619?"

He cocked his head and grinned at me. "Did you make a sex

tape?"

I snorted even as my face burst out a blush. "God, no."

"Shoot. All right, what's this video?"

I stumbled through telling him about it. As usual, I got choked up, and we had to pause for tissues. Would I ever be able to remember that night without feeling the world falling apart all over again?

When Roger reached for his phone, I stopped him. "No, please don't watch it now. I just…" I looked at him, hoping he'd understand. "Not while I'm right here."

"Okay." He put his phone away and patted me again. "No worries. I'm guessing there's been a response? Supportive, I hope."

"To the tune of thirty thousand dollars."

His eyes went wide and his mouth popped open. "You're kidding!"

I shook my head and bit my lip. I didn't really know what kind of person he was when it came to money. Would he think parties and shopping sprees?

"Damn, honey, you're set then." He reached over and shoved at my shoulder while smiling hugely. "Seriously, you'll be just *fine*."

"So you think I should accept it?"

He frowned. "What do you mean? I thought you meant it, like, went viral or something."

"No. I mean, I don't think it has." I'd have to check that. I didn't even know how that sort of thing worked. "But a journalist wrote an article about me and his own similar experience coming out, and then set up a fund for me. It's all donations."

Roger looked shocked again. "Holy shit." He covered his mouth. "Oh, my God, Mal. That's huge."

"I *know*. I have no idea what to do."

"Oh. Well. Same thing, right? Take the money."

"Yeah?"

He nodded so vigorously, he made his sunglasses drop down onto his nose. He set them on the table and said, "You need it, don't you? Your parents cut you off completely." He pointed at me. "And you said over the Fourth they were paying for your tuition and everything. How else are you going to do that on your own?"

"Yeah, my parents got their money back from the university last week." I told him about the deadline to pay and how I had a meeting with a financial aid person in a few days to talk options. "I'm sure I could get loans or grants or something."

Roger nodded with finality. "There. You take the money."

I nibbled my bottom lip.

"What?" he demanded. "Seriously, what's the hesitation? You want to go to school, you've got no money of your own... This is like a really fabulous scholarship with no application, you know?" He shoved at my shoulder again. "People are saying you deserve a chance and they want you to have it with their help. Take the money, Malcolm."

I sighed. "I just—"

"Honey, seriously, if me and my brother had gotten an offer like that, we'd have taken it. Anybody in such a situation would." He held up a hand. "Now I know Wes is loaded from his car thing and he could definitely take care of you forever, so if that's your thing, fine, do that instead. But if you want to get a hand up to be independent and all that instead, here's your chance. You can be Wes's little househusband, while also paying your way through college and, like, someday curing cancer or something."

That made me chuckle, but... Yeah, Roger was right. Maybe it was that nagging lack of self-worth making me think I couldn't possibly accept the money. That I didn't deserve it. Knowing Roger's story now, I wondered how many other kids out there had been or were in similar—or worse—situations. They'd take a helping hand. They'd save themselves any way they could. Why shouldn't I? And maybe someday I could pay if forward, too.

"I see that grin," Roger said and got up. "My work here is done. I rock."

I laughed and stood. "You want to stay for dinner? Wes should be back in a little bit."

"Oh, sweetie, as much as I'd love to take advantage of that boy's cooking skills, I've got a hot date. Like, seriously smoking hot and I'm pretty sure he's got a dick like a baseball bat." He fluttered his eyelashes and shimmied in place. "Mmm! I've got to get back home and fancy myself all up."

"You look perfect right now," I said more because I'd never really had to dress for a date—except an illicit rendezvous in a park—so I couldn't really see what he needed to change.

He smiled big and looped his arm around my neck to give me a hug and buss my cheek. "That is why I call you sweetie." He let me go and sashayed to the door. "I'll call you tomorrow, so we can start planning Wes's birthday party. I'm a fabulous party-planner. Ta-ta, sweetie!"

I watched him leave, my mind stuck on the fact I didn't know when Wes's birthday was. Holy crap, but that was something a boyfriend who's living with you should know. I looked at the calendar stuck to the fridge. It had all kinds of things on it, but no sign of a birthday this month. Was it after school started? I flipped the page to September, and then flipped the page again. But there was nothing written down all the way into next January to indicate a birthday.

When I let the calendar pages fall back to show August again, I saw little blue writing that said *W 25* on the Saturday before school started. Was that it? Wes turning twenty-five? Good grief, he could've made a slightly bigger deal about it. *Help a guy out, Wesley.* So I drew a red heart around it, and then added the event to my phone's calendar with a couple of reminders.

I'd need to shop for a gift. I groaned and rubbed at my eyes. Except... Well, maybe since I was accepting the donations now, I could use a little bit to throw a really great party and buy a really wonderful gift for the one person determined to stand by me no matter what. I smiled and started planning.

Chapter Twenty-Six

All Kinds of Attention

I wrote to the journalist and let Harlan know I wanted to accept the donations in the fund he'd set up. It hadn't been an easy decision, and it wasn't an easy email for me to write. Did I list all the reasons justifying why I was taking the money? Did I agree to let my real name and follow-up story come out now? In the end, with help from Wes, I sent Harlan an acceptance and a heads-up that I was going to make a new video. It felt like the right thing to do and, this time, Wes was in it with me.

We sat on the floor in front of the couch, my new laptop eye-level on the coffee table in front of us. My hands shook a bit as I made sure we were both in the frame. Seeing Wes on the screen watching me with a small smile on his face gave me a little boost of courage. I cleared my throat, pressed record, and leaned back shoulder-to-shoulder with him.

"It's been two weeks since I came out to my parents. If you watched my previous video, you saw how horribly that went and what a mess I was." I had to clear my throat again, and Wes put his arm around me. I smiled at him and said, "Things got better, though. Mostly because of you."

He gave me a kiss, making me sigh before I refocused on the camera.

"Before I knew what Harlan did in his article, and then so many of you did with your donations, I had my boyfriend and his family right there ready to help me. It took me a while to realize how lucky I was to have their support. That kind of thing was just so foreign to me, you know?" I sighed and shook my head. "My parents just don't show emotion and sometimes I would wonder if they even liked each other, let alone me. It was different when I was really little, but as a teen, any time I needed help, I was pretty much told to do it myself. Handle it. Be a man." I snorted at that. "Whatever that means."

I shifted, leaning more against Wes. His arm curled closer around me.

"I consider myself capable of independence and strong enough to survive, and I didn't want to accept the donations. I wasn't *that* bad off, you know? I wasn't homeless or alone. But a good friend recently helped me understand that when someone offers you a hand up, offers that help, it's okay to take it. To refuse seems…ungrateful and I'm really not that. I'm so incredibly grateful you guys heard me and wanted to help. I had no idea generosity like that was actually out there."

I took a deep breath and said, "So I'm going to accept the money from the fund Harlan set up. I don't need all of it to be safe and healthy, so I'll use what I need to pay for school and contribute to our household until I can get a job. The rest of the money will get donated again, this time to my local LGBT center."

Feeling a little freer for saying that, committing to that plan, I sat up and smiled at the camera.

"I'm Mal and this is Wes and we're really thankful you've helped us. I'm going to be okay, but others aren't doing so good. Help *them* now, okay? Donate to your local LGBT centers."

My throat hurt all of a sudden, but I pushed out the words. "Just, thank you. Everyone, seriously, thank you so much for all you've done to make sure I know it gets better." I forced out a smile before I leaned up and clicked the stop button.

Wes pulled me back and twisted around to kiss me thoroughly. It was the kind of kiss that usually ended up getting us naked and sweaty, so I was glad I'd stopped the recording first. Before I could swoon completely, Wes pulled back, grinning.

"You are amazing, Mal. I love you so much."

I chuckled breathlessly. "Yeah?"

"Yeah." He kissed my neck, and then stood up. "I'm going to go pay your tuition bill and get our books and stuff."

"Wes—"

"Nope." He held up a hand. "You can pay me back, right? So no fussing."

I rolled my eyes for his word choice, but didn't protest. He grinned with triumph and bent to kiss me again.

"Why don't you take a look at the other emails?" he suggested. "Skip anything bad, but there might be good stuff in there that you should see."

"Yeah, okay." I brought the laptop closer to me. "I'll upload this first, send Harlan the link, and then see what's what."

I could see he was excited to go spend money—well, to go secure my future as a college student, really—so I left him to it and did as I'd said I would. Seeing our video right there on YouTube for the world to watch gave me a hitch of nerves, but this time it was for a good reason. And people should have known they'd helped, that was important. By the time I'd sent Harlan the link, Wes was out the door with a grin on his face.

Trepidation returned when I let myself look through my email. There were a lot of notifications. I really didn't want to see anything hateful—I wasn't ready to deal with cyberbullying—so I did a search for nice words like *want to help* and *it gets better*. That resulted in a long list, but it seemed more manageable just knowing they were supportive.

After reading about another adult man who'd experienced being disowned by his family, but had gotten help and made the most of his life, I decided that I wasn't just going to read, but I'd also reply. It was inspiring and encouraging to know he, like Roger, had made it—that I could, too. So I thanked him and told him I appreciated his words. Everything about all of this was even better now.

As I was getting into the next email, my phone rang.

"Hi, Mrs. Kinney," I said as I answered.

I almost told her Wes wasn't here, but she'd explained last time that if she called *my* phone, she wanted *me*. It was still so strange to be…included. Would I ever get used to it? I almost didn't want to because it made me so warm inside every time I realized it.

"Hey, honey," she said, but didn't sound like her usual happy self. "Everything okay?"

"Well, something's happened over here and I wanted to check in with you about it before I responded myself."

My heart rate kicked up. "What's happened?"

"Your mom came to see me. She—"

"My mom? She did?"

Good grief, why? I mean, I knew there might come a time when they could change their minds. Or… Well, it really hadn't been her so much as him who decided to throw me out. She hadn't stopped him, that was the thing. I remembered not wanting to go to her for help or comfort that night, but now… I wasn't sure how I felt about her.

"She wants to visit you," Mrs. Kinney said, "and asked me for your address and phone number. I didn't want to give her anything until I'd talked to you."

"She wants… Why?"

"She mentioned seeing you on CNN."

I'd wondered if she would. My mother watched CNN's morning show every day before she went to work. She'd probably seen the bit they did about all the people who'd helped me in a segment they called *The Good Stuff*. Or someone she'd known had seen it and told her. It had probably gotten picked up online, too.

"Oh," I said lamely. So what if she'd seen me? It didn't change anything.

"Honey," Mrs. Kinney said, "I don't want to speak out of turn, but it's possible she wants to reconcile."

I opened my mouth, but couldn't speak.

"Mal?"

"I— Are you sure?"

"No, I'm not. But she seemed concerned for you." She sighed. "Your mom strikes me as a very private person, so I didn't want to push her for too much and do any harm before you two could even get started. You understand?"

I nodded before realizing I'd have to speak. "Yeah, I do and she is really private. I guess they both are. They'd never talk about this to other people." Mostly because they'd fear the backlash from their über conservative acquaintances or colleagues, but that could make it a privacy issue for them.

"I could ask her for more details about what she wants. Tell her you asked me to ask?"

Did I need that? Was I being overly cautious? She couldn't do much worse than letting my father kick me out. And I was getting better in so many ways that she couldn't touch. I felt a little sick to my stomach anyway, just for the potential emotional confrontation.

"You can give her my number and address," I said to Mrs. Kinney. "I can handle...whatever happens."

"Okay, honey." She sounded resigned. "There's nothing wrong with having some support there with you. Wes or even me, if you want. I could come over with her."

My first instinct was to say that wasn't necessary because my mother wouldn't be comfortable. But you know what? It wasn't her comfort I needed to worry about, was it? This was my home and I was allowing her into it. There could be any number of reasons she might want to meet with me, including trying to get me to stop being gay so they could accept me again. Fuck that.

"Yeah," I said and sat up straighter. "Don't give her anything, actually. You can bring her over, like, tomorrow or something. I want you and Wes here. With me."

"You got it, honey." Now she sounded pleased. Maybe proud? "I'll set everything up and let you know."

"Okay."

"Is Wes there?"

"No," I said, and then told her about making the new video and him gleefully running off to pay bills and buy books. She already knew all about the donations and my decision to accept.

"You know, Mal, he's really proud of you."

"Wes is?"

"Oh, yes. He can't say enough how strong he thinks you are."

"Me?"

Wes still thought *I* was strong? I remembered back in the beginning how he'd said that after I'd told him about my experiences being bullied. When he'd told me about that kid he'd known in high school. But that Wes *still* felt that way was a little hard to believe. I'd been falling apart almost daily.

"He thinks—" Mrs. Kinney cut herself off. "Actually, honey, you should probably ask *him*. I think it'll be beneficial to both of you."

"Oh. Okay."

"So, let me give your mom a call and get that ball rolling. I'll let you know."

"Thanks, Mrs. Kinney. Really," I said, realizing I should've before now.

"Of course, Mal."

We said our goodbyes and disconnected, me feeling a weird mix of curiosity and trepidation. To distract myself until Wes came home, I went back to the emails. That worked well since so many of them were well-wishes for me and my future, praise for Wes and his family, and a few more shared stories of good things that came to those who needed them once upon a time.

When Wes walked through the door with two big bags of books and an even bigger smile, some of that worry returned even as I grinned back at him.

"Did you clean the place out?" I asked.

He dropped the bags, locked the door, and rushed over to the coffee table. "You finished with this?" he asked and tilted the laptop's lid down.

I shrugged. "Yeah, for now."

Wes closed it, putting the laptop to sleep, and then bounded over to haul me up under my arms. I laughed at him and how we wobbled as he got me on my feet, only for him to encourage me to fall back on the couch. A second later, he pounced on top of me.

"What's gotten into you?" I asked on a laugh.

He framed my face with his hands and looked me in the eyes, a smile so bright and wicked on his face. But his words were serious. "You're going to college. We're living together. Everything's going to be okay."

My sweet, sappy Wes. "Everything's going to be *great*."

"Oh, yeah, baby," he said, his voice dropping to growly. "Great is all we do."

Well, regardless of whether he thought I was strong, Wes definitely thought I was sexy enough for an afternoon quickie on the couch. And as distractions go, he was exceptional.

He maneuvered himself in between my thighs, groins pressed close, and his kisses were deep and hungry. With his arms braced near my shoulders, I had clear access to his back and ass. Being the kind of guy I now knew I was, I immediately reached down and shoved my hands inside his jeans. Since he didn't have any underwear on, I got two handfuls of firm buttocks and held on.

Wes hitched my legs higher, wider, until I gripped under his ass with my ankles. Hands still down his pants, I felt every flex of his butt and held on tight as we rocked hard and fast against each other. He'd lift his head enough to let us gasp a few breaths before angling the other way and kissing me breathless again, his tongue delving deep while his whiskers scratched at my lips and cheeks. I shivered, knowing this sex frenzy would leave marks.

Every thrust of our hips against each other pressed on my cock or wobbled my nuts until it just didn't matter that we both still had all our clothes on.

After one particularly forceful pound of his hips, I realized... *Oh, God.* I was going to have to ask him to fuck me soon. There was just no denying it anymore. No shying away. I wanted it desperately, this act right here proving that yet again. All our clothes might be on, but I could absolutely imagine his cock sunk inside me as he rocked in and out.

"Yeah," I said. "Do it. Oh, yeah." Because my imagination was a seriously powerful sex toy. Wes *was* fucking me...in my joyously wicked mind.

Body strung tight, I peaked first. Scratching at his bare ass and breathlessly silent, I arched up and came, wet heat flooding my groin. I sucked in a breath and bellowed it out, Wes still rocking hard against me. Panting, I blinked open my eyes and watched him jerk and grunt, hips snapping, as he came, too. I was pretty sure Wes had felt like he'd fucked me and that, right then, was him coming inside me, bare, marking me.

"Holy fuck," I whispered as my muscles spasmed one more time. Yeah, I needed that.

Chapter Twenty-Seven

The Truth Comes Out

My mother wanted to meet with me alone. At first, I opened my mouth to tell Mrs. Kinney that was fine. I paused, though, and realized this was…mine. Everything about us even speaking was mine to control in every way. I doubted my mother would become violent or anything, but if I didn't want to be alone in a room with her, I didn't have to be. So, I asked Mrs. Kinney if she could bring my mother over and stay. Even if she and Wes hung out in the kitchen while my mother and I talked, I wanted them there.

Mrs. Kinney was great about it all. I'd felt a little bad about using her as a go-between, relaying messages, but she was happy to help in whatever capacity she could. Being a chauffeur and witness or whatever was fine with her.

Wes, on the other hand, was acting like my bodyguard. I'd cleaned up around the apartment, and he'd hovered as if the dust cloth might have an agenda. Now that we were minutes away from the arrival of our mothers, I was fidgety and trying to control my breathing. Wes stood slightly behind me, arms crossed over his chest and glaring at the door.

I sighed and turned to him. "Sprinkles."

His eyebrows shot up. "Huh?"

"If it was my dad coming here right now, I'd want you as badass as you could be." I moved over in front of him. "But it's my mom, and I kind of just need that smiley guy I met earlier this summer who's really great at...cuddling."

Instantly, Wes's arms were around me, holding me tightly against his chest. This time, when I sighed, it was with relief. He was warm and solid, letting me lean and relax for the next few minutes.

"Sorry," he whispered into my curls. "I'm worried about what she's going to say. She's been so fucking tight-lipped about 'it's a private matter' that it's driving me insane. She could be planning to say anything."

Mrs. Kinney had tried to get a sort of summary out of my mother on what she wanted to talk about, but Mom was holding on to her privacy. I didn't get it. This wasn't private, hadn't been since Harlan spread the word online and a bunch of others news media outlets had picked it up afterward. Sure, what we'd say here today was between us, but the cat was out of the bag as far as the reason we had to meet like this at all.

"I guess," I said, "I'm giving her the benefit of the doubt and believing your mom's idea that this is an attempt at reconciliation." I shrugged. "I have a lot of questions, though, and if I think about it too much at once, I get seriously pissed off. But that's where I'm starting from, a reboot of our relationship."

"What if she wants you to come home?"

I leaned back to look at him. "I am home."

His smile asked for patience, and then he kissed me just as a knock sounded on the door. We both took deep breaths before Wes went over to let them in.

My mother had on slacks. That was the first thing I noticed because it was so out of character. She wasn't wearing a skirt and no ruffled blouse either, but a cute, yellow top. She just looked...liberated.

Mrs. Kinney came in looking like an ad for a beach resort in a flowing skirt and tank top, sandals on her feet. Like Wes, her hair kept getting more blonde as she spent time in the sun. "How would you like to do this, kiddo?" she asked me.

I avoided looking at my mother and said, "I think you guys can wait in the kitchen or something." Still in the apartment, but not in the room. It was a compromise of sorts.

Smiling, Mrs. Kinney got hold of Wes's arm, all but dragging him into the kitchen. "We'll be right in here, if you need us." She gave me a drive-by kiss on my cheek as she went.

And then I was alone in the room with my oddly reborn mother.

"You look...different," I said.

"I've moved in with a friend from the office."

I frowned at her. "You what?"

"I left your father. What he did to you that night was the last straw."

Last straw? There had been straws? And she left him? I couldn't process anything she said.

"Would it be all right," she asked, "if we sat down?"

I blinked a few times, trying to reorient myself. "Yeah, okay."

I sat down the couch, and she sat at the opposite end. With her purse at her feet, she looked around for a moment. I let her look at what Wes and I—mostly Wes—had achieved in a home. Her hair was down. Well, not completely, but she had it in a ponytail instead of a bun. I hadn't known it was so long.

Who is *this woman?*

She took what looked like a fortifying breath. "Malcolm, there are some things I need to tell you about your father and me. I know you won't understand given...who you are now, but we both had our reasons for everything we did. And, back then, everyone involved thought we were doing the right thing."

I couldn't even imagine where this was going. Had we been in Witness Protection? Were they spies? Was I adopted? Discovered in a ditch in Kansas beside an alien space pod? It felt like anything was possible after statements like those.

While looking at her knees, fingers absently touching the seams of her pants, she said, "I met your father when we were at Bible Camp the summer we turned eighteen." She smiled faintly. "It felt like a torrid affair, but was absolutely innocent. We were both from very conservative and religious families."

"Okay, I did figure out the conservative part eventually, but religion? I've never been to church. Did you go without me?"

"Could you..." She looked over at me, her eyes pleading. "I'd like to get through it all and, perhaps, answer questions afterward. All right?"

I swallowed hard and nodded. Dread warred with my curiosity.

She nodded back and returned to watching her fingers on her knees. "Toward the end of the summer—just days before we were set to leave—I followed your father into the woods. He'd gone in alone and seemed very determined in his path. I'd thought to surprise him, reiterate our plans to keep in touch and…demonstrate my affection for him." She cleared her throat. "Instead, I discovered your father with someone else, the two of them in a desperate clench, kissing and crying." Her eyes cut to me and then away. "He was with another boy."

I froze. I didn't know for how long, until I had to gasp. I stumbled up onto my feet and away toward the window. No idea why. I just had to get up, get away.

Was she telling me my father was gay? That the man who'd beaten me and kicked me out, abandoned me for being gay, he was gay himself?

I must have asked that aloud because she said, "Yes, he is."

I looked out the window, my hands over my mouth. It was such a nice day out and yet the world was breaking apart in here. *My father's gay.*

I was shaking, my knees threatening to buckle. This was insane. All of it. But no, I didn't know *all* of it.

"If he's gay," I said, "why'd he react so violently to me being the same?"

"Malcolm, I said we thought what we did was right. *Everyone* thought it was the right thing to do."

My temper spiked. "What the hell did you all do?"

"Your father's parents sent him to a conversion therapy clinic in California. He went willingly. We were all so hopeful they could cure him. We *believed* they would."

"But they didn't," I said, my voice sounding flat. "They couldn't because there's nothing to cure."

"I know." She nodded. "Now, I know."

I snorted. "I'm guessing he does, too, huh? Except he's not one of those guys who'll embrace their truth, right? He's pissed it didn't work."

"Malcolm, you have to understand—"

"No." I crossed my arms. "No, I actually don't have to understand. I know it, but I don't have to understand any of it. I don't want to."

"All right," she said quietly. "You should know then that he was a different person after he left the clinic. After they said he was cured and released him, I mean." She looked up at me, and I could see a plea. "He wanted to be the best man he could be. Do right by his parents, his church. He was desperate to be *good*."

A small part of me clenched in sudden sympathy. I could almost imagine trying that hard to be... Well, shit, I didn't have to imagine. I'd been going out of my mind all through high school, trying to fit in and be what everyone wanted me to be. I'd been aiming at being liked and accepted. Apparently, my father had wanted to be...normal, a word I'd so casually assumed gay people couldn't be before I'd learned the truth that we're all normal in our own unique ways.

I'd learned. My father hadn't.

"But," she went on, "after we married and a few...encounters happened, he changed. He turned away from the church, stopped speaking to his parents, refused to engage with mine... He grew so angry, but I know most of it was aimed inward. He never talked about it with me, but he felt like he'd failed." She gave me a watery look. "He thought he could do things right with you, and I believed him."

Oh, God. Rubbing at my forehead, I asked, "So, everything about how we lived and how you both raised me, that was a result of his 'failed' conversion? 'No weaknesses, be a man, don't coddle him,'" I said, quoting my father's favorite lines. "That was to make sure I couldn't be gay, too?"

"Yes," she said. "Again, Malcolm, we thought we were doing the right thing." She sighed and this time it sounded defeated. "I was so wrong. So naive and blind." This time the plea in her eyes wasn't for understanding. "I'm so sorry, Malcolm." Her chin quivered. "I'm so sorry."

My eyes felt hot and my throat tightened, but I wasn't done being angry. "What are you sorry for exactly?"

She swallowed hard. "I—"

"Are you sorry for cutting me off from all forms of affection? Making sure acceptance and unconditional love were completely foreign to me?" I clenched my fists at my side. "Are you aware of the fact you both did such a great job that when I actually get those things, I question why anyone would bother to notice me let alone care about me?"

She was openly crying, her breath hitching in little sobs. Tears cascaded down my cheeks, but I didn't feel broken by the truth of all this. I felt...vindicated. There wasn't anything inherently wrong with me; I was a product of my mother's idiocy and my father's self-hatred. And their fears, really, because I had no doubt they'd tried to make sure I turned out all butch and straight in the most emotionless way possible. Well, I'd showed them by being fully in touch with my every emotion and undeniably homosexual.

Fuck it. My anger drained away with my every breath. It was over. My mother knew she'd screwed up big time. Wasn't like we could go back in time and clue anybody in on what they were doing wrong. Time to move forward. But which way was that?

I looked up and discovered Wes peeking around the wall. He raised his eyebrows and glanced at my mother, now quietly sniffling, and back to me. I nodded so he'd know everything was basically fine, no need to intervene, but said to my mother, "I think it's time for you to go. I need to think about all this."

She sniffed loudly, cleared her throat, and stood. Taking a couple deep breaths, she brushed at her immaculate slacks before looking at me again. "I wrote down my new contact information," she said and picked up her purse. "You can reach me whenever you want. Carol has it all as well."

I took the piece of notepaper she handed to me. To contact her through Mrs. Kinney would feel kind of cowardly or maybe just insincere. If I was interested in talking to my mother, I'd deal with her directly. "Thanks," I said and set the paper on the side table beside the dock where we charged our phones.

We hovered near each other and the awkwardness returned. I couldn't really look at her, and she seemed to have the same trouble.

Finally, she said, "I'm making changes in my life. I'm not certain of everything yet, but I know what went on before isn't how I want to continue." She stepped closer and reached out, gently grasping my forearm. "I hope you'll give me a second chance, Malcolm. I do love you."

And that was the end of my battle against crying. No longer angry, self-righteous, or defeated, I stepped away from her, covered my eyes and gave in flushing everything out with tears. A moment later, I heard two sets of footsteps cross the room, just before strong arms enveloped me.

I stayed huddled into Wes while Mrs. Kinney murmured indistinctly and no doubt guided my mother out of the apartment. I heard the door open quietly, and then close firmly, all sounds dimming down to my shaky breathing and Wes's steady heartbeat.

"She's gone, honey," he whispered.

I nodded, but didn't want to move yet. "Did you hear what we said?"

"I'm sorry. I couldn't help it. Mom kept smacking my arm, but I eavesdropped on the whole thing."

I snorted a laugh. "It's okay. I'd rather not have to rehash it."

"How about we lie down? Or a bath?" He rubbed up and down my back. "We can talk or not, your choice, but let's be comfortable."

I sniffed and stood straighter. "A bath sounds great."

Several minutes later, we were in the tub full of warm and sudsy water. I liked a shower for getting clean, but oh, having a bathtub big enough to bob in was divine. We sat with my back to his front, legs relaxed but not completely able to stretch out, and all kinds of stress slipped away. I leaned against Wes and let it all go.

"I never would've guessed," I murmured while he dipped the washcloth in the soapy water and glided it over my chest again and again.

"What?" he asked.

"That my dad's gay. Actually, that they had any of that history together. The whole thing is so far out there…"

"I wonder sometimes," he said, "if the fathers who can't accept their sons are dealing with their own sexual issues. Or trying not to deal with them." He shrugged. "They always say same-sex interest is way more common than anyone wants to actually admit."

I hummed, thinking about that. Was that Rick's problem? Why

he lashed out at me originally and every time after that? Could it stem from attraction? Resentment? Nobody developed hatred on their own; he probably had someone who'd shown him gay wouldn't be tolerated in the Lockhart family. I almost—for just a second—felt sorry for him.

"Mal?"

"Hmm?"

"Do you want to reconcile with your mom?"

"I… I don't know." I sighed. "Right now, I'm kinda done, you know? Exhausted. But I bet I'll get curious. That I'll want to know more."

He rested his chin on my shoulder and hugged my chest. "I get it. You can take as long as you need."

I smiled, the act feeling strange after almost a whole day of not doing that. My days included near-constant reasons to smile now. Talk about things getting better. So I smiled and tipped my head back to kiss Wes's cheek, making him smile, too.

Chapter Twenty-Eight

Happy Birthday, Wes

I'd accepted—and received—a boatload of cash from the fund Harlan Urban had set up *and* I'd gotten the most shocking news of my life from my mother. I still couldn't quite get a handle on either. So when Roger called to let me know my only job for Wes's birthday party was to get Wes to Brian and Jean-Louis' lake house, I could've cried in relief. No need for me to attempt whatever it was one had to do to throw a twenty-fifth birthday party for one's boyfriend in a brand new apartment.

I was *saved*.

But, since I'd woken up that morning and taken a very thorough shower, I'd had sex on my mind for hours. I'd cleaned places in ways I'd never imagined needed that much cleaning. By late morning, when everyone at the house went inside to change into swimwear, I was aching for a fuck.

No doubt our friends would wonder when we didn't come down again, but I meant to get what I'd been fantasizing about so much. Standing naked and half-hard from thinking about it, I heard Wes come up behind me. Equally naked, he fit himself against my back, the warm length of his cock stiffening against my butt cheek.

I grinned and bit my lip at the same time. We were so doing this.

"I thought the front of you was beautiful, Mal." His voice was deep and growly as he ran his hands down my body from shoulders to waist. "But the back of you is truly inspirational."

I braced my hands against the dresser in front of me and widened my stance. When he fit himself tighter to me, all down my back, I moaned, tilting my hips, pressing into his stiff, hot cock.

"If you keep doing that, I'll have to—" he cut himself off with a groan.

"What, Wes?" I had to ask, needed to know. "Tell me what you want." Because if it was what I wanted, I wouldn't have to say it out loud.

He chuckled behind me, the sound dark and wicked, and then his thumbs spread my cheeks apart. Heart hammering, I bit my bottom lip just before the long length of his cock was wedged between into my crease. He hummed his pleasure as I gasped mine. This was it. He did want it, too. His dick wasn't down between my thighs, but up, straining, like it wanted…in me.

"It's okay Mal," he mumbled against my neck as he kissed me there, his hands sliding around to hug my chest. "I just want this. Don't worry."

He moved, his cock rubbing against my hole, making my cheeks clench because of the friction. God, that felt good. And when he moaned, clearly enjoying my instinctive reaction, it felt even better when he did it again and again.

I gulped when his teeth raked my neck, his tongue following. It was time. I had to say it.

"Please, Wes. I need you to. I just do. It's been driving me *crazy* wanting it. Everything you do there feels phenomenal, and I want *more*."

He stopped rocking against me and rested his chin on my shoulder. "More what exactly?"

I took a shaky breath. "I want you in me *so bad*. And…I looked it up online and, um, I'm all, you know, *clean*…there. We can do it. Now. Okay?"

He stepped back, and I worried for a second, but then he encouraged me to turn around. Immediately, he held my face in his hands and kissed me, deep and lingering. I fitted myself all down his front, pressed so close, and held him tightly.

He lifted his head enough to say, "You know it's okay if you don't really want to do it this way, right? Or if you're not ready or want to talk—"

"Wes, it's about all I've been able to think about for weeks." I blushed, saying that, but couldn't hold back any longer. "I've just been nervous and some of the things I've seen have made me more nervous and others made me more horny for it and I'm just... I'm so..." I looked up at him for help, hoping he understood.

He smiled so sweetly. "You're ready."

I nodded, fingers biting into his hips and cock straining toward him. I was so fucking ready. "Don't make me beg. I'm seriously close to doing it, but I'll never forgive—"

Grabbing the back of my neck, he slammed us together again, his mouth devouring mine. I clung to him, desperate and moaning for more. Too quickly, he backed off again, but this time spun us toward the bed. A couple quick pulls and he had the covers pulled back to the sheet.

"Hands and knees," he said in that bearish voice and gave my ass a squeeze.

I forced down a sudden nervous uprising in my gut, getting on the bed and assuming the requested position. Deep breaths helped, as did reminding myself that I sincerely did want this and I'd lose my ever-loving mind if I didn't get it soon. But... Well, my ass was in the air, and Wes was totally looking at it.

When I peeked back at him, he chuckled. "What? I've been fantasizing about this since we worked on Ted the first time."

"Really?"

"Yes, really. Every time I turned around, there was your ass." He started stroking his cock slowly. "And those damn low-riding jeans of yours?" He groaned. "Took everything I had not to hook a finger in them and help them fall."

I chuckled, a snort slipping out. A little part of me was all a-flutter to know he'd been into me from the very beginning. And, okay, if he wanted to look—admire—I didn't feel like stopping him. It was a compliment.

So, instead, I bowed my back to lift my ass higher and spread my legs, trying to look more enticing. We'd already established we both liked the butt, so I figured he'd like this view. His sudden, deep groan made me laugh with success.

"Tease," he said.

"Then c'mon."

His grin got really wicked. I might've just poked the bear one too many times. I was in for it now. But oh, how I *wanted* it.

Would he smack my butt? Would he use his tongue? Would he come all over me? I shivered remembering everything I'd seen. Would he like being inside me even half as much as I'd loved being inside him? Would he come *inside* me?

I really hoped so.

Wes moved out of my line of sight, making me think he was getting the lube from his bag. But then his hands were on my ass, spreading my cheeks, and I bit my lip. Apparently, he really wanted to look at me. A blush burned my face, but I didn't move. Well, not until something thick and wet took a lap around my hole. That was Wes's tongue. Licking me. I flinched, but in a good way. In an oh, my God way.

Oh… Oh, it felt good. Like last time, his tongue on me felt sort of ticklish, making me want to squirm around. Actually, it felt a bit like when he licked the head of my cock. A sensual tease. I clenched and flexed my fingers against the sheet, my eyes slowly closing as I focused on that feeling. Did I really taste that good? Did he really like doing this rimming to me that much? Because the both of us were moaning while his tongue worked on my hole.

He thrust his tongue into me, and I tightened on it. "Yes," I said. "More of that."

I didn't get more of his tongue poking, but his finger swirled around in the wetness before easing inside me.

My face met the sheet and I moaned into it, focusing in on that feeling of being penetrated by Wes. It came with some stretch, but that was just a definite sign of having him *there*, giving me what I'd asked for. When he pulled back, I protested feebly, but he came back slicker than before. Lube. Damn, I loved that stuff.

When Wes was sailing his finger in and out of me, my body rocking to meet him, and little flickers of sensation and awareness darting through me, he pushed in a second finger.

I gasped. Okay, that burned in a bad way.

"Easy, baby," he said and rubbed along my lower back. "Deep breaths and try to stay relaxed. You're doing great."

I moaned into the bed, rubbing my face against it, because while, yeah, there was pain, there was also a pleasure I hadn't known before. He spread those long fingers apart, stretching me, making me gasp again. He started easing his fingers in and out, and it was all so…conflicting. I wanted him in deeper but also to get out; it felt so good, but it also made me ache enough to frown.

But then he pushed deeper still, wiggled around, and I jerked and grunted some unintelligible phrase that meant *holy fuck, what's that?*

"Malcolm Small, meet your prostate."

He rubbed, and a deep, animalistic noise tumbled out of me. I could barely breathe for the pleasure suddenly screaming through me. His damn fingers left for a moment, I snarled, he chuckled, and then more slick fingers came back.

"Oh, fuck." How many fingers did he have in there? "Jesus," I said, panting now, not able to say that I really, really needed him to find that spot again like right fucking now. "Please," I said and heard that I whimpered.

"Damn, Mal, you make the best sounds," he said and thrust those fingers deeper.

Oh, there! His fingers never stopped rubbing that amazing, hidden gem inside me as I thrust my dick into his fist and growled into the bed. Each breath left me with a cry, my body shaking, tingling, seconds from orgasm, and then— He pulled his fingers out and everything came to an abrupt halt.

"Wesley!"

"You wanna come without me? I'll keep going if—"

"No. You're right." I wiggled around, ass high and waiting. "Do me now. Yeah. Oh, fuck, Wes, come on."

He got up on the bed behind me, and then he draped himself over my back. I gasped at the sensation of being covered by him, by this bigger, stronger man. He was my Wes, though, and being under him felt devastatingly wonderful. I was thrilled we were doing it this way. I wanted him to hold me down and fuck me. In a loving way, but... "Dammit, Wes, *please.*"

"Hold on, honey. Listen to me," he said and made me get back up onto my hands. "This *will* hurt, and you might hate it, so if it gets to be too much, tell me. We'll go slow, but we can stop, too. That's fine. Okay?"

My sigh had some grumble to it. "You're not talking me out of this, are you? Now? When I could come any second just from what you've already done?"

He chuckled. "Just want you to be prepared." He lifted off of me. I missed him completely, but then heard him slathering his cock in lube.

"Oh, believe me," I said breathlessly, "I'm prepped." My new laptop was full of links to my favorite porn videos. Right now that was practically educational research.

"Then here we go," Wes said.

I didn't tense up anywhere when the broad head of his cock kissed my hole. I did gasp, though, when he pushed inside, making me spread around his fat glans and let him in. The pain was sharp this time and it radiated outward. Muscles tensed all over me involuntarily, and I tried to make them relax. I bit back any complaining words or sounds because I didn't want him to stop. I needed this. To be connected to my Wes, possessed by him as completely as he could have me.

"I know, baby," he said, rubbing my back again. "Just relax and breathe. Stroke yourself. Feel that pleasure until this feels better."

I took deep breaths, trusting that the pain would ease, and touched myself. That helped change my focus and, since I was still hard, still wanting, I moaned and felt myself sort of opening inside to let him keep going. He sank into me. Wes, inside me. The pain faded to a throbbing backbeat, and I moaned.

"That's it. That's better, huh?" It sounded like he was smiling.

"Yes," I sort of hissed. I gasped a breath, moaned, and leaned back, bringing him deeper.

Wes waited and went slowly, giving me time to adjust, but I was so full, full of him, and then to have that thick dick rubbing against that magical nugget of pleasure inside me and sliding past it... I gasped. "Sweet Jesus."

"Mal?" He was draped over me again, his hands planted beside mine.

I stared his corded forearms, suddenly realizing— "You're all the way in me."

His chuckle was a little strained as he rotated his hips against my ass. "Balls-deep, baby."

I laughed a little shakily at that ridiculous phrase. Then all thoughts fled my mind when he moved, withdrawing and returning in tiny bursts, seeming to work his way out more than he came back in.

"Don't leave!" I tightened my ass on his cock, trying to hold him inside me.

"Jesus, Mal."

"Don't leave," I said, though I relaxed again.

"I'm not, honey. See?" And he thrust back inside in one long stroke.

I couldn't speak to tell him that—oh yeah, sweet God—I saw. There were stars and bursts of rainbow-colored lights and I wondered if I could die from pleasure. He did it again and again, thrusting, making the whole world fade away as my absolute focus centered on this moment, this feeling. Nothing mattered but Wes and the very deliciously perfect pleasure he gave me.

Finally—*finally!*—I had what I'd wanted so much. We rocked against each other. He did things with his hips I couldn't figure out but that felt so fabulously hot. I was burning up from the inside out, sweating and panting, losing myself in the carnal pleasure of Wes fucking my ass.

I came hard, muscles tensed to the point I couldn't gasp or shout. I squeezed my cock in my hand and clenched tight on his buried inside me, frozen in orgasm for blissful moments. When I could drag in a breath, I think he slammed it out of me with his final thrust. His shout of pleasure made me smile and I sworn that was the heat of his cum coating my insides. I belonged to Wes.

My arms shaking, I tried to stay where I was, not wanting separate just yet. I'd finally gotten him where I wanted him, so I couldn't collapse immediately. But then he slowly eased upright, the cool air hitting my sweaty back and making me shiver. We groaned together as Wes took his time pulling out of my body. The throbbing returned and I was really open back there. Not the most fun feeling.

"C'mere," Wes said before he flopped on his back on the end of the bed.

I smiled and shuffled over to him, feeling very much like I just had the workout of my life. I hadn't realized every muscle would be involved. I didn't think I'd felt this worked over after topping him. Good, though. Really good. And Wes was flushed and panting, but there was a twinkle to his green eyes and a grin on his lips.

I collapsed half on top of him, and his arm rested across my back. Feeling like I could happily slip into sleep, I figured I needed to speak now or it wouldn't happen.

"That was everything I'd hoped for," I said.

He pressed his lips to my forehead, a sleepy kiss. "Me, too. Love you."

"Mmm... Love you."

Our sweet serenity was suddenly broken when Roger hollered, "Did you guys survive all that?"

I gasped and sat up, looking to the door, but... No, he'd sounded like— "Oh, shit. The window's *open*."

Wes started his surprised snort-laughing, while I buried my face in my hands against the bed. And there was the wet spot I'd made when I came all over it. While practically screaming. Or maybe there hadn't been anything "practically" about it if they'd heard us all the way down by the water. I groaned, but sat up again when Wes got off the bed.

Bold as you please in his birthday suit, Wes sauntered over to the window with his fists raised over his head. "Happy birthday *to me*," he hollered down to all of them.

Their cheering was immediate and loud.

Even though my blushing took on a new level of intensity over seventy-five percent of my body, I grinned and laughed a little. I'd sort of wanted people to know I was with Wes, that he'd chosen me. Now I'd definitely gotten that wish...and I was kinda proud of myself.

Chapter Twenty-nine

It's Just the Beginning

"You ready for this?"

"No. I mean, yes. Of course." I gulped hard.

Wes one-arm hugged me as we walked away from the parking lot on campus. It was the first day of classes and, while I knew where I was going and when to get everywhere…it was the first frickin' day of frickin' classes.

"You've got this, honey."

"Yeah," I said on a sigh.

He stopped walking, and I stopped with him. This was where we had to part ways, our first classes in opposite directions today. Tomorrow, we'd be on different floors of the same building. While I didn't want to do any of this on my own, I knew I couldn't treat my boyfriend like my security blanket. He'd helped me soar up to this moment. It was time I flew solo.

I wouldn't crash. Totally wouldn't.

Uh-huh.

Wes gave me a quick kiss. "Call or text whenever you want. I'll keep my phone in my pocket and answer when I can. You've got my schedule, and we'll be meeting for lunch in a couple of hours."

Suddenly, I resented the reassurances. *Are you a kid or a grown-*

up, Malcolm? I squared my shoulders and stood up straight. "I can do this. Don't worry about me."

Wes grinned lopsidedly at me. I blushed, recognizing that look.

"Damn," he whispered, "you're sexy when you get all butch."

I rolled my eyes, but then took advantage by gripping the back of his neck and pulling him down for a proper mauling of mouths. Give him something distracting to take with him.

After a minute or so of intense heat, I pulled back, and he stumbled a little toward me. *Score!* I walked off a lot more confident. I probably swaggered. He laughed behind me.

It was only after I was walking into my building that I realized we'd done all that out in the open and in front of bunches of people, right there on the sidewalk. *Huh. Look at me be all out and proud.* I gave myself a mental fist-bump, took a deep breath, held my head high, and walked into my first class.

The room was packed. Instead of individual desks, there were long tables spanning the width of the room and several chairs crammed into the alleys between them. I gulped, quickly scanning for an open seat that wouldn't require me to climb over people to get to it.

Two rows in and beside the window, a lone guy with a mop of curly blond hair gave me a tiny smile and waved a hand at the empty chair beside him. A whoosh of gratitude washed through me as I walked over.

"Thanks," I whispered and scooted around behind him for the seat.

"No problem." He had blue eyes and freckles and looked as nervous or embarrassed as me.

The girl on the other side of me was actively engaged with her phone. The guy who'd let me in just sat there, and I realized he was at a loss as to what to do now. But I kind of knew what to do and wanted to do it.

"Hi," I said and smiled at him. "I'm Mal."

He grinned. "Me, too."

"You're kidding." I'd never known another Mal before.

He shook his head. "Malcolm Mackenzie."

"Malcolm Small."

We shared a chuckle. How weird was that?

"I know two Adams," he said. "And there were five Brians in my class in high school."

"Eight Madisons and four Ashleys. Six Anthonys, but they all had nicknames like Tony and Tino and stuff."

We were quiet for a moment, and my mind wandered to gay couples and whether guys with the same names got together very often. Then I went and blurted, "I guess I should be glad I fell for a Wesley."

I snapped my mouth shut and stared at this other Malcolm. *Holy bejeezus, way to throw the gay on the table right away.* I held my breath and hoped I wouldn't have to climb over people for that other open seat in the back after all.

He blinked at me, pink tinging his cheeks, but then he said, "Actually, the Adams are boyfriends. One of them is my twin." He cleared his throat. "The name thing made them hesitate to get together originally, but everyone could see they were gone on each other right away. It was inevitable." He shrugged, smiling a little again.

Slowly, a smile spread across my face, too. "I know how that feels."

He just nodded. This time, the moment of silence didn't feel awkward at all.

An older, rumpled-looking man shuffled into the room and toward the podium at the front. He had to be our composition professor. There were actual patches on the elbows of his sport coat. I couldn't help grinning at the academic nerdyness of him. I hoped he was nice.

"I bet," Malcolm said, "he's going to call us by our last names."

I groaned a little. Did anybody ever want to answer to Small?

"Well, you can be Malcolm," he said. "I'm fine with Mackenzie."

Suddenly, with that offer and the small smile he gave me, I realized I'd made a friend. All on my own and completely by accident—and in less than ten minutes, too—but I'd really done it.

"Thanks," I said. "Maybe I'll just call you Mac."

He snorted a laugh, probably as aware as I was that neither of us looked like anything that tough-guy name implied. But I liked that

I'd made him laugh.

Maybe this making friends thing wasn't so hard after all. I just had to put a little of myself out there and give the other person a chance to do the same. Scary, yeah, but possibly really worth the effort for everybody.

I took a second to get out my phone and text Wes. *You're amazing and I love you*. Because he was and I so did. I'd come a long way and I knew it was mostly due to my first summer with Wes. I smiled happily, suddenly certain other great things were yet to come for the both of us.

THE END

Please Review

If you enjoyed this book, please leave a review on your favorite social media or book distributor site so others can have the same experience.

Thank you!

About the Author

Missy Welsh stares into space a lot, has conversations with cats, takes notes while people-watching, records conversations (not the ones with cats), named her laptop Norbert and her phone Pushkin, has backups of her backups' backups, faints at the sight of a misused semi-colon, and will often ask socially unacceptable questions of strangers. Basically, she's a writer.

My Summer of Wes

Also By Missy Welsh

NOVEL:

Isherwood

*

NOVELLA:

Take Your Pick

*

SHORT STORIES:

KLT23

What

Hope Is Good

Yours Forever

Come Cuddle Me

*

Visit www.missywelsh.com for freebies!

Made in the USA
Charleston, SC
10 February 2017